If you want to find yourself immersed in a WWII story that will capture your heart, you'll love *Strong Currents*.

— *USA Today* Bestselling Author Susan May Warren

In her WWII novel, *Strong Currents*—the follow-up to her novel, *Books Afloat*—Dee Topliff highlights themes of heroism and hope. I appreciated how she incorporated historical events with her various fictional characters. some of whom provide a light thread of humor. Topliff also weaves in a sweet romance against the backdrop of one of the most storied wars in history

— Beth K. Vogt, Christy-award winning author of the Thatcher Sisters Series

In *Strong Currents*, Delores Topliff drew me in on the first page when Josh Vengeance washed up on the shore of a small island after Midway during World War II and kept me turning pages until The End.

— Patricia Bradley, *USA Today* Bestselling Author

In *Strong Currents*, Delores Topliff has once again brought to life a fascinating slice of little-known history. Compelling characters walk hand-in-hand with a plot that captures your imagination and makes you want to know all you can about what was going on in the Pacific Northwest during World War II. I love books that entertain me as well as educate me, and this series fits the bill nicely!

— Carrie Schmidt, ReadingIsMySuperPower.org
and author of *Getting Past the Publishing Gatekeepers*

A vivid story of struggle, courage, acceptance, and new beginnings. Sometimes we have to let go of what we thought we wanted and allow God to show us our true path. Topliff's novel, *Strong Currents*, is an immersive story about the power or prayer, the endurance of the spirit, and the meaning of love and friendship wrapped around a slice of World War II that captures the traumas and the triumphs all at once. With characters to love and root for and a plot that puts you right in the thick of things, *Strong Currents* has all the history and heart that readers could want.

— Amy Willoughby-Burle, author of *The Other Side of Certain*

Strong Currents, a WWII historical novel by Delores Topliff, releases February 21, 2023, with Scrivenings Press. In the hands of this talented author, the deftly drawn characters leap off the page and into your heart. Privileged to read the ARC version, the dialogue is masterful, the wide-flung settings evocative. The polished prose leaves one wanting to read future works by this writer. Although the novel begins in the South Pacific and Europe, the plot unfolds primarily in San Diego and Washington state and draws upon historic wartime events that affected the region. It's a story to savor the masterful blend of warmth, courage, chuckles, and heart-wrenching moments. One that stays with you long after you've reached The End.

— Sara L. Jameson, author of *Cruise to Death* and
Death in High Places

STRONG CURRENTS

Columbia River Undercurrents ◆ Book Two

Delores Topliff

Scrivenings
PRESS
Quench your thirst for story.
www.ScriveningsPress.com

Published by Scrivenings Press LLC
15 Lucky Lane
Morrilton, Arkansas 72110
https://ScriveningsPress.com

Printed in the United States of America

Paperback ISBN 978-1-64917-254-9

eBook ISBN 978-1-64917-255-6

Cover by www.bookmarketinggraphics.com.

All scriptures are taken from the KING JAMES VERSION (KJV): KING JAMES VERSION, public domain.

This is a work of fiction. Unless otherwise indicated, all names, characters, businesses, events, and incidents are either the product of the author's imagination or used in a fictitious manner. Any resemblance to actual persons, living or dead, or actual events is purely coincidental.

With every book I write I learn more completely that it is the Lord that gives us stories worth telling to target readers' hearts. I'm thankful for the journey and the amazing friends He gives along the way.

"Does not the ear test words as the tongue tastes food?"
Job 12:11 NIV

Acknowledgments

I'm grateful that the Lord has set me on a life journey of loving books and then writing them. That led to great friendships with other authors who mutually encourage, support, and polish writing. Thanks this time especially to Beth K. Vogt, Patricia Bradley, and Sara L. Jameson.

Sincere thanks for story elements drawn from college roommate friend, lovely Austrian-born Ingeborg Oberweger, (one who travels the upper road), for sharing her childhood story of survival in wartime Austria and Dachau, Germany, which gripped me from the first time I heard it. Thanks also to newer friend, Ute Weber of Nuremberg, Germany, for inspiring aspects of Erika Hofer's character in this book.

Warm thanks to my agent, Julie Gwinn, and my Scrivenings Press editors, Elena Hill and Linda Fulkerson. Elena removed rabbit trails to make this narrative read faster with greater intensity.

I'm very thankful for Liana George and the brilliant professional virtual assistants at The Author's Write Hand, who are also my friends.

Thanks to my sister, eagle-eyed proofreader Nancy Williams, and to Mike Topliff, PhD, who gave his expertise. Great appreciation also to early reader/advisors Dr. Paula Boire and her sister, Susan Pearcy.

I'm thrilled to have warm support from small-town library staffs and support groups. Those in Milaca, Minnesota, have become friends. They and my Amish neighbors made 2022 my best summer yet in central Minnesota. Expect some of them to show up in future books.

Thank you family and friends for understanding and loving me even when book deadlines don't have any give in them.

Thank you, readers for being so important in this process and telling me how my characters or scenes encouraged you. That's more rewarding than you know and a huge part of what this writing and life journey is about.

Chapter One

Mid-June 1942—An unnamed island near Midway, the Central Pacific

Naval Seaman Apprentice Josh Vengeance drew a ragged breath. And another. Blackness ruled as the cosmic clock slowed. Time hung in the balance and almost ceased until Someone eased the ticking clock's hands forward.

His lips parted as his tongue sought moisture, but only sand grains entered his mouth. Josh moaned. His head throbbed when he turned to spit out sand. When one eyelid fluttered open, he glimpsed a single grass stem with three tiny dry leaves. Small bugs tunneled through his ragged clothes and even into his ears. Droning mosquitoes in precise formations attacked every inch of his body.

Josh scrunched his eyes shut so he wouldn't see. Rather than finding serenity, he relived the deafening roars and bright flashes of torpedoes that fatally attacked the *USS Yorktown*. Portions of the deck buckled and broke away. Massive equipment shifted and crushed. Flames seared flesh as the mighty aircraft carrier went down. Bodies flailed and survivors swam through burning oily patches to get away.

Josh had expected to sink with it, but powerful waves carried him. He grabbed crewmate after crewmate, attaching them to debris, until the torn sheet metal slashed his hands. His aching eyes fluttered again. He remembered a monstrous piece of wreckage smacking his head but nothing more.

Unknown time passed and light returned, spilling down the sky like boiling water. And then he stopped moving. How did he get here? No waves rocked him now. Sand scorched his skin everywhere it touched. Scoured him and ebbed as water lapped his body and retreated—then lapped and ebbed again. He changed position enough to taste water and spit, its salt closing his throat and burning external raw places.

The empty ocean tossed—no land in sight. More water washed in. He must move or drown. Summoning every muscle's last reserve he rolled face up, legs and back screaming.

But water reclaimed him, tunneled the sand away underneath. He wasn't getting anywhere on his own. More droning mosquitoes in whining formation drilled his flesh before louder buzzing filled the sky.

Battered and dazed, Josh tried sitting up, but his world lost its axis, and he fell back. A Japanese Zero swooped low. His elbows scrabbled to dig beneath the hot sand to escape, but it was futile. Strafing bullets kicked up lines of grit as perfectly spaced as his mom's sewing machine stitches. Bullets cross-stitched his legs, making blood spurt as he jerked and stilled.

Was this it? Tears came now from inner pain. Annie. Why hadn't he told her she mattered instead of leaving things vague? It was complicated. But she knew, didn't she?

Lord, no. Not like this. Let me live to tell her.

The Zero swung back in a slow circle—dropped lower still. The pilot's dark eyes peered at Josh.

Our Father, who art in heaven ...

Mom's voice echoed in his addled mind, "Whom have I in

heaven but thee? And there is none upon earth that I desire beside thee ..."

The Zero sprayed more bullets, zigzagging the sand, spitting grit into Josh's wounds. After one last pass, its air whooshing like a charging lion's near miss, it pulled up its wings and grew smaller.

"... The Lord bless and keep thee, the Lord lift up his countenance upon thee, and give thee peace." Dad's voice—his favorite closing scripture...

Peace.

After a shuddering overhead boom, a fireball lit the sky as the Zero broke and tumbled, its crash scattering debris and sending shock waves through the ground beneath him.

He must roll or crawl to safety. First he closed his eyes against the brightness.

Something poked Josh. Then nudged harder. He yelped and his eyes snapped open. A brown foot rested at eye level. The butt of a spear poked his ruined shoulder. When he grunted, a little man jumped back but his spear aimed at Josh's heart.

"*Kshama tanga!*"

The half-dressed man locked eyes with Josh. Two other small, tanned men stood a step back, faces fierce, eyes white and menacing.

"I'm no threat." Josh's voice creaked like a rusty hinge.

The first man lowered his spear.

Relief mixed with fear. Josh dared to ask. "Where am I?"

"*Shama bataru!*"

More excited voices chattered words he couldn't understand. Not Japanese, but what? Some kind of natives. The men wore brief loin clothes over glowing skin. They clucked their tongues as gentle hands slid him across the sand like a loaded picnic tablecloth without spilling a dish. That movement scraped away additional skin. Relief and exhaustion claimed him.

He roused but couldn't gauge time. The hungry bugs near shore had abandoned him for better hunting. Someone had brushed sand and dry grass blades over him to partially block the blazing sun. A small man tipped Josh's head back enough to dribble fresh water into his mouth and onto his swollen tongue. An old woman pushed bits of mashed banana into his mouth. Arguing voices rose and fell and then slid him inside a small rocky cave. Cooler. An older man stayed, dribbled more water into Josh's mouth, massaged his throat so he could swallow. It hurt. So thirsty.

Soon, the burning breeze carried shrill approaching Japanese voices. The native people scurried out of sight. Only the gentle knobby man stayed and kicked more sand over Josh. He gasped for air. Was the man burying him alive? No, building a sand dune high enough to hide this small cave.

Boots marched by.

Dear God, I stink. Don't let them smell me. If they're going to capture me, let me die now. "*If I take the wings of the morning, and dwell in the uttermost parts of the sea; Even there shall thy hand lead me ...*"

Harsh voices barked and moved on. The sand dune worked.

Things quieted.

Several natives returned. Fed him more bits of soft, ripe fruits or fish. He slept.

New voices startled him awake. Americans?

"Peeyouu," one said. "What's that awful smell?"

"Smells like death. Look here."

"Is he alive?"

"Not sure. He's American, like us. Injured, almost dead and buried here."

The unknown speakers kicked more sand aside and swept Josh's body clear with their hands. Josh groaned at the rough treatment and opened his eyes.

"Hi, buddy," one said. "You're in rough shape."

"Yup." Josh's voice rasped as he focused on the two men and then tried to speak. He recognized their US Marine uniforms and shook with dry sobs.

"It's all right, fella. We've got you. Are those shreds of a Navy uniform?"

Josh nodded.

"Which ship?"

His vocal cords screeched from disuse. "*USS Yorkton.*"

"Gosh, she went down a while back. How long have you been here? How'd you even get here?"

"Dunno. Drifted I guess?"

"That's nuts." He pointed to the water. "There are sharks out there. And only small debris bits on the beach." One Marine lifted his hat to finger-comb his crew cut. "I guess miracles still happen."

"The natives—hid me from Japs."

"No kidding? And risked getting payback? Decent!"

The other soldier slipped outside. Hand to his forehead, he surveyed to his right and left before scrambling higher up. "Come look, Tex, he's right. The boot prints up here are Japanese tread, not ours. And no bare feet or sandals."

"Wow, close call." The first man raised Josh's head to dribble in more water from a canteen. "Look at you, you've had it super rough. Even got shot up."

His hand groped around Josh's neck. "Where are your dog tags?"

Josh tried to move but his arms wouldn't work. "Dunno. Gone?"

"Do the natives have them?" They called the knobby man over. He mumbled and held out empty hands.

"He doesn't understand or doesn't want to."

Josh tried to answer, his words slurring, "Josh Vejenje, appren seaman, 128727."

"Good. I got that. Your uniform's burned but looks like US

Navy. If you're from the *Yorktown*, you've been missing since Midway."

"How long?"

"Around June seventh. At least a week and a half. You're skin and bones." The Marine pulled a chocolate bar from his shirt pocket, unwrapped the foil, and fed Josh a crumb. "You shouldn't have much at first."

Milk chocolate melted on his tongue. "Heaven!"

The other asked, "Where can we take him?"

"Not sure. Midway's closest, but their hospital got bombed. Have the lieutenant radio them and ask if they're operational."

"Will do. Hawaii's best," the other man said, "but their beds are full, and they're over a thousand miles away."

"He's not safe here. We have to move him." Strong hands slid Josh into a canvas sling and then into a mechanized, amphibious craft. Waves lapped and splashed as the vehicle sliced through the booming surf to a ship.

Lord, You're answering Mom and Dad's prayers. 'Yea, though I walk through the valley of the shadow ...'

He choked down the lump in his throat that nearly strangled him.

Chapter Two

June 18-June 19, 1942
from Kellinghusen, Schleswig-Holstein to Munich, Germany

Erika Hofer hunched in the rail car disguised as her own grandmother. She must find Dietrich Bonhoeffer. The coal-burning passenger train huffed and puffed from northwest Germany's lowlands past farms and forested hills to Bavaria's highlands and finally its capital, Munich. If God helped her, Dietrich would be there.

The young woman's heart pounded beneath her old-style dress. She had not told Mother her plans to escape lest she be forced to betray her to the *Gestapo*. Father was gone. But before he departed, he had removed two small scraps of paper hidden inside the earpiece tubes of his glasses and unrolled them. "You will both need this now and for the days ahead."

Erika smoothed out her paper. It held numbers and abbreviated words in tiny, cramped writing. When she peered closely it said, *Directions to Uncle Dietrich*. Father had sketched a map on a napkin before wadding it up and burning it. She and Mother committed their rolled paper contents to memory and did the same, watching the scraps flame and burn to ash. Uncle Dietrich mattered too much to let carelessness jeopardize him.

Aboard the rocking train, Erika pulled up her dress's long sleeve to check her watch. The Munich Express was on time but stopped at so many dairies, it should be called a milk run. Should she have contacted Dietrich before coming? No, but every beat of her heart prayed he would be there. A lost country-bumpkin grandmother could raise suspicion wandering in downtown Munich. His information was cunningly hidden disguised as an embroidered flower on her dress's cuffs.

The locomotive slowed and belched less smoke as it passed more farms. Cows grazed in fenced fields near fog-draped hollows along the Elbe River. It lurched to a halt in a village of picturesque homes and shops where one lone church steeple pierced the sky. A *Gestapo* agent leaned against the railroad station wall with his arms crossed, eyeing every traveler leaving the train.

Erika shuddered. Thank God this wasn't her stop. Passenger tickets were punched on departure. The train had barely resumed speed when a police inspector entered her car.

The man swayed in the aisle, clutching the seats before and behind the young woman sitting a row in front of Erika.

She wore a colorful scarf wound around her head, and her long purple skirt trailed into the aisle. Soft snores drifted back. The young woman couldn't have been more than a teenager. Erika scrutinized her smooth face and gaping mouth. Her head dropped against the red fabric-covered seat.

"*Fräulein?*" The inspector raised his voice. "Documents, *bitte*." He pushed the young woman's shoulder lightly—and then more forcefully.

Why didn't he move on? Or return to check on the young woman later in the journey? He shook her shoulder again, demanding documents until her eyes startled open. Frightened.

"Asleep or not, *Fräulein*, I need your documents."

"*Ach!*" She sat up and plunged her hand into a voluminous

pocket. She dug into a second and third pocket before extracting folded, wrinkled papers she thrust forward. "H-here, sir."

The inspector took them but shook his head.

"You're mistaken, *Fräulein*. These are wrong. Look again."

Frantic, she searched more pockets and produced a half-eaten sandwich and two coins.

"That's all?" He scowled and tipped his hat lower over his forehead. His terrifying eyes glared down at the girl.

"No, you don't need train money. Just your *kennkarte*—your identity paper." When he pushed her hand away, she shook worse.

"You don't have it?"

"*Nein.*" Her lips quivered. "At home."

"You can't travel without it." His face became stone. He reached over her head and pulled the yellow cord strung above the windows. The engine braked and screeched, sending ashes and cinders swirling. The train glided toward the border sign for Schleswig-Holstein. The guard hut came into view, and the iron horse stilled.

The policeman took the young woman's arm. "Come. You must get off here."

She jerked, trying to get away. "No, please. I only travel a little farther, *Herr Inspektor*."

Passengers craned their necks to gawk.

When the policeman gripped her arm again and pulled her to her feet, she grabbed a stained cloth bag next to her but it fell from her fingers.

He snatched, peered inside, and thrust it into her arms with a look of distaste.

"Come along. We don't let vagabonds or criminals ride our train. You will talk to the Order Police. They handle your kind and will find out what you're up to."

"Nothing. I promise."

When she entered the aisle, she was barefoot. Her tears flowed. "Please. I'm going home to my child!" She shoved the man's chest like a terrified mouse leaps to scratch the face of the cat cornering it.

"You she-devil," he screeched. "You want to be arrested?" His slap left a handprint on her face. She would have fallen except he half-supported half-dragged her to the car's stairs. She stumbled onto the platform and into the hands of the waiting guard.

Erika trembled. As the train's wheels turned, the guard dragged the kicking and flailing young woman inside the hut. Erika pressed her face to the window to see more, but they sped past.

Father in heaven. Help that unfortunate. And help me!

Reentering the aisle, the inspector wiped his face with a large hanky. With that girl's seat empty, Erika was next.

"Terrible." He shook his head. "We have at least one criminal each day. I hope it didn't upset you, *Großmutter*. So foolish. They can't get away with it." He gave a weak smile. "Your Identity Card, please."

"How sad and troubling for you." Erika pitched her voice higher to make it squeak. "You must get tired."

"Exhausted. It makes a man old before his time. Two more years and I retire."

"So young? Still, I understand." She clucked her tongue in sympathy and opened her leather wallet. She removed her *kennkarte* and didn't have to pretend to shake with age as she handed it to him—her hands were trembling sufficiently.

Erika Hofer, born in Kellinghusen, Schleswig-Holstein, July, 1867. She favored her grandmother greatly. Thankfully, it was a typical poor government photo.

"My cousin was born near there," the man said. "She loves the area."

"Yes, it's very beautiful."

"So she says." He returned the card. "Thank you, Frau Hofer. Everything is in order. Enjoy your trip."

As he moved on, Erika released the breath she'd held. She pressed her hand to her stomach, and let her head drop back.

Her disguise had worked—she'd drawn charcoal streaks on her forehead and covered them with cosmetics to look much older. She'd dusted flour through her hair to whiten it though only a little peaked out from under her flowered *babushka* scarf above the dowdy dress. The empty bags and baskets she carried suggested she was a granny eager to shop in Bavaria's capital.

Dietrich and the brethren would return the card to her grandmother immediately.

Praise You, Jesus, that Großmutter and I share the same name. Thank you that she is a wise believer who loves me and doesn't ask questions.

At dawn, the train chugged into Munich's main station. Stiff from the long ride, Erika had no trouble appearing as tired and bent as a granny should. Stooped over her bags and baskets, she hovered behind a large family descending the railcar steps as if she belonged to them. She sighed as she left the station without incident, despite passing many *Gestapo* and other policemen posted around Old Town.

Remembering Father's instructions, she followed signs to *Marienplatz,* across the wide fitted-stone pavement, admiring imposing buildings and the soaring towers of the famous *Frauenkirche.* Soon she reached *Viktualien* Market, where the tantalizing smells of colorful fruits, sausages, and herring made her mouth water. Food must come later. First, Dietrich.

Two blocks farther, she blinked as she recognized a young man standing outside a bakery. His bicycle basket was filled with fresh loaves of crusty bread. They smelled so good her stomach clenched. He had been a seminary student accompanying Dietrich when they came to celebrate her seventeenth birthday. Was it really three years ago? Germany and the entire world had changed since then.

Erika passed street vendors to track the young man's every

move. He turned into an alley, parked his bike, and offered his hand with a smile. "Welcome back! I hope you had a good trip. Give me your baskets."

"How did you—?"

"Never mind." He gave a quick embrace and whispered in her ear before releasing her. "Lower your bundles and greet me. I'm Fritz. Do you remember?"

"I wasn't sure of your name, but yes, I'm glad to see you."

"I love seeing who God brings our way and when. Sometimes no one. Other times, treasure—like you." He tied her baskets to his bike, and they walked arm in arm.

"You've come to see Dietrich, of course."

"Yes. Is he here?"

"You're in luck—he is. Have you eaten? Have this bread." Fritz handed her a small loaf from his basket.

"*Danke*. I'm weak with hunger, and this smells wonderful." She broke off a piece of crust and ate as they walked. "Mmmm. Delicious."

Fritz pointed toward a massive building. "He lives in a dormer at the top. He only came home yesterday. It's good I spotted you."

"Gracious, it is. I prayed hard!"

"It's tricky getting up there. His garret space is hidden—only accessible by using folding stairs in the ceiling. Dietrich rarely goes out. We can't reach him by doorbell, but he expects me at this time on the days he's in town."

"Goodness. I'm even more thankful you found me."

He flashed a smile. "More than you know. He'll be happy to see you."

They crossed one last street and faced the magnificent edifice of the central *Stadtsparkasse* Bank.

Erika tilted her head to take in all four floors, both towers and ornamental arches. "Dietrich has impressive taste. How I wish Mother and my grandmother could see this."

"Ha ha. The Lord has excellent taste, and Dietrich is His

guest. There's no better place to house a priceless man of God than in the city's oldest, richest bank."

"As long as he's safe." Her eyes measured the sprawling expanse. "It looks like a palace."

"It was at one time. An armed security officer guards the entrance."

The tall, burly man in uniform stood at full attention.

Erika quaked. "How do we get past him?"

"A friend down the block runs a cleaning service and will equip us." Fritz pushed his bicycle forward whistling a cheery tune.

Erika stayed quiet but her heart prayed, *Lord, help!*

Minutes later, they approached the uniformed guard without the bicycle dressed as two janitorial workers. Fritz carried two buckets and brooms while Erika balanced mops and a stack of cleaning cloths. Fritz doffed his cap to the guard. "How are you, Heinrich?"

"*Ach*, overworked as usual. If you're here again so soon, you must be overworked also."

"Yes. Always." Fritz shrugged. "But extra work means extra pay. Today my grandmother has come to help."

The man's gaze darted to her face, and he tipped his cap. "Welcome, *Großmutter*. You claim this rascal?"

"*Ja*, if you're pleased with him and he behaves. Otherwise, maybe no."

"Ha. Well, he's a good lad most days. You can be proud." The guard turned and swung the barred door open. "Don't work too hard."

"We won't. Thank you."

They trudged up the stone stairs, darted inside the maintenance room, and after making sure the area was clear, locked the door and lowered the folding stairs to Dietrich's hiding place.

Fritz folded the stairs back into place as soon as they climbed them and rapped three short knocks on Dietrich's door. "Special delivery," he said, and stepped aside.

It took only seconds for Uncle Dietrich to recognize Erika.

"May God be praised. You're a sight for sore eyes!"

His welcoming arms comforted almost as well as Father's. Tears stung her eyes.

"How wonderful you've come! But seeing you here tells me all is not well. Come in, both of you." He stepped back. His eyes surveyed her from head to toe. "Why are you dressed like your grandmother?"

"Because I need to be her on this trip." She laughed but more tears followed. "Do you not know of Father's death or that Mother was ordered to Berlin?"

"What?" His horror-stricken face gave full answer as he reached out. "Dear girl. That's terrible. Please stop and go slowly. When did this happen?" He handed her his handkerchief. "Start with your dear father. I worried when no word came recently."

"*Ja.*" Teeth chattering and her body shaking, Erika's breath came in short gasps. "When the order came for him to join the *Wehrmacht*, he told them he was a d-doctor, not a s-soldier. He'd never held a gun—didn't know how to fight or want to—but they wouldn't l-listen. They said placing a doctor with the troops would raise morale."

"And they did that?"

Erika gripped one hand with the other but the tremors didn't stop.

"Father told them he could care for people in local towns and still serve soldiers in military outposts, but they were determined. Two weeks ago, he was killed in combat tending wounded soldiers."

"Oh, Erika, how terrible." He reached for her hands. "Such a tragic waste. If they had been wise and saved his life, he could have given years of excellent medical service. They're desperate because they're losing." He clucked his tongue. "When tyrants rule, they make stupid decisions. But all their orders and regulations can't birth a new *Reich*—only God can do that."

Her sobs lessened. "How I wish God's kingdom would come."

"Yes. Sometimes it seems overdue. And your dear mother? She's gone to them?"

"Yes." She lowered her eyes. "It still doesn't seem real. Days after Father's death, the War Office ordered her to report to Nazi Headquarters in Berlin or assemble munitions in a factory. That work is brutal, and Mother is not strong. She hoped if she went to Berlin, perhaps *Günther*'s father would get her reassigned. He's a brother in faith, but it's hard to trust him these days."

"I've heard reports, and I'm sorry. We must pray for him. It's hard to resist strong pressure."

Erika raised her eyes in a fierce glance. "Yet you do!"

"We can't compare. I've had years to deepen my convictions. I have a fiancée but no family to support."

"But you wouldn't waver."

"Erika, none of us knows until the time comes."

"I agree," Fritz said. "I'm seeing weak men stand strong and strong men weak. It's impossible until we face such moments."

"You're gaining wisdom and growing old fast, Fritz." Dietrich clapped a hand on his shoulder. "You'll be getting gray hair soon."

"I hope not." Fritz brushed his fingers through his hair, alarm wrinkling his face. "I hope not."

"Well, perhaps not right away." Dietrich smiled.

"I understand what you're saying." Erika managed a watery smile. "Mother's orders said instructions were coming assigning me to Berlin, too, but I came here before those arrived. I didn't even tell Mother my plans, so she'd be innocent of involvement."

Standing next to Dietrich, Fritz's face grew darker. Empathy shown from his eyes. "I'm so sorry. That's terrible news. I know how I'd feel if those were my parents. My father died from illness, but the loss is the same."

Dietrich waved them to his small table. "Rest both of you. I only have water and a little cheese, but I share that willingly."

"I have fresh bread to go with it." Fritz's face brightened. He uncovered his fragrant loaves beneath clean dusting cloths and presented them with a flourish.

"*Danke!*" Dietrich laughed. "I thought I smelled something wonderful. My mouth is watering."

Erika raised her gaze. "I-I wanted to work with you in the underground seminary, but since it's closed—help me know what's next."

Dietrich sliced the bread and arranged cheese pieces on a plate. "We're not sure. We're waiting on the Lord to hear next steps, but you know recent reports are not good."

"I do."

Fritz leaned forward. "There's even worse news this morning. Hitler boasts he will crush all opposing him and names you, Dietrich, as someone he will capture soon and hang."

Uncle Dietrich took a deep breath and filled a water pitcher for the table. "Ah, well. He's said that for some time. His noose is tightening, but he can only do what God allows." He studied Erika. "I'm concerned about your mother. How is she coping? How is her mental and spiritual strength?"

"She's crushed but doing the best she can. I've had no word since she's gone to Berlin. I hear there are other believers in that same office. I'm praying they connect."

"I'll join you." When Dietrich glanced at her hand, she covered her naked ring finger.

"Wait. What does your *Günther* say about all this?"

"My *Günther?*" Erika shuddered. "Nothing these days."

"I thought you two were engaged—or had a committed relationship from that summer you both helped host our kids' camps."

"We did." Her shoulders slumped. "I don't understand him

now. He's required to take *Wehrmacht* training in university. You know he loves to succeed. Each promotion makes him eager for more. He's playing a dangerous game but thinks he can benefit from Nazi training without compromising himself."

"That's impossible." Dietrich wiped his brow. "Men like Hitler long to own prize specimens like *Günther*. Can his father help him see how serious it is?"

"He could, except he's not seeing clearly himself. *Günther* Senior troubles me more than his son." Erika twisted her hands. "He was hired part time as a *Wehrmacht* recruiter and agreed because of his low village clerk income, but now he's accepted full time. We were shocked when he served the papers ordering Father to active service and brought us the news of his death."

"I'm sure." Dietrich bowed his head. "Father in heaven, our world is going mad. We must strengthen each other in these terrible times." He paled. "I'm shocked by your news. Now I know why I haven't heard from your father either. His death is a dreadful loss to us." He took Erika's hand. "He was my dear friend and confidant. We won't find his kind again."

"Thank you. He treasured your friendship."

"His death doesn't seem real. If only they'd identified the wrong man and Dr. Erik Hofer would walk in here brimming with life like always."

Her eyes filled. "I'd give anything for that. When he left, he hoped to search for my brother, Klaus. We don't know if he had that chance."

"Klaus is still missing?"

"Yes. There's been no word."

"When I pray for him, I sense he's alive somewhere but in hard circumstances."

She clasped her hands. "I hope you're right. That's what Father said too. But with things in chaos, we can't be sure of anything."

"I'll keep praying for *Günther*, and Klaus, reassignment for your mother, and the Lord's clear words for you." He tapped his chest. "Tell me what's most inside your heart."

She sighed. "I'd wanted to help with the seminary but also loved working with Father in our clinic and learning. I delayed too long, and they closed it."

"It's good you weren't there when they did. You might be in prison."

"Father agreed. After his death, I thought of running our clinic alone, but I haven't earned my full license, so the government won't allow me. I know this, though." She tossed her head. "I won't do anything to help the *Führer* in Berlin or anywhere else. I'll die first."

"Erika, that's the point." Dietrich laughed softly. "I see the fire in your eyes. Many of us may die, but I don't believe that's your destiny. We must get you out of Munich."

"Out? Why?" She lifted a foot and smacked it down so hard, it sounded like a gun firing.

"Shhh," Fritz cautioned. "No noise."

"I'm sorry." She lowered her voice. "I can teach Bible classes and encourage small groups. Don't tell me it's dangerous. Father would want me to help. I will stand to help show the world that German believers oppose Hitler's evil."

Dietrich's eyes blazed. "While that's true, we each must hear our instructions from the Lord. Here in Munich, our days are numbered. Stay a day or two for rest and fellowship but not longer. Before Hitler only wished to close us down. Now he will exterminate all who disagree with him. There's no point in you being sacrificed. You can accomplish wonderful things beyond Germany's borders."

She reared back. "But this is my country and people. Mother is here."

"For now. The truth is, she's not safe. Neither are you. We must find a safe way for you to leave."

Erika scrunched her eyelids shut. "It's impossible to leave Germany these days. And where would I go?"

"The Lord will show us. And yes, it's impossible under most circumstances, but there are ways."

She rose from the table to stand full height. "Do you think I'm afraid? Is that it? I'm a Hofer. I'm more afraid of not obeying our Lord."

"Well said. I expect no less. Keep that determination. You will need it in coming days." Dietrich also stood. His gaze did not waver.

Her resistance faded. "Forgive me. My whole purpose has been to find you. Now that I have, you won't let me stay."

"But for good reason. You understand what I'm saying, don't you?"

Fritz tiptoed to the window and peered out the curtain.

Erika joined him. "Those pedestrians milling around the paved courtyard are like ants on an ant hill. They probably think their lives have purpose and direction, and yet—" She dropped her hand. "How strange that life can appear to continue on the same as before, when these days nothing is the same at all.

"You're right. But I fear far worse days are coming." Dietrich motioned to the table. "*Bitte.*"

Fritz sighed. "Frankly, everything is in crisis. We must clothe ourselves in God's spirit, but staying peaceful is hard." His eyes questioned her. "When you last heard from Klaus, did he give any clues where he was stationed?"

"Nothing." Her shoulders sagged. "Only rumors and fears. It nearly killed our parents. Now that I'm safely here, I wish I could send Mother word so she does not fret about me too."

Dietrich flinched. "That's risky. There would be a postmark, and—"

"I'm sorry. I mean by our brothers and in code. Before the war, our family agreed on code words for sharing information without others suspecting—though we hoped we'd never need to use it."

"You were smart." Dietrich's brow furrowed. "I wish all families had emergency plans."

"Father knew the importance." She jumped up again, flinging her arms around him. "Uncle Dietrich! You're a guiding star to our family and all Christians here. You must save yourself and not let them destroy you!"

"Erika, please—"

"No, listen. Let me stay. I'll fight harder with Father gone. Let me take his place. Even if our bodies fall, we must do everything to stop Hitler from making Germany a godless place."

"I hear you, but martyrdom is not your calling." His pained look melted her. "I believe our Lord wants you to live His plans for you to bring your earthly and heavenly fathers credit."

Her eyes misted. "Is there such a place on this planet?"

"Possibly. Your Father regretted not immigrating to the United States years ago when warning signs first appeared and others in your family left."

She twisted her handkerchief in her fingers. "We had that same conversation. He said one relative in particular had accomplished good things for America. Johann Hofer should be around Father's age, and Father believed he might be on America's West Coast." She rubbed stiffness from her neck. "I wish I had listened and paid better attention. But how could I find him among so many strangers there? And even if my heart could survive it, how could I leave Germany?"

His eyebrows quirked. "Staying here is too dangerous. Hitler and his henchmen are setting many traps. Any day now, one may snap shut on me. It's a miracle we've stayed free this long. My love for your parents is the reason I cannot let you stay."

"Cannot?" She gave a painful cry.

"Yes. If you did not hear me before, hear me now. Please consider." Dietrich raised his palm and counted points on his fingers. "You are well-qualified. We need witnesses to show the world that Christians here oppose Hitler and his unspeakable evil. True light must increase until it swallows this darkness."

"But surely the world already knows." She glanced up hopefully. "This madness must end soon, don't you think?"

He sighed. "Not soon enough." He draped an arm around Fritz's shoulder. "Can you take Erika to your mother tonight and bring her again tomorrow morning to finalize travel?"

Erika stared. *He's serious. This plan is going forward.*

"Yes," Fritz answered. "Mother will like that."

"Good. As much as I'm happy to see you, it's wise to go before dark. Prepare your clothing please, Erika." He pointed to one muddy spot on her dress skirt. "Wrinkle your dress a little more, so it looks like you've been working. Slosh sudsy water in your buckets and add dirt from this houseplant in case anyone stops you." He donated some dirt from a pot.

"I can do that." She plunged her hands in the bucket and warmed to her task.

Fritz did the same. "Yes, this will work fine. Mother and I know how to play the role. May God also guard you, Dietrich." Fritz rested a hand on his mentor's shoulder. "You know I'm prepared to stay and fight too."

"I do. We'll pray to discern what God has for each one of us."

After Fritz and Erika prepared their clothing, they descended the folding stairs, unlocked the maintenance room door, and after making sure no one was nearby, hauled their cleaning paraphernalia down all four flights of stairs. They fit in well and drew no attention.

Erika followed Fritz across the stone pavement to exchange the cleaning items for his bicycle and her baskets and luggage. Then they hurried to Fritz's mother's home.

Lord, You're arranging my steps differently than I expected. After only these few hours in Munich, my life is upside down. If You're truly closing this door but opening another, please make me sure. And help me survive it.

Chapter Three

Josh listened to the voices around him, exhausted and motionless. Where was he? The pad or mattress he rested on meant he was no longer washed up on a sandy shore. God had sent rescuers. Josh vaguely recalled his journey to Midway's hospital.

"It's shocking." Josh recognized the deep bass as the doctor's voice. "This man has suffered explosions, falling debris, shrapnel, blunt force trauma, burns, severe sunburn, infections, parasites, prolonged hunger—you name it. There's no reasonable explanation for how he reached shore, let alone survived. Nurse, do we have a name yet?"

"No," a pleasant voice answered, "At times, he's semi-conscious and mumbles but nothing coherent. His dog tags weren't on him or in the rotting rags clinging to him when they brought him in."

"Strange. Maybe the medical transport team knows something about them."

"I'll ask. And I'll start a chart. How shall I label it?"

"John Doe for now."

Josh struggled to rise from crippling fog, but it was too thick

"Well," the doctor said. "The more he rests, the faster he'll recover. Check him for identifying marks."

The nurse's cool hands skimmed Josh's body. As she brushed both ears forward, she said. "There's a one-inch scar behind his left ear."

"Noted." The doctor's writing implement scratched. "He's been through rough stuff even before these injuries. Record everything. Any moles or other distinguishing marks?"

"No more that I see."

"Fine. I'll send an update to headquarters of his approximate age, height, weight. Some family's waiting to hear the good news that their son's alive. Having a last name should help someone claim him. Unless he has no family."

"Doctor, no. That would be too awful to think about."

Josh ordered his body to move, but nothing. He could not surface again. He was as entombed in sleep as if he'd been handcuffed inside a coffin. Did trauma do all this? Or had the medical team given him sedatives? Muscle relaxants? A treatment-induced coma?

"What are the odds of this man's recovery?" Concern edged the nurse's voice. "Will he return to normal?"

Josh focused. *Yes, answer her question!*

"That depends on many things. There's always a chance. At least he's alive. His lack of alertness concerns me. What medications is he on?"

"Just morphine." Papers shuffled before the nurse continued. "Goodness, his admit slip says the evacuating medics gave painkillers too. I'll note in his chart that he got a double dose."

"Make sure that's not repeated. I'll check his pupillary reaction." The doctor lifted Josh's eyelids one at a time and shined a penlight into each eye. "He's deeply under. I'm not seeing a response."

"I see slight constriction. That would be a good sign, right?"

"Yes, if you truly saw that." The doctor hesitated then repeated the action more slowly.

Josh's insides screamed. *Yes! See me! I'm here. I'm alive.*

He heard the nurse's voice again. "I thought I saw—but perhaps not."

"Well, keep checking. His overall condition is improving," the doctor said. "I see no physical cause preventing consciousness unless there's brain damage we can't see. Have you seen any signs of alertness?"

The nurse hesitated. "I'm not sure. Yesterday, when metal shelving fell, he flinched, so he's hearing. Twice when I brought water to his lips, he swallowed small sips."

"Really? That's remarkable, but it might be instinct."

"Sometimes he moans but with indistinguishable sounds. There's little involuntary movement, but if he's over-medicated—"

"Yes, that complicates things. We'll reevaluate him soon." The doctor snapped his clipboard shut. "Keep up the good work, nurse. If he becomes conscious and remembers anything at all, he should have quite a story to tell. Somebody upstairs protected him. If you see any changes in his condition, let me know." His voice faded as he stepped away.

"Yes, doctor."

The nurse's cool, comforting hand brushed Josh's forehead once again. His mind calmed and he slept.

Chapter Four

Saturday, June 20, 1942
Munich, Germany

Erika's fists clenched. She must try once more to persuade Dietrich to let her stay in Germany to fight. After all, she was another Hofer determined to oppose Hitler's Third Reich. She would stay and resist, even if it meant being sent to a concentration camp or facing a firing squad.

Erika was shocked to see all the hustle and bustle in the city streets on a Sunday morning. Were they going to churches? Or to parks and coffee houses? Fritz had told her to age herself using charcoal and flour and other things before they set off for the massive bank's towers and arches.

Today a different guard stood outside the heavy embossed doors. Fritz walked up whistling a happy tune, and Erika followed, nodding and smiling. The guard whisked them inside. They reached Dietrich's dormer garret without incident.

He swung the door open at Fritz's first knock and smiled.

"Welcome, you two. You look like quite efficient cleaning people."

"We are," Erika said. "Did you see us cross the square?"

"I was watching and praying God's protection." Fatigue lined his eyes. He'd probably had little rest for many nights. He wore a tailored dark suit and well-polished shoes.

"You look ready for travel," Erika said.

"Yes. I believe the Lord has given a travel plan." A smile tugged his lips. "I'm to accompany you."

"Wonderful!" She raised her eyes. "As much as I hate to leave Germany, if you escape to safety, I'll leave gladly." She leaned on her mop to keep from falling and moved to the small table to sit. "How soon do we leave and with what plan?"

"*Gut*." He and Fritz exchanged looks. "That's the response I hoped for. Fritz, please sit also. I've gathered these maps of Switzerland, Portugal, Spain—even Mexico for you to study. We may add more nations."

Fritz unrolled several maps and poured over them. "How am I involved?"

"Just logistics this time. Probably actual travel later. Last night, several meeting here with me agreed that Germany's days of freedom are at an end. We're already on borrowed time." His eyes warmed as he studied Erika. "Today's situation is like winter ending and seasons changing. We hardly notice ice gradually melting until one day the temperature rises just enough and then —" He clapped his hands. "Great gobs of ice choking streams crack open and rush out in torrents."

"It's more dangerous than people realize," Erika said. "Last year one of our neighbors fell in and only survived when a few of us made a human chain to reach him."

"That's what escaping Hitler is like these days," Dietrich said. "It takes all of us pulling together in a human chain."

"Very true," Fritz said. "I'm sorry to say another informant reports Hitler will unleash a new *blitzkrieg* this week to charge Christians with treason if they don't join his national church."

Dietrich bristled. "He already knows we will not."

"And he's more determined to round up and destroy the Jews."

"A number of us have been on his list a long time," Dietrich said. "Now we're also more involved helping Jewish people escape."

"*Gut.*" Erika scooted her chair closer to the table. "Hitler's troops must not take you."

Dietrich and Fritz's eyes met again. "We seek God's will for all important decisions," her uncle said. "It's still possible to cross into Switzerland or slip undercover into some eastern countries. Although there are opportunities, many of us believe our place is here."

"No!" Erika nearly shouted, "You promised to go with me if I would leave my homeland. If anything happens to you, I won't need charcoal and flour and special items to make me look old."

Fritz raised a finger to his lips. "We can't be loud."

Her voice dropped to mourning as the fight went out of her. "Without you, our people would be lost sheep without a shepherd."

Dietrich pursed his lips. "It's not as bad as all that. Hardship teaches us to hear our Master's voice. Last night when the other elders joined me, friends of your dear father, we talked and prayed until we were sure."

"Thank you." She tented her hands. "And your peace is to send me away?"

"It's not your calling to languish in prison or worse."

"And for those like Mother who are already in bad circumstances?"

"We pray for their protection and will do our best to help them. This war will end, but not soon enough. May God protect her from harm like He kept Daniel safe though enclosed with hungry lions."

She shivered. "That's a good comparison. Nazi appetites have increased, They need more scapegoats."

"I watch the streets," Fritz said. "The number of *Gestapo* doing surveillance has doubled, plus they're enlisting more Secret Police. They're increasing the reward to traitors."

"To make us all Judases." Erika's head dropped. "I was heartsick when *Günther*'s dad betrayed Father."

Dietrich took her hand. "I'm praying he and *Günther* will wake up before it's too late."

"I hope you're right. I never thought he would fall. Many times, he was the one keeping me strong."

"*Ach*, dear one, that makes it hurt worse."

"Yes." Erika swallowed down tears.

Dietrich tapped the maps. "International Red Cross workers around the world help displaced persons reach safety in amazing ways when they have to flee." His finger marked a spot. "Their world headquarters is here in Geneva. The Nazis have left the route south open for now."

She could do this. She would be the means to save Dietrich. Erika clasped her water glass so tightly her knuckles whitened. "I hate the thought of leaving Germany, but it's so important for you to go and be safe, I'll trust the Lord and take the risk."

His face firmed. "I'll travel with you to Switzerland. Your path will continue on from there. We hope there will be another Hofer safe in the United States before long."

Her mouth dropped. "As Father hoped?"

"If you have peace in your heart, I believe the Lord wants you far from here. Contacts in America should help us find your Hofer relatives and arrange refugee status."

"Goodness. My head is whirling. When do we go."

"I'm giving you information now for our practice run. We'll leave tomorrow morning."

Chapter Five

"Rise and shine, sailor. Your silver sky chariot just landed!"

Josh stirred. He had slept deeply. Or maybe he was recovering from too many drugs. Had he imagined the buzz of a cargo plane overhead and its whining scream as it landed? Facts and sounds ballooned into fiction weaving in and out of his dreams. In slumber, he confused buzzing planes with the swarms of malarial mosquitoes dive-bombing with disease payloads. They even lined up on mosquito nets, waiting for a puff of breeze or his careless movement to shift a net enough to enter and feast. Josh shivered.

Two planes last week had raised his hopes but then crushed them. Delivering ammunition and rations were priority needs for men on land or at sea. Supply crews loaded cargo planes, leaving little room for passengers or patients. Josh was lower on the shipping list than goods to be delivered.

"Do you hear me, sailor?" The orderly removed Josh's sheet. "Today's your lucky day. You're out of here." Joy filled his voice.

"There's a slot with your name on it. I'll pack these toiletries the Red Cross gave, because you never know if you'll get more."

"Okay." Josh blinked awake and struggled into the summer uniform the Navy issued, every movement a slow-motion marathon. Perspiration dripped. "Thanks for helping." He positioned his crutches. "Give me a chance to get there on my own steam."

"Negative, sailor. Not allowed. We're responsible to deliver you." The orderly maneuvered a wheelchair into place. "All transfer patients leave this way. We don't take risks. Your next stop is where miracles can happen. You can strut your stuff there."

Josh glanced around to make sure he hadn't forgotten anything, but he'd had little to forget. "Do you know where I'm going?"

"Nope. To a larger hospital with an empty bed and bigger rehab team to get you mobile. Your pilot will drop off cargo and munitions at a few more bases but arranged a bed space for you. He'll tell you where you're going. Or watch out the plane porthole and enjoy the surprise."

"Yeah, sure." Josh grimaced as he dropped into the wheelchair.

Long hours of flight over blue-green tropical seas and coconut palm-dotted islands brought him to a medical depot on Oahu.

Sure nicer seeing the ocean from above than bumping along on it while getting shot at.

Josh couldn't quit smiling. Big place. People rushing around. "We're top of the line," the medics said.

Thank you, Lord, for getting me here. Fix me up and get me ready to go back to help win this war.

He'd been strapped into a berth for safety, but air travel was exhausting. He strained to hear what was causing commotion with the intake staff at the medical center. He couldn't see the personnel on the other side of the partition, but he heard them loud and clear.

"Who sent him?" a woman's voice asked.

"Midway. They're bombed to pieces. But many bases are sending their wounded to Oahu. We're buried alive, can't do anybody justice. Besides, do you see his list of injuries? He's beyond our scope." The man sounded exhausted, frustrated.

"You're sure?" The woman again. "Nothing we can do?"

"Basic maintenance, no improvement. It's not fair to him. Read the full report."

Josh heard papers rattle.

"Major infections, parasites. Possible surgeries. I understand."

"Yes, he needs mainland care. Phone the Rear Admiral's office. See when the next troop ship sails. Get him on that list."

"Will do. So we offer maintenance until then?"

"That's right. Plus pain management and hitting the infections hard. No sense in starting what we can't finish."

A younger voice spoke. "Lucky duck! This guy will see California's coastline and reenter the USA in days!"

"I wouldn't call him *lucky* with all those wounds."

"Well, *lucky* to be alive."

"That's true."

Josh let his breath leave him. They were sending him to the mainland. Farther from the action. Away from where he wanted to be. And there was nothing he could do about it.

Erica allowed Fritz to escort her to the main train station at the end of business hours as Dietrich requested. Many *Gestapo* and special police milled about, their presence enforcing order. Erika feared they would hear her thundering heart, but they conducted random inspections of others and passed her by.

Near the railcar steps, after a conductor validated her one-way ticket for Geneva, Erika hugged Fritz goodbye. "You and your mother have been so kind. I will constantly pray for your safety."

"And we for yours. God bless you!" He lifted his hand until she boarded the train.

She found Dietrich in the second car with the window seat he'd saved for her.

"Ah, there you are. Here, take the window seat." He stood to let her pass. "I'll let you enjoy the scenery again on your way home."

"Thank you, Uncle." Although her stomach fluttered, she relished this first travel beyond Germany's borders. After the train started, she showed him the food package. "Aunt Tilde sent our supper." She shared the bread, sausage, and cheese, and settled back to absorb the trip as they lurched, rocked, and rattled southward. Dusk settled like a cloak. Even when dusk became velvet night, she pressed her face against the glass, savoring the sparkling stars wheeling overhead, except for where the silhouettes of massive mountains blocked the sky.

"*Magnifique!*" She practiced useful words for the French part of Switzerland. She must also rehearse common German-Swiss words and phrases until they came to her as easily as their High German counterparts. They were less similar than she expected and with considerably different pronunciations. Dietrich had been to Switzerland numerous times. She would rely on him.

A conductor gave each passenger one postcard displaying mountains and lakes. She longed to reach out to Mother. How she wished she could send Mother her own forged passport and ticket and write, "Flee. You must come too." Did she dare tell her about traveling with Dietrich?

Recalling the code their family devised long before Klaus and Father went to the front, she started writing.

Dear Mother,

*After you left, Aunt Genevieve sent word she had suffered a
sudden illness. I will nurse her back to health and then visit
Cousin Portia. Don't worry. I'll send details later. Please water
my houseplants and spoil my cat. Spoil yourself also.*

Love, Erika

They had no Aunt Genevieve. Mother would recall it meant Geneva. But what was Erika thinking? The code was too simple. The *SS* troops would have no trouble deciphering this message. Erika slid the card into the bag at her feet. She would keep its lovely scenic photo as a souvenir. And trust God to show another way and time to contact Mother.

As the train thundered toward the border, an exhausted Dietrich slept while Erika wrestled with leaving her beloved people. *Lord, this is hard,* she whispered. *Yet it's what You did, too, when You left heaven to come to us!* She lowered her head, but sleep was impossible.

When Dietrich roused, they chatted to maintain the ruse of an ordinary trip.

His smile matched his banter, although weariness marked his face. He clearly didn't get enough sleep, plus bore the heavy burden of the church daily.

"I'll prepare you for the frontier crossing," he said quietly. "We'll stop at the German side where they'll check our documents again. Once we're approved, we leave this train to walk across the border and board a Swiss train. Others will transfer our baggage for us. I'm thankful so far it has gone smoothly."

"I'm glad you are with me."

He gazed out the window.

"If only Mother could be here." *Help her trust You and not worry that I can't contact her. Protect her from all enemy attacks. If she needs to disappear, show her where, when, and how.*

The Lord could also keep Mother safe in the center of any storm.

According to the map posted at the front of the car, as the sun rose, the train rumbled nearer to the frontier. Erika ached to record this scenic journey with photos but she must not. Smaller individual maps were provided in the seat flap. If only she could make a scrapbook with diary entries. Instead, she tried to commit every detail to memory.

Verses from Psalm 139 echoed inside. "Whither shall I go from thy spirit? Or whither shall I flee from thy presence? If I ascend up into heaven, thou art there: if I make my bed in hell, behold, thou art there ..." *Making my bed in hell* ... was life under the Nazis. She would listen for the Lord's plan.

Father often marveled at how the Lord kept the universe spinning on its axis while giving every individual exactly the attention needed. Dietrich napped. At least he was at peace. Erika found it hard to breathe as the last kilometers of German soil slipped by. Had her luck run out? Would the *Gestapo* be waiting for her at the border? Had they discovered she'd fled and were pursuing her even now? She pulled at a hang nail on her finger until it bled.

Lord, thank you that I will never be beyond Your care.

Chapter Six

Late June 1942
Oahu, Hawaii, to San Diego

Days after the intake doctor placed Josh on the urgent medical care evacuation list, he was assigned a berth, loaded up, and sent from Hawaii on a ship to San Diego. Orderlies pushed anti-nausea tablets down him with sips of water before covering his feverish body with a light sheet. This ship was far bigger than the *Yorktown*. Before Midway, he'd managed to overcome constant seasickness. Now his battered body forgot how to cooperate and couldn't keep anything down.

At times, he longed for the sea to swallow him whole. Then Dad could call him Jonah—half-digested in a great fish's belly. Like Jonah, would Josh learn to lift his hands in praise and surrender?

Days passed in the same routine—medicine, water, and sweaty sheets changed. Finally, Josh requested, "Take me on deck."

The troop ship surged through over two thousand nautical miles of tossing Pacific Ocean waves. Blue water crested and foamed to far horizons and sloshed back until at last, on a day like so many others, radiating heat lines solidified into California's coastline. The ship's captain slowed his engines and ordered depth soundings as they churned through strong waves to the Naval base at Coronado. Horns blasted. A pilot boat guided them past a few rocky shoals to their assigned berth where they dropped anchor.

Onshore, a brass band played. People swarmed, and waved, and hugged. An orderly pushed Josh through the crowd in a wheelchair.

"Welcome home, sailor." A young recruit with peach fuzz on his chin reached out and extended a hand. "Do you need help?"

Josh waved him off. "I'm okay." Recruits grew younger every day. Or he had grown older.

"Uh, sure." The young Seaman snapped off a crisp salute. "Thanks for your service."

"My pleasure." Josh winced. Where had those words come from? He'd parroted Mom's good manners instead of speaking from his heart. Yes, he'd willingly served, but this tour had been agony. So many sailors wouldn't return home. At least, many Japanese pilots wouldn't either. Josh was grateful to breathe and maneuver in a wheelchair.

Medics came and took wounded soldiers to assigned hospital spaces based on their treatment programs. One rolled him along an antiseptic-smelling corridor in a long low building. When he opened his eyes, his tiny private room had the whitest sheets he'd seen since leaving home. *Mom, you'd smile if you could see me now.* Sinking into comfort, he prayed for dreamless sleep.

Each night, he had fewer nightmares of burning ships and fewer screams of injured, dying crewmen, along with his own cries, as he'd struggled through flaming waves. He always washed up on that distant beach where he became food for malarial mosquitoes.

It was the first time since Midway, he'd slept without fierce muscle spasms or haunting nightmares. Vivid memories of swallowing dirty, oily water gagged him.

He'd asked God to hide him from the Japanese, and the gentle brown people had done it. Mom and Dad's prayers blessed him more than he deserved. Dad taught him to tune in to spiritual things. He sensed peace here.

He was farther from the war and his shipmates than ever, but alive. He would work hard enough to walk again and rejoin them. That's what he wanted more than anything in the world.

Lord, You keeping me alive was a miracle. If You see a purpose, please show me."

June 23, 1942
Geneva, Switzerland

The border guard waved them through. "Welcome back to Switzerland, Pastor Bonhoeffer, and welcome home, Miss Hofer."

She marveled at how easily she slipped into a Swiss identity. And it was sheer joy to accompany Dietrich. The train ride lasted ten hours. A second locomotive was added to climb the steepest parts of the Alps, but then they breezed downhill past green hills and lush fields where bells jingled on every dairy cow. Finally, they reached the vast vineyards surrounding the shining lake to enter Geneva itself.

"So much history is here," Dietrich said. "John Calvin built a unique city showing how the church can govern secular things well. You must see the sites."

"I'd love to."

"We have a meeting scheduled with the International Red Cross director, but first I'll take you to my favorite café for cheese fondue and the nation's famous apricot custard tart."

"How lovely that treats can still be found in wartime," Erika said.

"Not everywhere. There are severe shortages, but somehow

this place manages. As a neutral country, Switzerland functions as international moneychangers and bankers for all of Europe."

"I know little about that," Erika replied, "but I'm eager to learn."

The colorful flags of many nations fluttered above the boulevard leading to the International Committee of the Red Cross building itself.

"That gorgeous structure reminds me of the *Stadt Sparkasse*," Erika exclaimed. "It's as sturdy and lavish as a fortress. What a shame I can't send photos home."

"Perhaps in coming days."

She discovered many people inside the offices were familiar with Dietrich and his work.

"When I came twice last year, I visited here as well," he told her. "What a delight this time my trip includes helping you."

She completed forms to update and validate her Swiss resident status. She expected Dietrich to request similar paperwork.

Instead, after passing a gauntlet of two guard-dog lesser secretaries, he spoke with a distinguished-looking man in a large private office overlooking the gorgeous lake and mountains.

"Erika? Meet Oskar Kündig. Besides being top director of this organization, he is a brother in the faith."

Dietrich confided how the Nazis had ordered her brave doctor father into battle although he was not a soldier and how he was killed nine days later.

"I am truly sorry to hear that. I met him at a church conference years ago and had the utmost respect for him. I am devastated to hear of his loss."

Erika bowed her head. "Thank you. So are we."

Dietrich also explained her situation, her need to leave Germany.

"That must not happen." Oskar expanded his chest. "I admired your father and will not let a second tragedy occur." He took Erika's hand. "Thank God, you're here. Let me consider what might be possible."

"I suspect they might try to capture her even here," Dietrich explained.

"We have had some abductions." Oskar's voice was stern.

"Hitler hates to lose. By working closely with her father, Erika possesses medical skills they desire."

"They must not have them."

Erika interrupted. "More than medical skills, I'm a Christian wanting to make a difference. When Hitler took control of Germany, Father desired that the rest of the world know German Christians oppose Hitler, even to the point of risking our lives."

"Bravely spoken," the director said. "But you are outside of Germany now. If we can keep you safe, are you content to resist from here?"

"I would, except for Father's last words to me. A branch of the Hofer family immigrated to America a generation ago. He didn't know many details, but believed a cousin was well-established there."

"*Gut*. It might be difficult, but we could try to find him." The director jotted something down.

"Besides desiring our safety, Father wished us to be testimonies of faith, opposing Nazi darkness. I believe the Lord wants me in America. Will you help me?"

The director wove his fingers together, resting his hands on his desk. "You're asking a complicated thing. I won't say it's impossible during wartime, but it's challenging. Dietrich, don't you need help reaching safety as well?"

Dietrich's dark eyes blazed. "I do not."

Erika startled. "But you must. The Nazis have boasted they will hunt down Christian leaders and named you."

"My life is in the Lord's hands." Dietrich rested his hand on Erika's then turned to the director. "My concern is for her. Is she safer traveling with a Swiss or German passport?"

The director beamed. "The truth is, some Hofers have lived in our region long before borders were divided. The phone book shows many living in Geneva."

Erika sighed. "Excellent. Then I can keep my last name?"

"Definitely. There isn't time to contact local Hofers now, but since we're a neutral nation, our Swiss passport is best. In terms of travel, some routes are closed, but the majority of emergency flights delivering humanitarian supplies and workers get through. Other neutral nations cooperate with us."

"Good. Could I travel as a humanitarian worker?"

Director Kündig's eyebrows knitted. "Here's what I think. If you stay in our guest houses for a few days, we can find you the right train, ship, or flight to a safe destination. It may take a while, but you could travel west to reach the United States."

Erika leaned forward. "Which routes are best?"

"There's no single answer. Whichever one opens first. With so many nations at war, we receive constant requests for food and emergency supplies. You could go to Portugal, the Azores, Mexico, or some other place, but we'll trust the Lord to take you where He wants you. Keep your bag packed. Stay ready."

Erika's fingers fluttered. "You're saying it could be anywhere at any time."

"Exactly. The first transportation space available will decide your destination. We won't have much notice, but the Lord will guide you as surely as He does His birds in migration."

"I like that!" Erika beamed.

"Are you at peace?" Dietrich asked

"Yes ... But I also want you safe."

The director opened his hands. "Yes, Dietrich. Please make plans for yourself. Surely you see the handwriting on the wall if you're in Germany."

"I do, but don't have peace to leave my brethren."

"Y-you said—" Erika's voice trembled. "You let me believe you were coming."

"I said I would accompany you to Switzerland. And I did."

His eyes glistened. "I did not promise to go farther. I can only do what I hear God speak."

She twisted her hands as tears spilled. "I will pray fervently for the Lord's direction to safeguard you."

"Thank you, dear one. We only want the Lord's will."

With a hand covering her heart, Erika faced the director. "I so appreciate your kindness. I hardly know what to say."

"Wherever you go, I know you will make the same good contributions to those around you as your brave father and this fine man."

The director clapped Dietrich's shoulder and pulled Erika's paperwork to him.

"Please one more question, Herr Kündig?" Erika asked.

He raised his head. "Of course."

"As you complete my travel papers, can you also prepare a set for Dietrich in case … the Lord persuades him?"

"That is something I'm very willing to do." Oskar lifted a second application packet from his desk drawer.

Chapter Seven

In the back seat of a government car, Erika twisted her gloves as Oskar and Dietrich drove her to a small airport outside of Geneva for the first leg of her flights west. She would accompany Red Cross staff from country to country on planes and ships. When it was time to depart, Oskar placed a crisp green paper in her hands.

"What is this?" Erika held up the paper.

"An American five-dollar bill to help you on your way." He folded her fingers around the currency.

"This is too much."

"I wish it were more. I don't know where you'll arrive." He also pressed a white envelope into her hand. "This is a letter for a chaplain friend of mine assigned to a major hospital on the west coast. I'm hoping you meet. If not, the Lord will bring someone your way able to help."

She held both items and took a deep breath. "Thank you for these. Now ... Well, I worry about my mother and wonder—does the Red Cross publish a report or newsletter you regularly mail to subscribers?"

"Yes—once a month to people around the world."

"Even inside Germany?"

"Yes, even there."

She handed him a scrap of paper. "Then would you please send Mother your newsletter and at the end in small writing add, 'You have a pleasant daughter.'"

His eyes crinkled. "Only that?"

"Yes. That is all I dare. More could endanger her."

"I understand." He draped an arm around her shoulder. "God bless you, Erika. It has been a pleasure. I know the Lord has good things ahead. I won't say *auf Wieder Ehen*, goodbye. Only *wir wieder treffen*—until we meet again."

"Thank you." She boarded the small plane waving as ground crewmen spun the propellers.

One day, she would tell Mother how God arranged each part of her trip. Surely this war would end soon and they could reunite. For now, widowed Frieda Hofer would be comforted by any clue of her daughter's whereabouts and any organization helping her.

The plane bounced into the sky and threaded its way among towering clouds. They reminded her of the pillar of fire and cloud that led Moses and the Israelites from Egypt's slavery to freedom—that same divine power leading her now.

As day faded and sunset's last colors lit the mountains. Geneva's city lights slid beneath the plane as it winged toward mountain darkness. She noticed a few scattered lights, but most areas were under blackout.

Goodbye dear homeland and loved ones. Goodbye war-torn church. May God preserve you until we meet again.

Dietrich's parting words of blessing rang in her heart. *"The Lord lift up His countenance upon you, And give you peace."*

Lord, strengthen me for what's ahead.

The drone of the plane's engines continued for hours. Then they lost altitude and the plane touched down to refuel. There was no moon and few ground lights. When the pilot opened the outside cabin door, warm flower-scented air rushed in. The co-pilot wouldn't let anyone disembark or say where they were. Two hours later, they visited another island and changed to a much bigger aircraft. By runway lights, she read C-47 but no other identifying mark. That flight lasted all of a long day and into darkness until the pilot directed, "Prepare for landing," and the wheels bumped down.

After long travel, Erika was eager to know their destination. She asked again, "Where are we?"

"I'm sorry, we can't say." An officer stood in front of the cockpit. "Please surrender all papers in your possession for shredding except your passport. We'll handle suitcases. Wear sensible shoes."

This long runway was in the middle of nowhere—with no visible airport or other buildings. Only the expanse of flat beige sand in every direction beyond the runway dotted with cactus, tumbleweeds, and other sparse bristly plants.

A large van different from any in Germany raced across sand to the runway. There weren't enough seats for everyone so some sat on the floor, but it carried her, and the passengers, and the flight crew some distance. Then the driver parked and waited in the late afternoon shade to avoid shimmering heat. Their clothing stuck to their sweating bodies. The driver distributed water, but it wasn't enough to slake their thirst. At sunset, they carried small bundles and shoes to ford a wide slow river. On the other side, men in plain olive drab uniforms helped them climb up the bank, one by one.

"Go to the security structure on my right for citizenship clearance," the next official said in English and Spanish.

"No need. That's covered in this document." The van driver handed over a long paper.

"Welcome to the United States of America," the official said.

"The river is our border. You'll have varying travel arrangements from here, some by highway, others by rail."

"What is our destination?" Erika asked.

"Please be patient. Your group will be divided for two destinations. But first we'll give you some food and water."

After eating, she was ushered into another van. Despite her determination to resist sleep to absorb every clue about where they were and why, she slept. When she awoke, the van drove a long day except for food and restroom breaks. At dark, they finally stopped at a small ranch miles from anywhere.

"Rest and be refreshed in this safe house," the van driver said. "We'll get an early start in the morning for the final leg of your journey."

Erika again didn't want to sleep, but the desert heat had drained her.

Before sunrise, they were on the road without complaint. Three hours later, the buildings of a sprawling city loomed to the west. Eyes questioning, Erika and the other passengers tried to make sense of the scene. Horns blasted and vehicles whizzed in every direction before the van entered a secondary road bypassing most of the noisy, crowded thoroughfares. Their final exit took them past a checkpoint to a military barricade.

The sentry left his guard post to poke his head in the driver's open window.

"Destination and purpose of your trip?" His eyes X-rayed each occupant in the van.

"Red Cross volunteers to help in the medical facility." The driver handed over a stamped paper. "Here's my Confidential security clearance."

"Yes, sir." The man saluted and lifted the barricade to a large, well-organized base.

They drove forward for a minute before Erika asked, "Now can you tell us where we are?"

"Sure. It's time. This is Naval Base San Diego, headquarters for the Pacific Fleet. My orders are to deliver you to the Red

Cross director at the medical center. He will welcome and process you, and assign you to your roles."

"Th-thank you."

The riders in the van peered in every direction. "After today, will we see each other again?" another passenger asked.

"Not guaranteed. It's a huge complex. I can promise you'll get to rest soon. It's been a long trip," the driver said, "but we're finally there. I know you're beat, but this is almost paradise." He waved a hand. "Over there's the Pacific Ocean, with waters that stretch to Japan, China, and beyond."

Erika thrilled at the ocean's rhythmic blue waves rolling to the horizon.

"The causeway to our left connects this coastline with our bases on Coronado Island. The complex is so big, I carry a map so I don't get lost."

Several blocks into the park, towering palm trees and sweeping lawns opened to a confusing network of hospital buildings. Sailors and Military Police held rifles in position, some accompanied by guard dogs. She shuddered. *Have I come this far to end up on a military base?*

July 2, 1942
Naval Medical Hospital, San Diego

Excruciating water therapy sessions gradually made Josh's scarred skin pliable enough to stretch over the worst burns. Too many weeks had passed since his Midway injuries for skin grafts to take effect. Tight puckered scars partially released. Low-impact exercises woke up some muscle groups, helping them remember to move again—but it all took time.

Questions hammered his mind. Who were the brown people who helped him? He hoped they hadn't paid a price. Headless bodies tied to stakes had been found in some places. Where was that barren island? How were his fellow sailors from the *Yorktown?* What was happening in the war during the days he'd lost?

Dear Lord, who's winning in Europe and across the Pacific? Help me leap out of bed to rejoin my fleet. Get me on my feet and out of here.

Would they treat him in this facility or send him elsewhere? Why hadn't Mom and Dad contacted him? Did they not care? Day after day, no one came but the staff delivering meds and meals. No one had come to see him, not even the chaplain. Had God given up on him too? He tuned into the all-consuming darkness.

Late one afternoon, a breathless, red-faced officer rushed into Josh's room and pointed to the name tag on his uniform. "Chaplain Eugene Merritt. I can't believe I've missed seeing you until now. This room is hidden past an odd bend in the hallway from their last hospital remodel." He held out his hand and Josh shook it.

"That's par for the course," Josh growled.

The man opened a chart. "Seriously. It doesn't line up with hospital hallway room numbers or show up on the revised floor plan."

"I'm not surprised."

"We'll fix it. Please confirm your name young man. I want my records right."

"Vengeance. Naval Seaman Apprentice Joshua Gideon Vengeance."

"Good. This says initially at Midway they mis-identified you as John Doe when you were incoherent and later wrote *Ven Jenz*, until they found there's no Navy enlisted man named that. They corrected your last name to Vengeance in Hawaii but kept the wrong one for your parents."

Josh jerked. "What do you mean?"

"Take a look." The chaplain helped Josh sit up to see the chart. "It's still V-E-N J-E-N-Z for them."

"That's nuts—not their name. That might explain not

hearing from them yet. Even the last two numbers are reversed in their phone number. How can we win a war if we don't get the details right? Do we have idiots working for the government?"

The chaplain tried to hide a smile. "Maybe we shouldn't ask that. Whoever started your chart made mistakes. People under stress do that."

"I hear you. Dad's a pastor. He'd say the same."

"What should your parents' phone number be? I'll fix it now. But the town is right, correct?"

"Vancouver, Washington? Yes."

"This may explain a lot. Several families are contacting us asking how their sons can be missing when most are accounted for."

"I guess things like this explain it. Frankly, it makes me feel a little better." Josh gave a slight smile. "Mom and Dad won't be happy."

"Not at the delay, but they'll be thrilled to get the news you're present and accounted for. I'll contact the proper authorities to get your records fixed. The sooner we start, the faster we'll finish."

"Thank you."

The chaplain started for the door but turned again. "Washington state? Interesting. I just read a news release from there. Something about a gal on a floating library boat intercepted and boarded by an I-25 Japanese sub that invaded the Columbia River. Can you believe that?"

Josh froze. "Actually, I can. It sounds like a friend of mine. Do you know her name? How did it end?"

"A major showdown. A mechanic onboard got wounded making the Japanese mines go off early. He sank the submarine but it meant the library boat had to go down too."

Josh jerked. "What? Are they dead?"

The chaplain's reply took forever. "No, they're alive. I don't know more except it was a narrow escape. The Japanese didn't make it. The Americans were wounded but saved the day. Pearl

Harbor was bad enough. We don't want Japan invading our mainland."

"For sure. That's why I have to get strong and out of here." He tugged a bedspread thread harder and it snapped in his hand. "You said a houseboat library?"

"Yes. Sounds interesting. I'll try to find out more."

"Please update me if you do."

"Sure, though they may keep it hush-hush for a while. I'll contact your folks and work on your paperwork. Don't go anywhere. I'll be back."

"Look at me." Josh spread shaking hands. "Does it look like I'm going anywhere?"

"Not yet. It's a figure of speech."

"Chances are when you get back, I'll still be here trying to absorb what you just told me." Josh ran a hand through his hair. "I think it's my friends."

"That would be a pretty small world, but if it is, it sounds like God protected them and they'll recover."

"Yeah, but it still makes me shiver."

"Understandable. I'll try to learn more."

Chapter Eight

End of June, 1942
Naval Medical Center—San Diego

Erika sat next to the van driver in the front passenger seat. As they neared the entrance to the facility, he used his travel guide voice. "Here we are, folks, final destination, Naval Medical Center, San Diego—biggest and best military medical facility on the West Coast."

She loved the huge insignia displayed at the top of the building combining the Hippocratic oath staff with a Naval ship anchor, but the strong military presence of men standing guard with rifles sent chills down her spine. It reminded her of Hitler's Germany. She trembled, and the van driver noticed.

"Don't be afraid. We're here by permission, and you've done nothing wrong. This is a good place. Red Cross Orientation will get you situated soon enough."

"Can our group stay together?"

"Probably not. We'll know soon. At least you should pass each other occasionally and see a friendly face."

After a cafeteria meal, the base commander's staff presented assignments. "There's no obligation," one liaison said. "But after checking your backgrounds, we've chosen volunteer assignments we think are good starting places for each of you. Try them for a few days. If they don't fit, come in and request something else. Erika, with your medical background, we're starting you in the patient care sector. My assistant will take you to the chaplain in charge. He's a great guy."

Erika followed the assistant to the next building. When she saw the chaplain's name on the door, she dug in the leather wallet she guarded to find Oskar Kündig's note. The names matched. This was the Navy's largest West Coast medical facility so perhaps it was the same man.

The assistant knocked on the open door. "Chaplain Merritt? I'm pleased to bring your newest volunteer."

The man pushed back from his desk and stood, his warm blue eyes giving immediate attention. "Come in and welcome."

Erika extended Oskar's note. This must be the right man. "Sir, I bring this from a friend."

The chaplain accepted the envelope. "Oskar Kündig? Wonderful. He's a good friend. How is he?"

"Fine." She smiled to the depth of her toes. "I just saw him recently."

Erika told her story of Dietrich taking her to meet Oskar.

Chaplain Merritt listened attentively. "I don't know Bonhoeffer well, but I've met him. It was during my first visit to Geneva before the war, when I was still a student. That's when I met Oskar too. Those were both divine appointments. We've stayed in touch since." He opened the envelope. "Let me see what he says."

Except for his American accent being hard for Erika to understand at first, she found Chaplain Merritt almost as easy to talk to as Dietrich. Dietrich looked older than his thirty-six years because of his burdensome care of the church. She couldn't guess this chaplain's age. Streaks of gray threaded his blond hair, but his crew cut made him look boyish. So did his cheerful green eyes edged with crinkling laugh lines.

The chaplain finished the note and looked up with a smile. "Oskar says you have good medical training but need to get to the Pacific Northwest if I can help you. Why is that?"

"I'm trying to reach a relative who I hope will sponsor me for residency. I don't know many details yet or how long it might take to find him. Here's what I do know." She filled him in.

"You're on a Swiss passport?"

She paused. "Yes. It's complicated."

He lifted a hand. "Most things are, but if Oskar worked it out, that's good enough for me. I'd be delighted to supervise your volunteer work here."

"Thank you, sir. I'm pleased."

"I'm sorry that despite your strong background, without US licensing you can't provide medical care here. You could deliver meals and patient supplies. That's what I suggest for now."

"I understand, and that's fine."

"Meanwhile, as you tell me more, I'll try to initiate a search for your family member."

"I'd be very grateful." Her cheeks warmed. "I'll do everything asked of me to the best of my ability."

"I'm sure you will." Chaplain Merritt handed her the paper clip holder from his desk. Exquisite white mountain lilies with golden centers were painted around the rim of the blue cup. "Does this look familiar?"

"*Edelweiss!* Her voice rose with delight. "How do you have that?" She immediately pictured *Günther* bringing her fresh flowers from the high peaks.

"I loved its beauty when I was in your country. Seeing it reminds me to pray for people and situations over there."

"That's wonderful and helps it seem less far away." Then she smiled and gestured toward his window. "But it's so lovely here with this warm air and gorgeous trees and flowers. It's almost paradise. If I didn't feel called on a journey to find my relative, I'd be content to stay."

"That's fine." Chaplain Merritt removed his eyeglasses, rubbing smudges from the lenses with the fabric of his shirt.

"It's hard keeping these clean," he said. "You're fortunate to be young and not need glasses."

"Not yet." She cocked her head and studied this smiling man. "Yet you are not old."

"Tell that to my bones sometimes." He laughed and slid his glasses back on. "When this war ends, I'd love to visit Germany again. Perhaps I can meet your mother and Dietrich and his group."

"That would be wonderful, but his group is hit hard. May God protect them all."

"Yes. Meanwhile, I'll begin thinking of how I can look for your relative. If I succeed, you can request U.S. residency with his endorsement. Even if it seems hard, when God is in a plan, He moves mountains."

"Yes. When do I go to work?" She stood at attention.

"If you're content to serve meals to patients in a hospital setting, I'll have the kitchen staff introduce you to our system, and you can start later today."

Chapter Nine

Josh faced the hospital wall letting gloom settle around him. Word that a library boat had sunk a Japanese sub on the Columbia River—his home ground—rattled him. What would it take to get more details?

That young woman onboard had to be Annie. What was going on? Was she on the river alone? All boats needed a support team. The chaplain mentioned a mechanic. Who was that? His best friend, Ted? He was ready to write Annie to tell her what she meant to him. He should have done it before now. He'd eaten nothing, but his stomach was nauseous. He wanted them safe, but didn't like Annie and Ted being together too much without him being there too. His jaw tightened. His pulse trip hammered to an insane rhythm.

Just then, he heard light footsteps and a knock on his open door. Dressed in a simple blue dress with a red cross stitched over her heart, an attractive young blonde woman entered his room and offered him a paper and a pen. She wore a boat-shaped white hat similar to beginning-level Navy recruits.

"Dinnertime," she called. "I must ask you to check your preferences for future meals on this card."

"Preferences? I don't have any. I'm not hungry." He ignored her and faced the wall again. "Leave me alone, please."

"No. You must eat." She cranked his bed several turns to raise him higher and rolled a food table into place over his legs.

"I said no, thank you."

But she. didn't listen. She was dedicated. Food smells drifted from her cart. Spaghetti and meatballs—usually a favorite, but not now. The heavy, greasy aroma made his stomach churn.

"Will you eat spaghetti now and choose your other meals later?" She sounded European. Her *W's* and *F's* were close to *V's*. Maybe Sweden? Or Norway?

"No."

"They pureed these noodles and tomato sauce to make it easier."

"I said no. I can't eat. My stomach's messed up. I don't want it." When he turned away, she stepped closer.

"They made it especially for you. At least taste it."

Why wouldn't she quit? He scooted to the back of the bed and lifted a hand, turning down the plate she was offering. He'd had enough.

"I said no!" His fist pounded the movable table so hard everything bounced. The table rolled, and the loaded plate flew.

Pureed spaghetti and red Marinara sauce decorated everything including her face and dress.

"*Ach. Himmel.*"

She rattled off foreign words. German? She definitely said *dummkopf*. Horror filled her eyes. She grabbed a napkin to scrub off all she could, but the damage was done. "That was not nice!"

"I-I'm sorry," he stammered, "I didn't mean—"

"Yes, you did. You haven't eaten. How are you strong enough to pound the table that hard?" She whirled away. "Never mind. I will call a janitor."

Josh stared, open-mouth, unable to speak. Most of the

pureed noodles and sauce landed on the girl, but red sauce also stained his fingers like blood, as if he had murdered someone.

Soon a burly janitor stomped in, pulling a rolling mop bucket and an armful of cleaning rags.

"What's the matter, sailor? You don't like pretty young ladies bringing you food? Or you don't like our cooking?" He questioned Josh from beneath heavy brows.

Josh's face heated. "I told her I can't eat. She didn't listen. It was an accident."

"Sure. The plate flew on its own. No help from you."

The janitor read him like a book. He swirled his mop around the floor.

"Be more careful next time. I guess there's no real harm done. Most of it cleans up with soap and water, but find a better way to express yourself. You hurt the gal's feelings." He moved his bushy eyebrows. "It will be a while before she brings you food again."

Josh hung his head. "I don't blame her, but I warned her. It was still an accident."

"Sure, buddy. Just don't do it again."

"If only I could see the young woman and apologize.

Lord, I messed up. No matter who she is or where she's from, she didn't deserve my anger. Help me fix this. Just because I'm hurting, doesn't mean I should hurt others.

Dad had taught him Bible verses could be spiritual vitamins. *If you tune in, the Lord brings the right ones for any situation.* Josh waited until Psalm 46 washed over him. *Therefore will not we fear, though the earth be removed, and though the mountains be carried into the midst of the sea ...*

The *Yorktown* going down had been like that. He tossed his head like a wounded bear. Mountains, landmarks, and too many shipmates had slipped beneath the Pacific. He could never be the same again.

Erika scrubbed a long while but couldn't get all the tomato stain out. Scrubbing food out of her uniform seemed like a ridiculous part of her war effort. What was wrong with that sailor? He said it wasn't deliberate, but he'd looked very angry. Yes, he'd suffered terribly in the war and seen teammates die while being severely injured himself, but couldn't he see she'd been trying to help? She shook her head. What price was Klaus paying? *Dear God, let him be alive.* Hopefully he didn't face anything so silly. She couldn't even afford to think about Mother and what she might be facing. She scrubbed harder at the stubborn stain.

Americans were supposed to be nice, weren't they? Maybe not. She should report this incident to her supervisor except he was so busy. No, she'd handle this problem herself. It would be a while, though, before she'd enter that patient's room again.

Chapter Ten

July 2, 1942
Naval Medical Center - San Diego

Josh tossed and turned all night. Finally, two hours before dawn, fitful sleep came, and he was grateful for a reprieve from his usual muscle spasms and living nightmares. But concern for his childhood friends plagued him. Rather than his constant living memories of swallowing dirty, oily water, he saw Annie and her floating library boat crew explode in flames.

Lord, am I imagining this? Did those things really happen?

He didn't know, but every time Josh's memories turned to Annie, he pictured Ted too. What were the other two musketeers doing back home without him? Even though he hadn't written, surely she understood how much she meant to him—his hopes to have a future with her.

Why had he never told her? The three of them were best friends through high school. But when he and Ted flipped a coin to see who would take Annie to senior prom something had changed.

He laughed remembering. It was good to win the coin toss because Ted didn't dance. Ted could be here with him now if the

Draft Board hadn't labeled him 4F for flat feet. Or if Ted had joined the navy, he might be dead like so many others.

Josh shuddered. *I don't wish that!* Tears washed his cheeks. *It's my fault, Annie. I should've shown you my heart. I just hope I'm not too late.*

Chapter Eleven

July 2, 1942
Naval Medical Center, San Diego

Josh saw men in all stages of injury and recovery during his first week in San Diego. Two veterans worked every day building up strength on parallel bars. Another gritted his teeth while learning to walk on artificial legs, but he got farther each day. Impressed with the well-equipped exercise rooms and capable staff, Josh soon understood why Hawaii had sent him to San Diego. If there were answers to improve his condition, they would be here.

Brad, his cheery physiotherapist, read Hawaii's brief report and started creating a personalized patient evaluation and treatment plan for Josh. "Yes, you have serious injuries, but congratulations on making it home. At least you have both legs attached. One amputee here lost his fight with a shark but lived. His buddy didn't."

"That's awful. We saw sharks circling, but there were so many dead and wounded in the water, the sharks—"

"That's okay. You don't have to tell me. Horrible. I can tell something or a few things smashed your back and legs, but you're lucky to have all four limbs. That's a good start right there." He took measurements and started a second page of writing.

"Seriously." Josh fidgeted. "You're writing a lot. Tell me straight. Will I get better?"

"You should, but that depends on you." Brad leveled his gaze. "You'll get better if you do the work and don't give up."

"I'm no quitter." Josh clenched his teeth. "Tell me what to do, and I'll do it."

"That's clear. You're determined or you couldn't have gone through all you have and still be around." Brad picked up another measuring tool and angled Josh's legs to different positions, stretching them farther each time. 'Let's see where we are. I need a starting point to chart your progress by. Don't get discouraged if results are slow." Brad lined up a circle and ruler with Josh's bent leg.

Josh cranked his head around to watch. "What are you doing now?"

"Documenting your flexible rotation to determine what you can and cannot do. The numbers will increase with time."

"But you're taking a lot of time and writing a book. Am I worse off than I thought?"

"Not at all. You survived a massive explosion. Most of your injuries will respond to treatment, but in small steps." He worked a tight knot out of one leg, kneading hard.

"Yow!" Josh flinched and gripped both sides of the treatment table.

"What's wrong?"

"You're killing me. I definitely feel that."

"That's good. You're supposed to. Your nerve endings are connecting when you feel pain."

"They're connecting, all right! Rub harder, and I might break your table."

Brad let up a moment. "No need to go that far. What's your pain level now?"

"What's your highest number?"

"Ten out of ten."

"I'm at least a nine."

Brad stood back. "I'll give you a short break, but gains come at a price. No pain, no gain. If you want to advance from the wheelchair to crutches and then canes, it's going to hurt."

Josh clenched his jaw determined to keep silent as Brad tortured his shins, calves, hips, and back for each hard-won degree of movement to return to normal. At times this ranked with the pain of being wounded, but he'd gladly master crutches and do the work to advance to canes and one day leave even them behind.

Brad moved around the table to change positions. "I must be doing a fine job. You're in a sweat."

"I'll say." Josh wiped his face. "But you don't have to be so cheerful about it. You're as bad as my dad."

"What do you mean?"

"He's a pastor and claims pain is good for the soul."

"I see parallels. There's probably truth in that. Just remember, even if it takes a while to earn the improvement you're after, you're steadily moving forward every day."

Josh unclenched his jaw. "I'll take your word for it. I'm glad to know you're trying to help. Otherwise, I might want to hurt you back."

"Fight that urge." Brad moved on to the next exercise. "Only five minutes of this, and I promise it's good for you. You'll thank me before long."

"I'm thanking you now. Is it Brad or Bradley?"

"Bradley, Junior, to avoid confusion."

"Gotcha. My folks almost named me Bob, Junior. I like having my own name better." He sucked in a breath. "Except it's rough getting compared to a Bible hero."

"At least he was one of the best ones."

"I guess."

Josh tightened up again as Brad manipulated his legs until

they cramped and quivered. He followed that up with a final light pounding on Josh's back, thighs, and leg muscles, then wiped him dry with a warm towel before rubbing in pungent eucalyptus oil to penetrate and calm muscles.

"Ah, that's at least soothing. But how can this do me good when I'm drowning in sweat?"

"I'll let you answer your own question. Are you seeing any improvement at all?"

"I have to confess I am," Josh said. "And I only nearly came off your table five times today instead of ten like last time."

Brad laughed. "No matter how you feel, it is all progress. You are moving considerably more freely than when you arrived. Do yourself a favor. Don't look for progress every day. Instead check your numbers once a week. Then you'll be encouraged."

"Promise?"

"I do. You can take my word for it."

During the next day's session, Josh was determined to take everything Brad threw at him without complaint. He'd absorb all Brad gave to heal faster. He did fine until near the end when his upper calf spasmed and he groaned and bit his knuckle.

"Is it that bad?" Brad stopped kneading him.

"You're probably just doing your job well and hit pay dirt. That's the deepest place you've reached yet."

"You're right, but keep remembering that pain is your friend. It proves your muscles are alive. You've had terrible damage, but your muscles are alive and responding. That's miracle stuff," Brad said. "Stick with the program, push through the pain, and one day you'll walk again."

He grimaced. "You promise?"

"Yes. If you do the work, that's what you can expect." He held up two canes.

Josh eyed the spindly things. He could barely manage on crutches. "We'll see."

Brad handed Josh the canes. "Give these a try. See how you

do with them. This is what you'll graduate to. Lots of patients don't get this far."

Muscles tense and shaking, Josh managed three steps forward by leaning on both canes before he returned and collapsed into his wheelchair. *Lord, if You'll give me my legs back, I'll do whatever You want.*

"Plus, Here's some good news." Brad lit up with a big smile.

"What's that?" Josh grunted. "I can use it."

"Despite supply shortage issues, our top brass rounded up some pyrotechnics. We have fireworks to shoot tomorrow night for the Fourth." He laughed with excitement. "Prepare for a great show starting at sunset."

"That is good news, sounds terrific." Josh beamed a big smile. "We'll all enjoy that."

His wheelchair wheels spun a little easier heading back to his room until he recognized the blonde girl who he'd spattered with pureed spaghetti approaching. He wanted to make things right. "Miss? Excuse me."

She kept pushing her cart forward without breaking stride.

"Please? Wait, Miss," Josh called again. If he could stand for even one second, he'd get her attention. "Just give me a minute."

She braked her squeaking cart to such a sudden stop, she rocked on the balls of her feet—poised to run—but turned and faced him. "Me?"

"Yes, thank you." He took a deep breath and told himself, *Do it!* "I want to apologize for what happened."

"Which time are you talking about?" She cocked her head.

He gulped. He had that coming. "When I accidentally dropped the plate. I mean, I didn't intend to plaster you with food."

"Yes, you did." She angled one arm on her hip. "I think you're angry about what happened to you in battle, but it's not my fault."

"No, not at all." He hung his head and rolled his chair several feet closer. "I am sorry. You didn't deserve my anger or getting plastered with food."

She frowned less. "At least you admit you shouldn't have done it."

"Yes, I do know that." He nodded furiously. "And I guarantee it won't happen again."

"Are you sure?"

"Yes."

When her eyes searched his face, he smiled bigger.

"Maybe you weren't angry at me, but you were angry." Her eyes squinted. "It seemed best to leave you alone."

"I don't blame you, but I hope you'll give me another chance." She wasn't making this easy. He lifted a hand in entreaty. "I see you delivering meals to other patients. Would you please bring mine again?"

She tipped her head to one side again. "I'm not sure. I'll consider." Her mouth twitched with the hint of a smile. "As long as it's not spaghetti." She pointed to a dim stain. "Tomato sauce is hard to clean. I couldn't get it all out."

"I learned my lesson. That's the worst thing I could have thrown." His face felt like it turned tomato color. Now as her lips curved, he sputtered a squeaky chuckle and she joined in with a soft laugh that sounded like heaven's music. He leaned back, sighing his relief. "Please give me a chance to show you I'm not a jerk."

"Still considering." She rearranged things on her cart.

He scanned her uniform for a nametag. Most hospital staff wore them.

"I don't see a name badge. Are you a volunteer here?"

"That's right. Your hospital nurses are so busy, we Red Cross volunteers do all the support tasks we can." She pointed to a white patch with Red Cross insignia stitched onto her bright blue dress.

"So that's who you are, Red Cross. But I don't think you're from this country."

"No." She bent over her cart rearranging something else. "You'll like today's food. This prize-winning menu includes sliced turkey with mashed potatoes, gravy, and bright red cranberry sauce." She eyed the plate and then Josh. For a moment, the gleam in her eye made him think she might toss the food at him. Instead she lowered the plate back down to the cart and smiled.

"Thanks for not throwing it."

She opened her mouth and closed it again. "I thought about it, but I have work to do." She pushed her cart down the hall to the next patient's room.

"Wait." He spun his wheelchair to pursue her. "You didn't say if you'll bring my meals again."

She studied him as if she had X-ray vision. "Maybe. If you're nice. But if you're not ..." She drew a hand across her throat.

"Scout's honor." He raised three fingers in the Boy Scout salute until her blank stare told him that his gesture probably meant nothing to someone from outside of America. The Boy Scouts had started in England, but her accent wasn't British.

She pulled something from her pocket. "You need to fill in this card showing meal preference choices that you refused to complete before."

"I will. Sorry about that. I still have the one you brought me and will do it today." He reached out his hand. "Or I'll fill out that one right now if that's better."

"No. The other one is fine." She returned the card to her pocket. "Tomorrow morning will is soon enough. I may come then." She dipped her head and hurried forward. After she completed several strides, he turned the opposite way and rolled his wheelchair back to his room. If she brought tomorrow's breakfast, no matter what was on the menu, he'd be a model patient. He needed a chance to redeem himself.

Although Erika had only said she'd consider bringing Josh's breakfast—not promised—she rolled her cart into his room the next morning. He struggled to sit up as she cranked his bed three turns and positioned his food table.

"Thanks for coming." He gave a bright smile.

"You're welcome. But you may not thank me when you see what you have." She kept her voice upbeat because this meal looked terrible. Still, this might be a good test for him to pass. She removed the plate's metal cover with a flourish. "You have Cream of Wheat and toast, but I think the kitchen didn't mix the liquid proportions right. Look." She stuck his spoon into the bowl's middle. "This cereal is so thick, your spoon stands upright without quivering."

"That's impressive." He sat up the rest of the way. "I'll try it. I'm sure it will be fine."

She bit her lips to keep from smiling. "Don't you think you should taste it before you decide?"

"No. If the kitchen made it, it will be great." He spread his napkin. "They fix good meals here, don't they?"

"Usually."

"Thanks for bringing it."

"You're welcome." She stepped back in case he threw the stuff. It might be a good weapon. "How are you feeling this morning?"

He couldn't answer because he had put the first spoon of cereal into his mouth. And chewed. And chewed some more.

"Fine," he said and pointed at the Cream of Wheat. "It tastes like the library paste we had in school when I was a kid."

She held up a hand. "We had it in my country too. I'm glad I didn't make this."

He took a deep breath, ready for another bite. "I hope this makes me strong enough to return to the Pacific. Physio works me hard, but they're building me up." He ate a second spoonful and chewed longer, trying to look like it was delicious.

"You're going back to the war?"

"Yes. That's why I'm working so hard. We need to fight so this war can end and we can have peace again.

Watching Josh made her want to laugh. Not only had the kitchen sent him this bowl of solid library paste without enough liquid to do anything but chop it in pieces, they'd also added the tiny white flag on a toothpick that marked it as a bland diet with no salt or sugar. He must think he was being punished. He had every right to complain—she would. But Josh chewed and sipped water between bites and chewed some more and drank more water until he drained his glass. When he held it out, supplication in his eyes, she refilled it. After he swallowed the last bite, he looked up.

"You didn't set me up with that difficult meal, did you?"

"No." She tried to hide a laugh. "It's a tempting idea, but I didn't. I don't know what happened, but I feel sorry for anyone getting Cream of Wheat today."

"Me too but it should stick to our ribs all right."

And then he laughed, and she did, and the atmosphere warmed.

"Now that I've behaved better, may I ask you a question?"

"Yes. Anything. You've passed a test, but I'll decide if I'll answer or not."

"Fair enough. Where are you from?"

"Far away, in Europe."

Josh nodded. "Most of our ancestors came from somewhere over there. Did you mutter German words the other day when the spaghetti flew?"

She narrowed her eyes. "That spaghetti didn't fly by itself. You made it happen. And you're mistaken. I spoke German-Swiss from a free country which is very different. Is that a problem?"

"Of course not." His voice deepened. "But I'm interested in people. If you're from Europe, it must have been hard to come here in wartime."

She sighed. "You're right—very complicated. I don't even

know all the ways we came. But now I must serve breakfast to the other patients. And hope anyone getting Cream of Wheat will be as nice about it as you were." She grasped the cart handle.

"Wait a minute." He lifted his hand. "You're with the Red Cross but I don't see a name tag. Will you tell me your name?"

Her cheeks flushed. "I am Erika Hofer. My father was Dr. Erik Hofer, a good man and excellent doctor."

"You are named after him?"

"Of course. And proud he trained me in his field. I loved working with him to learn medicine."

"But you said he *was* Dr. Hofer? Past tense?"

"Yes. Because—Because." Her face tightened, but she would not cry. "He was forced into Hitler's Army. My father was a gifted doctor, not a soldier. He was killed in this awful war."

She fled before Josh could voice the concern his face clearly expressed.

Chapter Twelve

July 4, 1942
Naval Medical Center, San Diego

Josh had returned from an extra good mid-morning rehab session when a young communications officer he had not met before dashed in.

"Here's a teletype hot off the press marked *RUSH* with your name on it. Here you go, sailor." The young man grinned and hurried through the door again before Josh could say thanks.

It had to be from Mom and Dad. His hands shook and his eyes blurred. When he cleared the moisture away, he read Dad's name in the upper left corner as sender.

Thank you, God, they didn't give up on me. His eyes filled as the wavy black printed words expressed his parents' joys and tears.

Joshua! Son! Thank God you're alive. We never gave up hope or quit praying! No matter how badly you're injured, the Lord's in charge and will help. What's your prognosis? Can you come home soon? Or shall we come to you? We'll do whatever it takes. God answers prayer. We can never thank Him enough and love you always.

We told Ted and Annie you're found. Their floating library team had some crazy challenges. They'll write soon. Your chaplain says communications are complicated, but he'll try to arrange a phone call.

Strong hugs, Mom and Dad

The next words were Mom's.

I'm so happy, I can't quit crying. I'll save ration coupons until you're home so I can cook your favorite things. I'm sure you're thin, but at least you're alive. Do you want chocolate or white cake?

Josh shook his head. Some things never changed. What made mothers show love by cooking and feeding their kids until they burst?

He started thinking of his answer even before he finished reading. *Don't worry. I'm better off than most guys here. Some are missing limbs, and I have mine. I don't need cake or anything. I just want to see you both.*

But then Dad took over again. He could hear his voice in every word—as warm as a firm hug. Josh's shoulders heaved.

Your chaplain says you'll be there a while. Just get better. That's all we want. There's a tight lid on war news, but you're closer to the action so probably know more. We're thankful Japan has backed off from invading Australia and South Pacific islands. After losing Midway, they've abandoning most southern targets. You played an important part. We're proud.

Nuts. That part stinks. Josh slammed a fist into his mattress. *I didn't do anything.* But Dad still said more. Josh hoped this teletype was free. Otherwise Dad had paid a fortune.

Mom and I saw Annie, Ted, and crew in Kelso-Longview when Governor Langlie celebrated their team getting halfway on his challenge before a runaway log rammed them. Books Afloat had to being repaired, and then more happened. Will write more soon but want to send this now. Just get better! All our love.

Josh exhaled. "Good. Annie and Ted's *team!* Others are with them. It takes more than two people to run any boat. Maybe Ted's just being a great mechanic with nothing romantic going on. It's great others are along. But then again, Annie's tempting." He frowned so tight, his head hurt.

Time flew. Before long, Erika brought lunch, cheerful and smiling. He would not let his emotions ruin things this time. "Hello again," he said with a smile.

"I'm bringing your food first this time. You asked me questions. I'll answer, but you must answer too. Where are *you* from?"

"Washington state. Eleven hundred miles straight north from here."

Her blue eyes brightened.

"Are you aware of it?"

"If you mean between Oregon and Canada, yes! I may even have an uncle there."

"Really? That's interesting. What's his name? It would be crazy if my family and I know him."

She clasped her hands. "He is Johann but probably John Hofer over here. If he's found, I hope he'll sponsor me to be a resident and then a citizen of your country."

"That sounds very good." He nodded encouragingly. "My dad's a pastor. He and Mom often write letters for recommendations—whatever's needed to help people with things like that. May I ask them if they'll help?"

"If they wouldn't mind. Would they do that for a stranger?

"My parents are very kind. They will if I ask."

"Then yes, please."

Later that day he took out paper and wrote a letter.

Dear Mom and Dad,

Long story but a Red Cross volunteer here from Europe thinks she may have a relative in Washington state named Johann or John Hofer. Do you know that name? Could you search? If you do, would you consider writing a support letter for this young woman on my recommendation?

Also, please fill in blanks about Annie and Ted. Is he part of her library challenge? Or something more? I haven't heard from either of them for ages, but they didn't know I was alive. I know it's a miracle that I am. As much as I'd love to go home and see them, I'd rather recover and return to the war.

Chapter Thirteen

July 4, 1942
Naval Medical Center, San Diego

It was hard to know what to think about Ted and Annie. The more Josh tried not to think about them, the worse it got. Finally an hour before supper, he grabbed a paper and pen and tried to swallow the giant lump in his throat. *Lord, I don't know if you're telling me to do this or not, but I have to try.*

Dear Annie,

>*I don't know the details, but Dad says you finally did it. Got a library boat to deliver books all the way to the Pacific. Or maybe you're already there. He says Ted's helping. That's great. I miss you guys. I'd give a lot to be there with you both, so it could be us three together again against the world like old times.*

>*But it wasn't meant to be. The Japs sank my ship, killed too many of my crewmates, and caved me in bad. Navy docs say I'm lucky to be alive. I hope God shows me His purpose in saving me since I'm broken up. My rehab specialist says I have to give it time.*

An anguished growl rattled his throat. He wadded up that page and pitched it toward the waste basket across the room, but he missed. Just like he fell short in most areas he tried these days.

He grabbed a second piece of paper to start over but stopped and stared at the wall. *Lord, help. I don't have any right words at all. I'm not even sure You're there.*

Erika found San Diego intriguing and beautiful except she missed the long summer days in Europe's northern hemisphere. There, in mid-summer, golden light lingered until very late. Here, in late afternoons, the sun rolled across the sky but dropped quickly like someone jerking down a window blind after gorgeous sunset colors briefly painted the sky before darkness fell.

After serving supper, Erika pushed her cart along the corridor busy collecting dinner trays and refilling water jugs. As she passed through the main hall along tall banks of windows, suddenly, a massive explosion lit the sky. A deafening boom shook everything.

Beyond the big windows, whistling rockets flashed overhead in arcs like tracer bullets.

Her heart seized. Was this another Pearl Harbor? Was Japan attacking here? They had threatened to attack the mainland. In fact, they'd dropped bombs on an oil refinery in Santa Barbara. Around her, patients up and down the hall rushed to the windows shouting and cheering. Were they crazy? Many could be killed!

Her insides tightened in a knot. *Lord, help.* Fearful for her life, she crouched below a corridor window. From the corner of her eye, she saw Josh roll forward in his wheelchair, a smile on his face. Was he crazy too? He should stop and take care of himself. Everyone was at risk. She shrieked and dropped flat on the floor behind her cart, flinging her arms over her head for protection.

With her thoughts screaming, she sensed movement near her. Someone bent down or leaned forward to reach her. She turned her face an inch and saw Josh's hand on her shoulder. He said something, but everything was so noisy and loud, it took moments to understand.

"You're safe, Erika. Can you hear me? I promise. It's just fireworks. In America we celebrate Fourth of July this way as our freedom day."

"Celebrate?" she repeated in a terrified voice, every part of her body shaking. She peeked through her locked fingers but stayed flat on the floor. "You mean fireworks—like firecrackers?"

"That's right. Big colorful ones for a special display. What did you think it was?"

She sat up several inches. "War. I thought it was war, with people dying. Like Father. And maybe Klaus, and so many." She sobbed. Her body wouldn't quit shaking.

He bent down and patted her arm. "It's not real. Only fireworks. You'll be okay." She saw him speak more words she couldn't hear above the noise, but she sensed his kindness. No buildings fell. There were no attacks or dead bodies.

As the fireworks progressed, she sat up and hugged her knees. Pinwheel clusters exploded in bright colors across the sky. How dare they look beautiful, like giant blooming flowers when they sounded like explosions bringing death?

Josh had slipped part-way down, almost kneeling to comfort her, except he couldn't manage his injured legs.

"Your father's dead, but who is Klaus? Is he in this war?"

"Yes. My brother. We're not sure if he lives or not. Hitler also forced him to go."

"I'm so sorry."

Gradually, as they watched the rest of the brilliant display, her breath slowed and her heart calmed.

"The fireworks are pretty if you know what they are."

"But loud and frightening if you don't."

Kindness lit his face. He had suffered much and had anger but cared about people. He would make someone a good husband one day, but she shook her head to chase that thought away.

She made herself calm. "I knew America celebrated an Independence Day but not that it was with fireworks."

"It's named for the day in 1776 when our Declaration of Independence was signed and took effect."

She barely raised her eyes. "I understand."

The explosions reached a crescendo with dozens of fireworks exploding overhead in loud staccato bursts. Their fading colors rained down until everything quieted and was dark.

Sulfurous smoke and fumes drifted across the lawns and inside the buildings.

"It does look and sound like war," she said.

"You're right. Just like when my ship was torpedoed and broke apart."

"How did you stand it?"

"I don't know. I don't remember much at all except weapon bursts and screaming noise before I blacked out." He shook his head. "I have no idea how I reached land. I can't figure it out. I'm lucky to be alive."

She pulled herself up and dusted herself off. "It wasn't luck. God saved you for a reason. Always remember that. My faith usually keeps me strong, but these explosions shocked me. Thank you for helping me. I—I must finish my work now." She saw the compassion on his face but rolled down the wide hallway before he could say anything more.

Chapter Fourteen

July 4, 1942
Naval Medical Center, San Diego

Josh watched Erika disappear down the hall. Strange how the deafening explosions and spinning fireballs overhead that brought joy to almost everyone on the base left her badly shaken.

He frowned at his useless legs. His situation hadn't changed. He might never return to combat, but it felt good to help calm her when she was so far from home and loved ones. *Thank you Lord, for having me in the right place at the right time. Comfort her. Thank you that I was nearby when the fireworks started so she wasn't alone. And that my arms are strong enough to propel me down these halls to help someone.*

As he rolled back to his room now, his chest warmed. The wall calendar still read the Fourth of July, the good old red, white, and blue. As Brad promised, the fireworks did stir patriotic pride and got body juices going. Too bad there hadn't been a marching brass band and a loud rousing song or two, but by the looks of it, Erika had survived all she could handle.

He glanced at the calendar again. Why did the July page

show George Washington and men suffering in snowy Valley Forge? Josh licked his lips. Someone in Armed Forces Communications got that art assignment wrong, though a little snow would be great in this hot, beautiful place. So many men here were confined to wheelchairs or crutches. Many couldn't even climb out of bed without help. It cost a high price to keep nations free, whether it meant America's independence from England or preventing a post-card painting German egomaniac from enslaving nations and rewriting history with himself in charge.

Before entering Josh's room to bring lunch, Erika arranged and rearranged the sets of salt and pepper shakers on one side of her cart. Again. She needed to work up the courage to face this man. What could she say to thank him properly? How could she explain being so terrified by fireworks that she'd dropped flat on the floor to hide?

When she knocked on his door and he called, "Come in," in a cheery voice, she relaxed a little. When she opened his door and saw him smile, that was better yet.

"Hello," he said and put aside the paperwork he'd been working on.

"Hello yourself. How are you today?" She rolled her cart closer.

"Not bad at all. After someone else served my breakfast, I hoped you were doing well and would show up later. How are you today?"

"So much better!" Her face heated. "Please forget what happened last night. Yes, I've seen fireworks in Europe, but these were so loud and threatening. They triggered every fear I had. Those were like newsreels of Hitler's bombings and burnings. No wonder the Allies want to crush him. He destroys everything."

"The whole civilized world agrees. We will stop him soon."

She positioned his lunch table into place over his legs and sighed. "I wish the whole world understood that most Germans are peace-loving. We fear Hitler. He makes our men fight a war that's not in their hearts. If they resist, he arrests or kills them."

"Is that what happened to your father?" Josh sipped milk from his glass, watching her.

"It was terrible." She turned away from the shining in his eyes and removed the cover from his plate.

Today's lunch smelled delicious—chicken pot pie with fresh salad. A chocolate brownie for dessert. He raised his fork but listened instead of eating. "That must have been very hard. Doctors want to save lives, not take them. Medical men would have an awful time waging war."

"That's true." She shuddered. "It went against everything Father stood for." She straightened the sets of silverware along the edge of her cart that were already just right. The pieces clinked against each other. "Father hunted with his camera only. When he found a rabbit in our woods with a broken leg, he splinted it until it healed enough to release. He'd never held a gun until they drafted him. He went to the front caring for the wounded but was killed weeks later when Russian soldiers overran their position."

Josh laid down his silverware. "You're saying your father was in Germany—part of the army?"

"He had to be. He had no choice. Afterward, a *Wehrmacht* officer brought his belongings and a certificate thanking us for his service." She held a hand to her throat. "We wanted Father back—not a government paper."

"I'm so sorry. I've seen the ugliness of war. I can't imagine losing my dad like that. The Allies are fighting to stop Hitler and Japan's Emperor, but I also understand how desperate any families get when their husbands or sons go to war to win that victory."

"Thank you. You do understand. But look—" She waved her

hand. "I'm talking too much, and you're not eating. It's good food this time. I promise."

"I can eat and listen." He picked up his dinner roll and spread butter on it. "Keep talking."

"My brother, Klaus, is missing in combat like you were. We've heard nothing since he went with our Northern Army to Russia or Finland months ago—he couldn't say where. His only note mentioned birch forests and frost on the ground. He could be dead or a war prisoner. It's terrible not knowing. We trembled every time someone knocked on our door."

"I can imagine." Josh lowered his roll. "It's tragic. I told you my dad's a pastor. I'm not as good at praying as he is, but I will pray for you and your family."

Her lips trembled. "Thank you. Every prayer helps."

"I believe that." He wiped his fingers on his napkin. "For weeks, my parents didn't know if I was alive or dead. I hate to think how torn up they were. When the Marines found me, I was pretty far gone—didn't know where I was or what had happened. I'd been lying on a beach with bugs biting me. When a plane flew overhead, I didn't know if it was good or bad until it strafed the beach around me. I figured I was done for."

"What a nightmare. Yet you lived."

"I don't know how. And I'm not sure why when so many didn't."

"You must understand—it was God's protection. He has a purpose for you."

"Maybe."

She quit fiddling with the silverware. "What if Klaus faces a situation like that? Not a burning beach but extreme cold and starvation?"

"It's possible. But if God rescued me, He can rescue anyone."

"I think so. It's just so hard not knowing." She folded and refolded her small stack of white cloth napkins.

"Where's your mother now?"

Erika stilled her hands. "They ordered her to Berlin to work in the *Führer's* War Office. I left before paperwork arrived ordering me to the same place. I didn't tell Mother I was leaving or where I would go so they can't blame her for my escape."

"She didn't know? That must be very hard for her."

"I know, but it's too dangerous. If she had information but didn't stop me, they could do something terrible to her."

He pushed his tray aside. "How awful. Do you have a way to contact her? To learn how she's doing?"

"I'm working on it. If I write, it puts her at risk. I won't do that to her. She's suffered too much already."

"What about contacting her another way? Or having friends do it? After losing your dad, she must be frantic to not know where you or your brother are. My mom has strong faith, but that could just about drive her crazy."

Erika frowned. "I fear for Mother but can't send her details. I long for this war to end so I can see her again. I've asked the Lord to help her know I'm safe."

"Is she in danger?"

"All Germans are in danger—Christians most of all. My friends will check on her. They find ways to help even those in prison."

Josh nodded. "That's good, but your situation is truly hard. Thanks for telling me."

"Of course." She swallowed hard. "Thanks for caring." She poured the stale water from his bedside jug down the sink and replaced it with fresh. "I thank God for my Father's example. It's awful losing him. I'm thankful he trained me in medical work. I loved helping him—seeing broken bodies recover." She stilled. "It often seems Father's with me."

Josh's voice gentled. "We all want it to end. It's true war is ..." He left off the word in his thoughts, not wishing to speak it in front of a lady.

She checked her watch and gasped. "Forgive me, I've talked too long. I wanted to thank you for helping me last night, but I haven't even done that right." Erika turned her cart so abruptly it rattled as she dashed from his room. She trembled as she realized she had told him too much of her story—where she was from and of her brother and friends in the *Wehrmacht*. Posters everywhere warned against enemy aliens.

Lord, what have I done with my runaway mouth? Make Josh forget or think the authorities know my situation. She twisted her hands. *Save me from arrest.*

What had Erika confided? She was here on a Swiss passport but from Germany? The top officials on this base must know. In no way did she seem like an enemy, but this was serious. His Adam's apple bobbed. *Lord, she's likable and spunky, but is she up to something? Show me what to do. Who should I tell? Maybe the chaplain?*

He wrote a note and dropped it in the mail box next to the chaplain's door on his way to afternoon physio.

Chaplain Merritt,

I need to talk to you privately.

Josh Vengeance

He was barely back from a good workout when Erika brought snacks.

Her eyes pled. "What I told you earlier—you must please forget it. Several officers know. Others cannot."

"Thanks for trusting me. I'm sure you have the right clearance through necessary channels."

"Yes, I do. Much hard work went into getting me here, but that's all I can say. I trust you but should not have been so open."

"It's all right. You're safe with me, but it's wise not to tell others."

"I know." Her hand shook as she held out something. "There

aren't enough of these for everyone, but these treats were just served in the officers' mess. They gave our staff the extras. Please have mine for helping me."

"No, I don't need anything." He waved her hand away. "I was glad to help." But his eyes widened when he saw what she held. "Is that a Dixie Cup? I haven't seen one of those since I enlisted." He accepted the frozen treat and turned the lid to read the label. "Yeah, this is the real thing." He pulled the paper tab and lifted the round lid to read the underside.

"Look. You might not know it, but now they're showing America's Fighting Forces instead of athletes and movie stars. It says they'll feature more tanks, planes, and ships. Maybe mine, the *Yorktown*."

"But your ship sank, didn't it?"

"Sure did—from Japanese torpedoes." When she smiled, a dimple appeared in her cheek. "The war office says we lost over three hundred men in the attack, but many more are wounded or missing."

"That's terrible."

"Yes, it is." He unwrapped the flat wooden paddle-shaped spoon from its wrapper to bring a bite of ice cream to his mouth. "Mmmm. This tastes like a kid's birthday party, don't you think?"

Her face puzzled. "I don't know. We don't have these in my country."

"And you're giving me yours? I won't let you." He handed it back. "You must have this."

"No. Thank you for helping."

"I said I was glad to help. It made me feel less useless." He held out the treat. "You've got to try this. I took one bite from this side. Grab the clean spoon on my tray and taste it."

"You don't want it?"

"Let's share. Quick. Before it melts!"

Erika dug her spoon into the swirled ice cream where the vanilla and orange flavors met. "Mmmm, this is delicious. No wonder you like it."

They scraped the cup clean.

"It was kind of you to bring this, Erika. I really do thank you."

"You're welcome. I'm glad I could."

A silver cross dangled on a chain just inside her dress. Josh had noticed it each time she moved but now she pulled it free and clutched it.

He waved his spoon. "That's a beautiful cross."

"Thank you. My father had it made for me."

"That's nice. I've been a church kid my whole life."

"If Father hadn't entered medicine, I believe he would have served the church. I don't see how people live without faith. So many Christians in Germany risk their lives to show how much we oppose Hitler. That's the main reason I'm here."

"That took courage, but explain what you mean?" He laid down his spoon and wiped his sticky fingers.

"Have you heard of our Christian leader, Dietrich Bonhoeffer? He teaches us how to live in wicked times when monsters rule."

Josh's head jerked. "Bonhoeffer? Yes! My dad honors him! He's impressive."

Her eyebrows lifted. "How do you know of him?"

"From his radio broadcasts when he visited New York. Dad also has some of his books."

"Then you know he ran a secret seminary in Germany until the *Gestapo* closed it. He has courage but is in great danger." She tucked the silver cross back inside her dress.

"Yes, he's a true hero."

"I wanted to help his underground church, but he insisted I leave to stay safe. I hated to go, but ..." Her eyes filled. "He's like an uncle to our family. For years, his summer camp was near our home. Many young people came. Klaus and I and our parents always helped." She spoke more about their summer camps and Dietrich's seminary while she rearranged her cart. "I'm talking too much again."

"No, it's fine. I'm interested." Josh extended a hand. "Does it help you to stay in America if we find your uncle?"

"Yes, because he's my relative." She wadded up her used napkin and tossed it into the trash.

"Hey, good throw. You scored two basketball points."

She laughed.

"Wait 'til I tell Dad you know Bonhoeffer. Besides praying, how else can we help?"

"Praying helps most. And of course, finding my uncle."

Josh nodded. "That shouldn't be hard. Washington's not so far away—only eleven hundred miles north."

"That far? And yet that's less distance than I've already come. You make it sound easy." She studied him. "You're really from there?"

"Sure am." He sat taller. "Check my medical record. It shows my home state."

She opened his chart and sounded out the names. "Van-cou-ver, Wash-ing-ton." Her blue eyes sparkled. "What language is that?"

"English words, but we have native Indian names too—Yakima, Chehalis, Wenatchee, Walla Walla."

"Interesting. Maybe you know people acquainted with my uncle."

"Washington is a big state, but I guess it's possible. Maybe my chaplain could work with my dad to find your uncle faster and speed up your refugee request."

Erika startled. "That's a good idea. Do you mean Chaplain Merritt? He's my work supervisor."

"I do. He's a great guy. I'll ask him if my dad can help."

Monday, July 6, 1942

Erika knocked on Chaplain Merritt's partly open door and stuck her head in. "You sent for me?"

"I did. Come in." He removed his uniform jacket and pushed up his shirt sleeves. The overhead fan moved hot air around without lowering the room's temperature.

Erika shifted from one foot to the other.

He waved her to a chair. "Sit. You're not in trouble."

"That's good." She perched on the chair's edge.

"Someone passing by during the Fourth of July fireworks said the flashes and noise upset you."

She glared. "D-did Josh Veng ...?"

"No. An orderly said you looked frightened but someone was helping you. I'm checking to be sure you're okay."

"Yes. Josh Vengeance came along and helped. He explained it wasn't another Pearl Harbor, but a celebration." She leaned forward. "Did you know he's from Washington state where my uncle might be? He wonders if his pastor dad can help you and the authorities find my uncle."

Merritt tented his fingers. "Possibly. It's interesting he's from there."

"Yes, if my uncle's in Washington state like Father thought."

"It could help to have boots on the ground. I'll stop by Josh's room to hear more."

"Thank you, sir." She floated back to work. *Lord, You are ordering my steps.*

Chapter Fifteen

Josh had struggled since Midway when he saw himself in the mirror. He peered at his facial scars to appraise the damage. The two worst stitched purple areas had partly faded but showed up ugly and brighter whenever he got cold or tired. Then, they became as vivid as neon paint on a Frankenstein Halloween mask. Sadly, what the mirror revealed was no rubberized mask he could put on or take off.

He stared again and winced. His regulation crew cut did him no favors. His Brylcreem-resistant reddish hair bristled instead of lying flat, no matter how much goo he applied. He used to laugh that only desperate guys slapped on pancake makeup to cover acne or scars. But he'd joined them. Even thick makeup didn't mask the jagged shrapnel cluster star-burst scar trailing from his left ear to his chin. *You'd think I'd remember what caused that cut unless I was unconscious.*

This morning, the lead doctor walked in. "You're making progress, Vengeance. You'll plateau soon. It might not be long before you head home."

"Home?" Josh rocked back against the wall. "That's not what I want. Let me rejoin my *Yorktown* crew. They're regrouping, and I want to be reassigned." He pounded a fist into his other hand. "Let me go fight this war."

"Sorry, sailor." The medical man shook his head. "Not yet. Full recovery might be possible, but we're talking long term. Your slower responses now would jeopardize your shipmates. Give yourself time—permission to heal."

Josh's mouth went dry. "Do you always tell it the way it is?"

"I try. We need our seamen to be in their best fighting form, or step aside when they would be liabilities."

Josh's stomach dropped. He turned from the doctor's gaze.

"Don't feel bad," the doctor said. "Hearing the truth does you a favor. When patients know their limits, they take hold and recover faster."

"If you say so. You know I've been giving this my all. I'm getting stronger, but I guess not on a fast enough timetable." Josh tried to swallow his frustration.

"Your effort is impressive. We're still considering a corrective surgery—all the results aren't in yet. We'll fine-tune your physiotherapy to see how you progress. At least you're one of the lucky ones with four limbs."

"Yeah." Josh gulped. "I see that."

The doctor tapped his arm. "Keep up the good work, Vengeance. You're doing well, but your recovery might be managed just as well from your hometown."

"When will I know? Are you saying there's no chance I can rejoin my crewmates?"

"Not for a while at least." The doctor rested a hand on Josh's shoulder. "I'll run more tests and reevaluate in a few weeks."

"You know which option I want," Josh said through clenched his teeth and watched the practitioner stride down the hallway carrying charts to take hard truth to other patients.

Could he go home to Mom and Dad broken? That sure wasn't what he bargained for. They didn't deserve that either. Or should he request further treatment in another facility that might give a tougher accelerated program? His thoughts jumbled.

Lord, what are You saying? What do you have in mind? Go? Stay? Recover? Be a burden and embarrassment? Be thankful anyway?

He couldn't think. Holding a washcloth in his hands, he scrubbed away his pancake make-up and reapplied it again closer to how the personal care nurse showed them in class. Who'd guess applying the stuff was an art form?

He had to do something about his face. He couldn't have Mom scream when she saw him. Or Annie turn pale. He practiced a crooked smile for the mirror. *That's worse. I'm surprised the glass didn't crack.*

What would Annie do? It was hard to second-guess her. On days when his brain fogged most, he hardly remembered why it mattered. But deep down inside, he knew it did.

As Josh held pancake makeup in one hand and a brush in the other, the young communications officer walked in holding a yellow telegram with Dad's name at the top—not the longer black and white Telex transmissions that now came weekly.

"Hot off the press," the young man said. "But gotta go. I'm the only guy on duty."

"Thanks." Josh pulled the message close, opened it.

JAPANESE SUB BOARDED BOOKS AFLOAT. THREE INJURED SHOULD RECOVER. TED OUTWITTED JAPS, ADVANCED DETONATION. SUB AND CREW SANK. SMITTY SAVED TED, ANNIE, AND CHAR. TED AND ANNIE ENGAGED.

Ted's a hero on *Books Afloat*, Annie's library? They sank a Japanese sub? Their neighbor Smitty Young who lived near church? It had to be. His head spun. Ted and Annie engaged? Those words slammed Josh's chest.

Dad! Tell me more! He held the telegram to the light. Holes perforated the form where censors had blacked out portions, but the closing line clearly said, "Ted and Annie engaged."

No!

The words sliced his insides worse than the torn metal from torpedoes sinking the *Yorktown*. He dropped on his bed, head in his hands, and wept until his tears became deep groanings. When he was totally empty, he swiped a hand across his face.

Personal telegrams in wartime were discouraged, yet Dad got this one through. Maybe if he told the communications guy this was an emergency ... Josh drafted a reply.

"Thankful they're alive. Ted found action? Write more. Congratulations!"

After chopping it to nine words, his throat tightened. He tasted bile. He limped to his door and hung the Do Not Disturb sign outside.

Later, someone knocked. Erika? He didn't answer. It didn't matter anyway. Annie was engaged. A half hour later, he heard a louder knock. When he didn't respond, the knob turned and Chaplain Merritt stood there.

"I got your note. I'm not sure what you want to discuss, but we should also talk about finding Erika's uncle. She says your pastor dad might be able to help."

"There's a good chance." Josh sat up, trying to hold his composure. He described his parents' role in similar projects. "And there is something else I also want to talk about. You know Erika's going through many adjustments."

"Yes."

"The July Fourth fireworks really frightened her. Weeks ago, she said something that sounded like she might be from Germany, but I thought I must be wrong. After the fireworks, she clearly said she's a German Christian here on a Swiss passport. I don't know what's going on but figure the authorities here do. She's nice. I hope she's here legally."

"Thanks, Josh." The chaplain hiked his eyebrows and pulled up a chair. "In wartime, conversations are always serious. Erika should not have been so open with you or anyone, but I can say that our top rank Red Cross and Navy officers are informed on a need-to-know basis. She's cleared and vetted at high levels."

"That's good because it sounds like she's gone through plenty. I don't want her to find more trouble." Josh lowered his head. "I also know, we have to keep America safe."

"Roger that. She's here under special circumstances that need to stay hush-hush. For her to slip in a weak moment and discuss her situation is quite a sign she trusts you."

"I know. Amazing. Especially considering our first meeting."

"Oh? What was that?"

"Never mind." Let's just say I was having a bad day but moved past it."

"Good. Thanks again, Josh." The chaplain stood and extended his hand. "I'll have a gentle word with her."

They shook hands and although Josh did his best, he couldn't keep the nervous tic in his left eye from flickering rapidly or his right leg from jiggling.

The chaplain took a longer look. "Something more is going on. You're really hurting. Can I help?"

Josh's head dropped. "Thanks—I doubt anyone can." But then the dam broke, and Josh spilled his heart. "It's about a girl back home—And my best friend—Both heroes now—Engaged —And I'm stuck here."

"That's rough." Chaplain Merritt gripped his shoulder. "I'll pray, but things like this are usually something you have to wrestle through with the Lord."

Josh groaned.

The chaplain looked him up and down. "I also believe you're man enough to do it."

Josh flinched. "Then you've got more faith than I do. I think I'm done."

"Not a chance. The Lord hasn't given up on you either."

"You're sure?" Josh met the chaplain's gaze.

"Absolutely."

After the chaplain left, Josh heard every sound in the corridor amplified, the storm wind howling and screeching outside, and the labored pounding of his hurting heart. He couldn't stop Dad's words about Ted and Annie from replaying over and over. He sobbed, pounding his pillow and grinding his teeth until they ached.

By dawn, he didn't know if he had even a mustard seed of faith left or not. If he did, the sprout was puny, sickly yellow. Not healthy green. Things looked no better when the sun came up. Sudden rain lashed his window. A fierce storm battered royal palms and broken fronds littered the ground. Josh stared at the destruction.

He was thankful Ted was alive. He'd gone with Josh to their senior sports award banquet the night things got ugly. After eating a fabulous meal for their record wins, the baseball team captain had harped on Josh about drinking with the team until he'd finally succumbed to the temptation. And Ted had been there for him during the aftermath.

Now this morning, in San Diego, Josh jolted awake, that horrible memory as fresh as if it had just happened. Ted had held Josh's head over a bowl, cleaned up the mess, and opened windows to chase out the stink. How do you thank a friend who plays nursemaid? Nothing is good enough except not repeating your mistake. How could Ted not know he'd always been the better man, flat feet and all? He had saved the day.

Mom and Dad never learned about that night. Josh figured if they did, they'd think less of him. Who could blame them? Now inside this broken body from Midway, Josh loved Ted more than ever for standing up for him.

He ground his teeth. Why did things have to change between the three of them? Why couldn't he, Ted, and Annie stay three best friends forever? Except life wasn't like that.

For years, Annie had dreamed of having a houseboat library to take books up and down the Columbia to people without them. He had to hand it to her. Somehow she'd pulled it off. Plus, Ted had managed to go along to keep her safe.

Acid burned Josh's throat. Every boat needed a good mechanic, and Ted was one of the best. They must have been nearly to the ocean when the Japanese boarded. And now Annie loved Ted, and Josh didn't blame her. He loved him too.

He swallowed a sob. He needed to hear the full report instead of imagining things. Good old Ted, stuck at home, ashamed of his flat feet, but winning a battle and becoming a hero. And Ted winning the girl while Josh sat in a wheelchair, getting sent home broken. How could he face them?

Flashbacks of torpedoes and the blazing *Yorktown* going down.

God, if I lose Annie, why did you let me live? It would have been better to let me die out there.

Beyond the window, the sweltering sun rose, burning away the last of the storm. Heat waves radiated beyond the glass. Moisture drops beaded the jug of water by his bed. A house plant by the door drooped from heat, but Josh shivered, chilled to the bone.

He limped to the window. The storm had done extreme damage. Instead of a park, the grounds looked like a war zone. Why did life swing from one extreme to the other? He caught his reflection in the mirror. Today he resembled Frankenstein more than ever. If the head doc shipped him home, he'd better seriously practice applying facial makeup over his scars and pits. Otherwise, he'd frighten everyone. Even himself. He made a strangling sound and smashed the mirror with his fist. Shards of glass shattered and flew. Without cleaning it up, he climbed back into bed and pulled a sheet over himself like a body in the morgue.

Not smart, God. You shouldda let me die.

Chapter Sixteen

July 7, 1942
Naval Medical Center, San Diego

Erika brought Josh scrambled eggs and breakfast sausages on her early rounds, but he didn't answer her knock. After trying a second time, she opened his door. He lay motionless but then raised one hand with blood on it.

"Josh? What happened?" She rushed in, stepping around pieces of broken mirror on the floor.

His blurry eyes opened. "Don't ask. Had a pity party. Made a mess. Leave it—I'll clean it."

Her head bobbed. "You did. What's wrong? You didn't eat last night either."

"Don't worry. I won't throw the food. I'm past that."

"Do you need a chaplain? A medic? You look bad."

"Big surprise. What do you expect? War does that." He rubbed the stubble on his cheeks. "Guess I'd better shave unless a beard would hide these scars better."

"I don't mean your scars. You look sad."

"I'm fine—just worried about stuff back home."

She stepped closer. "We all have worries back home."

"I know." He licked his lips. "Can I have fresh water, please? My gut thinks I'm drinking salt water."

"Sure." She ran the faucet and filled his glass. "Are you fighting old battles?"

"Something like that. Hoping to win this time, but they always turn out the same."

She focused. "That doesn't sound good. Do you want to talk about it?"

"No point."

"There might be."

He drank the water but waved his plate away.

"Oh, oh." Erika gripped his plate with both hands.

"Don't worry. I've reformed. I won't make you wear it."

"Good thing. You had me worried." Broken glass clinked as she scuffed the pieces with her shoe.

"I said leave them. I'll clean them later."

"You've cut your hand."

"Funny thing. Broken glass does that. Nothing major. Just stupid. I've done worse." He dropped back onto his pillow and closed his eyes. "Need more rest is all. I'll be fine."

She returned his plate to her cart and covered it. "Maybe you'll feel like eating lunch. I'll be back later."

"Maybe. No guarantees."

She served the rest of the ward quickly to take an early lunch break. Chaplain Merritt had asked her to pick up paperwork at Naval Administration for her refugee application. She'd mention Josh's greater depression to him too.

She walked and felt refreshed by the rich variety of tropical plants in this place. She'd seen similar beauty in Berlin's Botanical Garden as a child.

There'd been talk of an underground bunker being built there to protect the *SS* Elite Corps. But if the *Führer* was winning, why should that be necessary? No beautiful gardens anywhere should be attached to war.

She took her favorite short cut across the square. This

morning's sudden storm had done damage, but the groundskeeper crew was already restoring order. Lofty coconut palms swayed in the breeze. Fragrant cream and lemon-yellow frangipanis drenched the air with sweetness. Royal poinciana trees displayed flaming red blooms, and orchids and hibiscus in all colors festooned the grounds while chameleons darted in and out of the foliage.

As she breathed in the beauty, movement behind one palm at the left of the square caught her eye. Several people had walked past. Perhaps lingered. Echoes of the ocean's roaring breakers hitting the shore filled the air. What a place. How could she describe the paradise here to people back home?

After several more steps, she stopped for another glimpse of the azure-blue Pacific. Someone dashed from the first palm tree where she'd seen movement to hide behind a nearer one. A young seaman with a mop of short red curls peeking out from under his hat. How did he avoid the Navy regulation crew cut? Or were his curls so tight that even a buzz cut missed the corkscrews on his head?

He peered furtively, holding a camera. She was thankful she'd brought hers today and clicked gorgeous shots including the medical center's skyline. Maybe he also wished to capture the wonder of the place. She couldn't blame him. The day was perfect.

But as she crossed the courtyard, he stuck his head out from behind a large Royal Palm. He aimed the camera toward her, and she heard a click.

"What are you doing?" she shouted.

He sauntered closer. "Taking pictures to prove you're a Nazi spy. I've heard your accent. You shouldn't be here. My pictures show you sneaking photos of our base installation. That will get you locked up for a long time and me promoted to the war securities division where I belong."

"Are you serious?" she snorted. "You'll get what you deserve, but not a reward. Who are you?"

When he didn't answer, she stepped closer and read the name stitched on his blouse—B. Dahlstrom, a Corporal with two stripes. She raised her camera and took his picture.

"Don't!" He raised his hands to cover his insignia but was too late.

"Why not? I'll show *my* supervising officer that I'm taking pictures of paradise on a lovely day, but you're a suspicious sneak. Show your superiors your film." She huffed out her words. "We'll see who gets believed."

His smile twisted to a sneer. "We will, won't we?" He stepped close as if he might strike a blow. "Our troops are fighting in half the world to get rid of your kind. My evidence will show what you're up to and get you arrested."

"I doubt that."

He smirked, spun, and stomped away.

Was he serious? Did he believe what he said? She shivered. The gorgeous surroundings faded. The sun still shone, but not for her.

More people must not learn she was the citizen of a hated land waging war. Until now, most she'd interacted with had been gracious, accepting her explanation that she was a German-Swiss citizen. But she'd be naïve to think there were no suspicions.

Lord, I need protection.

Slipping her camera back into her day pack to hide it, she hunched forward and walked faster, wanting to be as inconspicuous as the small chameleons blending into the background foliage. She picked up the papers Chaplain Merritt had requested from Naval Administration and rushed to his office.

"Thank God you're here!" Holding back tears, she dropped into the chair by his desk and poured out her story.

Josh's next letter from Mom and Dad said more about Ted and Annie. Japanese officers had boarded *Books Afloat* when it neared the ocean. Her brave crew, though wounded, had achieved victory while he was a messed-up sailor with a broken body. He'd never heal enough to be the man he had been. He frowned at his still almost-useless legs. Yes, some muscles were regaining definition, but Ted's flat feet were nothing compared to Josh hobbling on crutches. Next to Ted, he was a cripple.

Annie had hugged Josh goodbye and kissed his cheek the day he'd boarded the train to San Diego for boot camp. He groaned now and touched that cheek, remembering. He'd believed it held the promise of more. He would feel her kiss forever.

Images of Annie and Ted together flashed before his eyes. If they were engaged, they might wed soon. Annie would be a married woman—Ted's wife. No more three musketeers. That would all change. How could he spend time with them again? But how could he not? His head throbbed. *Lord, I don't know how to fight this. I can't imagine not seeing them.* His insides heaved. *We're joined flesh and bone. Why did You let this happen?*

Now every time Erika walked in the lovely park, she pictured a sneaking seaman hiding behind every tree. She carried her camera in case she needed to get proof of his stalking. Chaplain Merritt had said not to worry. It was hard not to.

It helped to picture Father's kind face. And Klaus's—except his was blurring in her memory. *Lord, don't let me forget those wonderful men. Is Klaus alive? You let Jonah live inside a great fish for three days. You can keep us anywhere. Whether he's on earth or in heaven, watch over him.*

Daily, she asked the Lord to shape the next links in her life's silver chain. Quality jewelry making required hammers and fire. If she could be patient, the Lord could fashion something as lovely as the chain fastened around her neck and supporting the beautiful cross Father had given her. He had taken her to watch the silversmith. She would never forget.

She clutched it now, remembering the cherishing words Father had spoken at her sixteenth birthday as he'd clasped it around her neck. That seemed a lifetime ago. The whole world had changed since then.

Lord, you are marvelous and your ways past finding out. I wonder what milk and honey will look like in Washington state.

Chapter Seventeen

July 10, 1942
Naval Medical Center, San Diego

"Josh, if we're talking about the same man," Dad's telex message said, "he's a local hero—a modern Robin Hood, doing good and helping people. Years back, he and our neighbor Smitty worked together in aeronautics. They and Ted deserve medals for their recent rescue during the Columbia River-Japanese crisis."

Wow, Josh thought, *how had the general public not heard more of this?*

As soon as the official Department of the Navy notice of Josh's survival had reached his parents, happy telexes and letters flew back and forth. In today's communication, Dad mentioned John Hofer. He might be Erika's relative. Josh wrote a short return message for Whiz in the Communications office to send back.

ASK HOFER IF HE'S RELATED TO DR. ERIK HOFER OF
GERMANY. HIS DAUGHTER ERIKA IS HERE VOLUNTEERING
WITH THE RED CROSS BUT NEEDS A US SPONSOR.

Whiz labeled that *Top Priority* and sent it clicking and whirling through the air waves.

Josh wouldn't tell Erika anything yet—no point in raising her hopes. Dad had cross-checked the Hofer name and it matched. There must be a family tie.

Erika hummed when delivering lunch trays today. One melody sounded familiar, but Josh couldn't place it. It was something Mom had the church choir sing at Christmas or Easter.

Did Christians sing the same hymns in Germany? And then he recalled the song—Martin Luther's, "A Mighty Fortress Is Our God, a bulwark never failing ..." Yes, Germans had written some of the best. How did Erika trust God when she faced so many losses and unknowns? He'd failed her too.

Josh was doing the hard rehab work to recover to be a hero sailor again. He built muscle daily by swinging on crutches to the exercise room, sometimes twice a day, mastering crunches, balance, and weight building. His weaker muscles took on definition. Not everything had improved, but he was getting stronger.

He logged almost an extra mile going back and forth to Whiz's office, and soon made himself swing along on crutches instead of using a wheelchair. *Even if my legs don't smarten up, I'll have fabulous arm muscles.*

He couldn't change world events, but he could control his body. Brad's demanding exercises took all Josh's grit, but he couldn't deny the results.

"There's a science to it," Brad said. "I have charts galore to show you which tendons and muscles control which movements. We fine-tune exercise road maps to produce flexibility and strength. When people sit around, they atrophy. You see examples all around you."

"For sure." Josh gulped. "No matter how hard it is, I won't quit."

His respect for therapists soared. Josh hadn't thought of

physiotherapy as a medical science, but it made sense. The practitioners worked miracles. How hard was it to become one?

Two days later, a telegram sang back across the air waves. Whiz skipped into Josh's room, and Josh prepared his heart. "What have you got this time?"

Whiz grinned. "Good news, I think. This one says, 'yes' and 'yes.' You didn't propose to some gal, did you?" He waggled his eyebrows. "Lucky you!"

"Nothing like that. You watch too many movies." Suddenly lightheaded, Josh sagged against the door jamb, making Whiz reach out for him.

"Oops. You okay?"

"Yeah. Just tired."

"I'd better head back, but if you need anything, let me know."

Once Whiz left, Josh hobbled to his bed to read Dad's words.

MET HOFER. YES, HE'LL CLAIM ERIKA, KNEW OF HER DAD.
HE'S OPEN TO SPONSORING ANYONE WHO ESCAPES HITLER.
HEROISM HAS EARNED HIM FAVOR WITH THE AUTHORITIES.

Dad didn't mention Ted and Annie, but this other encouraging news sent Josh swinging on crutches all the way to Chaplain Merritt's office. What had been physically impossible weeks back was easier now. When he showed Chaplain Merritt Dad's transmission, smile lines crinkled around his eyes.

"This sounds fabulous. I'll complete her refugee application and rush it to your dad."

Just then Erika's noisy cart rattled down the hallway with afternoon snacks, and Chaplain Merritt waved her in.

"Come in. We have news." The chaplain didn't hide his smile.

She read the message and teared up.

"I'm so thankful. It sounds like it might work. Should I laugh or cry?" She giggled while a tear ran down her cheek. She hugged Chaplain Merritt. And then Josh.

Chapter Eighteen

July 17, 1942
The Columbia River, Washington state

Hopping from one leather-clad foot to the other near a campfire in the woods by the river, Johnny Hofer crowed when he opened the telegram Smitty had just brought him.

"This says I have a niece on a Swiss passport who escaped Hitler and made it to San Diego." He stopped and read the words again. "I don't know how she did all that, but I'll find out. She wants to come here. Wants me to sponsor her."

"You have a Swiss relative in this country? Traveling here?"

"She says so. Anyway, Hitler is a cesspool of human infection hiding in that mountain fortress he calls the Eagle's Nest, but I call it a rat's nest if he's there." He slapped his leg. "I'll do all I can for any brave soul opposing him. This young gal says we're related. I've heard of a Dr. Erik Hofer, so could be. How exciting that this old coot might have a relative show up?"

"I'll say." Smitty chortled. "Congratulations, Johnny. No wonder you're all grins. It's like the stork finally flew low and found you. You should hand out cigars. But a niece showing up will change your bachelor life, won't it? Make you a family man?"

"Only for the better. I can adjust." He smoothed down his springy hair. "I don't imagine my life here is like anything she's known."

"Definitely not."

"I hope she's up to it."

"If she's a Hofer," Smitty said, "chances are she'll do fine."

"Hand me those steaks you brought. I'll get them on the fire."

"Good, I'm starving. What about our undercover work? Do we tell her anything?"

"We'll wait and see." Johnny pulled a packet of salt and pepper out of one pocket and sprinkled it on the meat as it sizzled. "We'll watch to get our questions answered. It shouldn't take long to figure out."

"That means we've got serious praying and listening to do." Smitty shook Johnny's hand. "But if she's related to you, she's probably amazing. This should be fun."

Chapter Nineteen

Erika waited with Chaplain Merritt as he knocked on the senior officer's door. When a muffled voice answered, "Come in," Merritt stood aside.

"Ladies first, Erika." He smiled encouragingly at her and saluted as they entered the office of Rear Admiral Bill *Horse* Jensen. Then they waited for the Admiral to invite them to sit. Jensen controlled all troop and supply movement to and from the San Diego base. No personnel traveled anywhere without his approval.

After a full minute of standing at attention, Merritt said, "Admiral?"

Only then did Jensen look up and grunt, "Why are you here?"

"For our scheduled appointment regarding this young woman's excellent volunteer service in our hospital, sir. We've found her sponsoring relative in Washington state and request transport so she can join him."

Jensen leaned on his elbows on his desk. "Washington state? Don't we have enough troops to transport without helping non-

Naval personnel? That's what the Red Cross and other agencies are for."

Erika studied the Admiral as he still left them standing. Was he forgetful or rude?

Chaplain Merritt shifted his feet. "If you would permit us to sit, sir, and give Miss Hofer a minute to tell her story."

"Very well, sit." The Admiral sat back. "But a minute is all you'll get."

Erika's throat constricted like she'd just swallowed a woolen sock. The squeaky sound she produced first would have made a mouse proud. She cleared her throat to try again.

Lord, give me Father's courage. Reaching Washington may depend on this man. After she presented the condensed Red Cross-approved version of her journey, Merritt immediately praised her excellent work as a hospital volunteer.

"Her paperwork is in perfect order," Merritt added, laying it on Jensen's desk. "Her temporary resident status is pre-approved by Washington's Governor Langlie because of her uncle's exceptional service to that state and our nation."

"Is that right?" the Rear Admiral boomed. "More than most people?" He tented his fingers under his chin, his steely eyes drilling Erika's face. She returned his gaze without flinching.

After a painful silence, Merritt spoke again. "Admiral? You've heard our case. Erika's residency approval is in place. She only needs one-way transport. Will you help?"

Watching the Admiral reminded Erika of volcanic eruptions. A vein in his neck pulsed. His jaw ticked, and his ears reddened.

"You expect me to help someone with a German accent travel on our dime?" Jensen asked in a gritty voice. "Not on your life. I don't care how good your report is, you might be spying for that guttersnipe. In fact, ..." He shuffled through papers on his desk and picked up one. "Here's a complaint lodged against her."

He waved the report by the sneaky seaman.

Erika's heart sped up. "But, sir, there's no truth in it."

The Admiral glared. "When I want you to speak, I'll say so."

She sucked in a breath. *Have I come this far to be stopped now?*

Merritt leaned forward. "Sir, I've learned that same corporal has made similar charges against other individuals. They all proved false."

"I'm aware, but we must consider the facts each time. Something he says may be true. Why would a foreign girl come here seeking US residency?" Jensen fixed her with a dead-fish stare. "Young lady, if you're doing anything underhanded or criminal, pulling a fast one on our great nation, I assure you I'll find out and prosecute. I hate everything German. I don't even allow sauerkraut, brats, or apple strudel to be served in our mess hall."

Erika shrank in her chair. *Dear Lord, this must be what it's like when the Gestapo interrogate people.*

"I don't care how much you've done for our hospital. It isn't enough, do you understand? Make your way north some other way—like hitchhiking or swimming." His lips curled above the shiny medals on his uniform. "I won't help."

"Admiral, please—This young woman has passed all surveillance checks and given dedicated voluntary service." He shot Erika a reassuring glance. "She has the full support of everyone she's met and worked with."

"Except mine." The Admiral sat as unmoving as a toad carved of stone. "And mine's the only one that counts."

Every instinct urged Erika to plug her ears and run. Instead, she gave no reaction except for gripping her chair with both hands. Was this bullying officer's hatred so different from Hitler's?

Jensen's jowls quivered. "No matter how hard you work, young lady, it's not enough. You've been heard speaking German. You could be a spy. We should ship you back where you came from."

"Are you serious?" Merritt's voice shook. "Why are you so resistant to this reasonable request?"

Jensen's chest puffed. "You question me? I don't owe you an explanation." He glared, spitting his words. "Don't ask me to help anyone or anything German. And that's my final answer. See yourselves out and close the door behind you."

Merritt saluted but his Adam's apple bobbed. "Thank you, sir. Good day, sir."

Trembling, Erika followed the chaplain into the hall. Her eyes burned, but she would not cry. "That man won't stop me. I will find a way to travel."

"Of course, you will," Merritt said. "We'll find other avenues. Even a cantankerous Rear Admiral can't stop a determined young woman when God is opening the way."

She jutted her chin. "I agree with you, but I don't agree with anything that man said."

"Neither do I. I don't believe he'll have the last word this time."

Chapter Twenty

July 22, 1942
Naval Medical Center, San Diego

This was more like it. Josh held the two-page letter on thin airmail sheets. Dad had come through again.

You remember our retired tugboat neighbor, Smitty? He's friends with Hofer so arranged a meeting. When we told him a niece of his made it here and wants residence, he lit up like a Christmas tree. 'Blood kin? A brave girl escaping Hitler? Good for her! I'll meet her when she arrives. I'll do the same for any relative escaping Hitler's rat hole.'

He's interesting, Josh. He doesn't look wealthy but must have some means to offer financial help. I won't forget meeting him downriver last week dressed in green and brown leather patches with a homemade cap.

Smitty says Hofer dresses that way for undercover work. All he needs is a bow and arrow to be a modern-day Robin Hood and probably has those stashed somewhere. Once we hear Erika's

*travel schedule, Smitty and I will also meet her so she's not
frightened by her uncle. Anyone seeing him in wilderness garb
would be shocked, but he probably doesn't always dress that way.*

Josh puzzled over the description. His imagination ran wild. How strange could the guy be? For now, at least, maybe he'd keep Dad's description of Hofer to himself.

Two days later, Chaplain Merritt called Josh to his office. He arrived on crutches at the same moment Erika did.

The chaplain waved them in. "Please sit down, both of you. Here's an update on Erika's travel options. It's true Rear Admiral Jensen handles all transport, but an officer above him approves all final departures. That's my friend, Bruce "Butch" Hotchkiss. We serve on humanitarian committees together. When I told him how Jensen had acted, he was *not* happy. He's decided to intervene."

"Was he surprised?" Josh asked.

"Not at all. Everyone knows Jensen's history of prejudice, but until now it hasn't affected operations. Hotchkiss will put a stop to it."

Erika leaned forward. "What can he do?"

"Give higher orders. And he explained how Jensen got his attitude. Turns out his only son, Bill Junior, is on a cramped subchaser in the Pacific. The men walk hunched over, crowded in like sardines because their passageway floors are stacked with canned goods under plywood. They're seasick most of the time. The Japs have sunk sixteen subchasers, and Billy said conditions are so bad, some men pray to be sunk too."

"That's awful," Josh said. "But I don't get it. Since his dad's a Rear Admiral, how come the son isn't at Annapolis?"

"That was the plan so he'd be career Navy. But when Roosevelt's draft bill passed, the day Bill Junior's Army draft letter came in the mail, instead of opening it, he rushed downtown to a Navy recruiter and signed up. There wasn't time to contact his dad. Enlistment put him on active duty at sea on a subchaser. That experience has been so bad, he's sick of the Navy. Says if he makes it home, he'll go so far inland, he can't see the ocean and learn a different profession, like carpentry."

Erika shrugged. "Is that bad if he's alive?"

"It is in his father's eyes. He wanted his son to follow in his footsteps. That's why Jensen hates Hitler and Germany and all enemies with such a passion. He claims it's ruined their family by breaking his heart and ruining his wife's health. He refuses to help anyone or anything connected to Germany, Japan, or Italy."

"I get it." Josh winced when he crossed his legs. "I'm glad my dad doesn't expect me to follow in his footsteps. I'm not a good fit."

Merritt scrutinized him. "I'm not sure of that. If not now, perhaps later. Or God may have a completely different path for you. Either way, I see fine qualities in you. But Jensen's story doesn't permit him to treat people that way. Hotchkiss is also investigating that corporal, Dahlstrom's, accusations. It turns out he's done this several times, but each complaint has been unfounded. He'll be called in to explain. I don't envy him."

"I don't either, but that's good." Erika unclenched her hands.

"Erika, I hope you know how pleased our hospital staff is with you," Chaplain Merritt said.

"Really?" she shrugged. "I haven't been here long."

"But long enough for them to notice. They recognize good service when they see it. By the way, Hotchkiss is also trying to find travel vouchers to get you to Washington state.

Erika choked up. "That's wonderful news. I'm amazed that people here are willing to go out of their way. That's truly kind."

"It is," Josh agreed. "I love it when officers go out of their way for ordinary folks."

"The good ones do. And Hotchkiss is top-notch." Chaplain Merritt turned his calendar pages to the coming week. "We get little advance notice before plane or train seats open up. They fill quickly on an as-needed basis. Hotchkiss says to keep your bag packed. That way, if there's an opening, you can grab it."

Her eyes brightened. "That's easy. I couldn't bring much with me, so I mostly stay packed."

Josh checked his watch. "Oops, I have a physio appointment I can't miss. Fill me in later on anything I miss."

Erika stood. "I have to go too."

"Stop by any time. God bless you both."

<hr>

Because Erika's transport could happen soon, Josh decided to hint at his dad's comments about her uncle. As she arranged dinner items on the tray table over his bed, he said, "Not today. Let's push the table aside. I want to eat sitting up in a chair like a healthy man. I've been an invalid long enough."

"Good for you." Erika beamed.

"But please take a minute to sit with me." He gestured to a chair against the wall.

"Just for a minute." She pulled the chair closer.

"I'm not sure what my dad means, but he says sometimes your Uncle Johnny dresses strangely for work assignments. He might look unusual when you meet."

She cocked her head. "Unusual? That could mean many things and maybe different here than in Europe. I guess I'll find out."

Josh picked up the letter. "He adds, '*Sometimes when needed, Johnny shows up looking like Robin Hood in a green fringed jacket and leather moccasins. Other times he might resemble a lumberjack or Indian scout.*'"

"Really? He sounds interesting." Erika hiked an eyebrow. "Creative and fun—not boring. That makes me want to meet him more."

Josh frowned. "What if it's hard to recognize him?"

"Since we haven't met, we may both be surprised. He'll probably have the flashing Hofer eyes. I'm asking the Lord not to let him be disappointed in me."

"I'm pretty sure that won't happen." Josh smiled. "In fact, I'm writing my folks now. But instead of mailing it through Navy channels, I wonder if you'd deliver it in person? My folks and a retired boat captain neighbor plan to meet you too. I'll bet a letter you carry will reach them faster than regular mail."

"Probably." She laughed. "That's a nice thought." She glanced at her arms. "Look. This trip will really happen. I'm getting goosebumps."

Chapter Twenty-One

July 26, 1942
Naval Medical Center, San Diego

In very early morning, Erika heard loud pounding on her door.

"Erika, it's Captain Merritt. Rise and shine. Your plane is waiting."

"What? Now?" Erika scurried about her room. When she opened her door, she stood fully dressed and ready.

"Good girl That was fast. Is your bag still packed? There's a seat on today's Skymaster, but we have to hurry."

"Really?"

"Guaranteed. They're warming up the engines right now, but they know you're coming. Grab your bag."

"Can I have another minute to gather toiletries?"

"Just one. I have your residency papers. We'll go straight to the airfield."

She latched her small suitcase shut. "I should pinch myself."

"Later. Come on." He grabbed her case. "I'm as excited as you are."

"Wait. Let me check my room once more." Her eyes swept in

every direction. She grabbed a pair of slippers partly tucked under the bed.

"You can buy more of anything where you're going."

"You're right." She paused. "I guess there's no time to tell co-workers goodbye."

"I'll do that for you." He grinned. "And I'll tell Josh. The US is huge, but with an uncle in Washington state, you'll probably see Josh again. I'm sure he'd like that too."

Her eyes scanned the room one last time. "Done!"

"Good, let's go."

She closed the door, hiked a small carry-on's strap over her shoulder, and climbed into Merritt's Jeep. She had barely shut the passenger door before he revved the engine and roared to the airfield.

"Are you ready to hear how you got this seat?"

"Yes. How?"

"It was Jensen's. He was scheduled for a top-level meeting in Seattle but on its way, the plane stops in Portland. Now he'll be traveling at least a day late if he makes it there at all. Last night he ate three portions of deep-fried squid and got the worst gallbladder attack our base doctors have seen."

"Truly?"

"Yes. He's in the hospital with our best surgeon standing by. Jensen's not going anywhere, so his seat is empty. Hotchkiss ordered me to get you to the plane in time."

He mashed the gas pedal so hard, she jerked back flat against the seat, unable to stop smiling. Soon, she'd be with Uncle Johann.

Every morning, seagulls and songbirds outside Josh's window sang him awake—different birds than back home in Washington state. He learned to identify them by their sounds just like he did the types of planes taking off and landing daily at the nearby airfield. The morning's Skymaster had departed on time, its noise just fading.

He flexed his arms and legs to get the blood pumping before climbing out of bed. He'd head to physiotherapy for his morning workout after Erika brought breakfast. Minutes later, a wheeled cart rattled across the corridor's tiles, except the footsteps behind it were not hers.

Someone rapped on his door.

"Breakfast."

Hearing a man's deep voice, Josh hobbled to answer. The orderly was someone new.

"Dark toast or white? Coffee or tea?" the man asked.

"Erika knows."

"That's fine, but she's gone." White teeth flashed in a happy face. "You probably heard her plane leave. She's on today's Skymaster. By now they have great views of the Pacific coast."

Erika had flown on planes in her travels, but on nothing this big or fast. She buckled the seat belt for takeoff, thoroughly enjoying Rear Admiral Jensen's comfortable spot near the plane's front. She stretched her legs and leaned against the window for its full view.

She heard words from Isaiah. *They that wait upon the Lord will arise on the wings of eagles.* Soaring high—like now—across each step God had arranged to bring her to this new branch of her family and life.

Another scripture song bubbled up, *The steadfast love of the Lord never ceases. His mercies never come to an end. They are new every morning, new every morning, great is thy faithfulness* ... As a child learning those words, she hadn't understood how true those promises were.

At takeoff she caught one last glimpse of Balboa Park with its coconut palms and azure waters along San Diego's sunbaked golden hills. She lowered her camera. No photo could do these scenes justice. Could heaven be lovelier?

They stopped once to refuel. They were halfway there. She clutched the seat's armrests so she wouldn't float up through the plane's roof for sheer joy.

She smiled each time she reread the telegram from her uncle that Chaplain Merritt handed her as she boarded the plane.

Dear niece,

I'll be so pleased to meet you. When you land, cross the tarmac to Visitor Arrivals. I'll be your handsome German-looking relative waiting there. If you have any trouble, contact Washington's Governor, Arthur Langlie. He's willing to help. Safe travels.

John Hofer

Despite not wanting to miss anything, she dozed above part of California's coast. The seaman steward moved along the aisle serving fresh coffee and sandwiches. Erika's stomach dropped as the plane hit air pockets, making her as giddy as a kid on Christmas morning—or someone about to be sick. She grasped her seat's arm supports tighter and eyed the air sick bag tucked behind the seat in front of her. *Lord, don't let me need that.*

In northern California, one cone-shaped snow-capped mountain rose taller than any in Germany. The steward identified it as Mt. Shasta, part of the Cascade Mountain chain of dormant volcanoes stretching from Canada to Mexico that could erupt again.

Erika shivered. *Not today, please.*

Finally, the plane began its descent in wide slow circles. Still glued to the window to see everything, she noticed a glittering river flowing from a tall silver mountain in the east to farther west than she could see. Soon the plane's engines changed sounds. Its wheels dropped and its propellers quit spinning. The wind shrieked as it raced over the aircraft's wings and the brakes engaged, letting the plane touch down and race along the runway.

Erika patted her hair and shaded her eyes at the top of the plane's steps. Her heart pounded so hard, it was hard to focus her eyes or even know where to look. Blue sky overhead, more gorgeous snow-capped mountains above forest-carpeted hills along the shining river. And people—one related to her, from the same bloodline as Father. A row of them stood in front of a low concrete block building. She gulped a breath and donned her brightest smile. There was no turning back.

Lord, thanks for each step. I still please need help every moment, but You didn't bring me this far to abandon me now.

She smoothed her travel-wrinkled clothes and swallowed down her fear. Carrying her small suitcase plus the carrying bag on her shoulder, she put one foot in front of the other and descended the metal stairs to begin the next stage of her life.

Chapter Twenty-Two

July 26, 1942
Portland Air Base, Oregon

As Erika approached the long low Portland Air Base building, she saw no one resembling Robin Hood or anyone unusual. Perhaps her uncle was downriver doing undercover work. Thankfully, Josh had also described his dad and their retired sea captain neighbor, Smitty. She recognized them right away even before they introduced themselves and gave handshakes and then hugs.

"Welcome to your new home," Bob Vengeance said with a smile so much like Josh's.

"Mighty pleased you're here," Smitty, the retired tugboat captain said and tipped his hat. He was older than Bob with neatly combed white hair and electric blue eyes that flashed intelligence and fun.

"You'll both be fun to know." Erika laughed as part of her nervousness fled.

Josh's father was a bigger, older version of Josh with deeper laugh lines. He grabbed her small suitcase while Smitty hoisted her shoulder bag.

"My wife and I feel we know you already," Bob Vengeance said. "Sue can't wait to meet you."

Smitty craned his neck. "Your uncle said he'd be here, but I don't see him."

Just then, a beaming dapper man in a three-piece suit gave a hearty laugh. He stepped forward holding a creased fedora in his hand. His thick wavy gray hair was nicely trimmed and his leather shoes polished to a high gloss. He bowed from the waist and extended his free hand to her.

"*Willkommen, Liebchen,*" he said in a pleasant voice. "I'll claim you as I see our family's bright eyes flashing humor. Except yours are blue and mine are dark."

Kindness glinted in his as well. He folded her into his arms in a hug as comforting as Father's.

"How great you've come so far. I believe I'm your uncle, John Gerhardt Hofer, but most folks call me Johnny. From what I can tell from Mother's Bible, your father is my grandfather's youngest brother."

"Good. That helps put things in place."

Josh's dad and Smitty turned and stared.

"Johnny?" Smitty's mouth dropped.

"That's me." Erika's uncle bowed again and courteously greeted his friends. "Fooled you two geezers, did I? Goes to show I can manage social niceties when I have to."

Smitty gasped. "Not only fooled me, Johnny. Left me speechless, and we've been friends forty years." He eyed Johnny up and down. "I've never seen you gussied up this much."

"I never had a reason but just goes to show I can." Johnny chuckled deeply again. "We're never too old to keep learning." He waved a hand. "Plus, I like keeping you two guessing."

Erika fidgeted. Why had Josh made it sound like her uncle was odd when he stood here quite presentable? Or did his friends' shocked reactions mean there was more to the story?

Johnny stepped to the side to let an attractive well-dressed woman join him.

"Nice to see you, John," she said, clasping his hand and then Erika's. "I'm Irene Pruitt, Governor Langlie's top aide. He wished to be here today; but state business detained him. He looks forward to meeting you soon."

"How kind. Please thank him for his support," Erika said.

"No thanks required. We're thrilled you're safely here. We appreciate your uncle and want to make your time here pleasant, beginning now." She held out a stiff gold-edged paper. "The governor designed this welcome certificate to give you free meals in our Evergreen Hotel for your first week plus local bus service for your first month here. It also provides a suite for the next three nights in the same hotel, our city's finest. Let us know if you need anything extended."

"He didn't have to do that." Johnny reddened.

Miss Pruitt glanced his way. "Of course, not, but he wanted to."

Johnny faced Erika, his ears still red. "Several of my homes need repairs and updating. I'm considering which is best to live in. Maybe I should let you look around and decide."

"Anything is fine, Uncle, I'm happy with any arrangements you make. And thank you, Miss Pruitt, for your kindness. I'm impressed and grateful." Erika ducked her head as one does with royalty.

As Miss Pruitt stepped aside to greet Josh's dad and Smitty, Erika surveyed her uncle more slowly. "You are not what I expected."

"In what way?"

Her cheeks heated. "I was told sometimes you dress simply or strangely for work."

"Simply or strangely?" He tented his fingers beneath his chin. "That's a nice way of saying *odd*. So, people have been telling stories. Ha-ha, ho-ho, that's rich, isn't it, Smitty?"

Smitty turned beet red.

They chuckled again before Johnny returned his attention to

Erika. "My dear girl, you're not what I expected either. You're better."

"Really?" Her shoulders eased.

"By far. I know few girls of any nation who could travel halfway around the world alone in wartime."

She shifted her feet. "But if it's necessary—"

"That doesn't make many able. I'm mighty proud. And neither of us had a photo to work from and probably wondered what we would find at the other end of the trip, but we've both done quite well."

"I'll say." She chuckled again.

"I'm happy to have genuine family here. It means a lot." The tear glimmering in his eye brought mist to hers.

"I'm sure you have tremendous stories about your travel here, and I want to hear them." He rubbed his hands. "We have years of catching up to do, so we'll need to start soon."

After retrieving Erika's bags from Josh's dad and Smitty, he took her elbow to guide her outside. On their way, a man carrying a camera stepped from the crowd and raised it. "Just a minute, Mr. Hofer."

"Not today." Johnny blocked him with an uplifted hand and then approached a sleek gray sedan and opened the car door for her.

"This is yours?" Erika asked.

"Yes. I'll let you drive it sometimes if you like. It's not my usual transportation but fine for town."

"That's kind, but I haven't learned to drive. Back home, we walk, ride busses, or take trains."

"Maybe I'll teach you."

Erika prickled with excitement as she took in these new sights. Vancouver on the Columbia River reminded her of Heidelberg on the River Rhine. Did she dare send Mother a letter now?

Could she mail a postcard to Berlin with coded words that she was enjoying days with the other side of the family? Mother might understand. Or was even that too risky? *Lord, protect her!*

For now, Erika loved exploring this scenic area. And getting to know her uncle.

"When did your parents leave Germany?" she asked over dinner in the hotel's elegant dining room. Their juicy roast beef reminded her of German *sauerbraten* except it hadn't been marinated and there were no juniper berries. If those grew here, she would gladly fix that special dish for Uncle.

"Our family sensed hard times coming and left over a generation ago," he answered. "My parents came separately as teens and met at church here. My father was a Hofer on your dad's side of the family."

"Father told me he was very sorry they did not understand the warning signs sooner. He greatly regretted waiting too long. That's why he was excited to recall you were here. He said if I ever had a chance, I must do everything possible to find our blood relative. And now, with the Lord's help, I have."

"Yes." Johnny covered her hand with his. "I'm thankful too."

"The Lord helped incredibly. One day I will share the scariest parts. I was given a Swiss passport, but that's not the whole story."

"I assumed that was borrowed unless you had married a Swiss with the same last name."

"No, I haven't married." Her cheeks heated as she redirected the conversation. "My fast acceptance here seems tied to you being a hero honored by America's government. What did you do?"

He cleared his throat. "I'm not free to discuss much of that. I don't know what Josh might have told you of his friends, Annie and Ted. They are the true heroes and deserve full credit for destroying a Japanese submarine. Smitty and I only picked them up later. They'll be home tomorrow. I'll let them share their story."

Erika leaned forward. "Josh speaks well of them but doesn't know details of their adventure."

"That's because the government wants to keep the facts quiet in case more Japanese subs try the same. We don't want them to know how we destroyed the first one."

She shivered. "If that happens, I'd like to be there to help."

"Not so fast. I don't want you near that kind of action." He closed his eyes. "I'm considering the best plan for you here and asking God to help your brother and mother too. Getting your permanent residence should also happen fast since we're related. If more in your family can come, I'll help them as well."

"Perhaps if they see me succeed, others will try." She'd love that to be true. If only there were a way, especially for Mother. As they visited, Erika sometimes lapsed into German until Johnny cautioned, "Our language isn't popular these days during wartime. I slipped at the airport but speak it only when we're together or for an urgent need. People fear what they don't understand. They may get suspicious."

"I will remember."

He patted her hand. "Let me explain more about how I live and where. Most of my residences are small and far downriver, hard to reach and not suitable for a nice young woman. I'll spruce up a town place some and let you remodel, but I have to keep a low profile."

Her imagination exploded with possibilities. "I want to be a blessing, not a burden. Let me fit into your life as much as I can to help you. Once I have resident papers, I can work or live anywhere."

"You're welcome to live with me as long as you want."

"Thank you. I also look forward to meeting Christians here —and more of your friends."

"That's easy. As you know, Bob Vengeance pastors a fine church. His wife Sue and everyone else there wants to meet you."

Her happy laugh joined her uncle's cheery one, except his

deep chuckle sounded like a bubbling stream splashing over rocks.

"The Vengeances are great people. Until I get a town place ready, they're offering you one of their spare rooms."

She worked to keep disappointment from her voice. "That's nice, but I don't know them."

"You will. They're easy to know. You and I'll see lots of each other while we do the remodel except for when I'm downriver."

"May I go with you sometimes?"

He paused. "I'm considering. That may not be easy, but I hope to answer you soon." His thoughts appeared to drift. "My family has stayed small. I never married, and now it's too late. It blesses me that the Lord brought you here. I'm listening for what good things He has in mind."

His gaze warmed her. She hoped he would say more.

"Like I said, Josh's best friends, Anne Mettles and Ted Vincent, should be back tomorrow. They're eager to welcome you and help you get settled."

"That would be wonderful. Josh thinks the world of them."

Johnny shot a glance from beneath his bushy brows. "Did he tell you they're planning to marry?"

She frowned. "I don't recall. I'm sure I'd remember if he did."

"He may not know, but it's wonderful they survived and can plan a future together. They're so happy, they look like they swallowed the moon."

"Swallowed the—?" Erika shrugged. "Americans say such funny things. I think you and Captain Smitty helped save them too."

He cocked his head to slant a grin. "It's like a potter working clay. You need good material to work with. Gritty, sandy material falls apart, but once the rough stuff gets kneaded out, the rest is smooth and sticks together. Annie and Ted are the best."

She loved the humor in Uncle Johnny's dark eyes. They made him look younger, like a playful elf. That might be a Hofer trait.

Father's eyes were a similar shape but blue with gray tones, like Klaus's eyes—and her own when she glanced in a mirror.

Where else had she seen eyes that easily revealed someone's thoughts? Clear and honest? Josh's face and his gray-green eyes flashed into her memory. At first, his eyes mostly brooded, but now they sometimes sparkled. She shook her head. Josh was a patient. She must only think of him medically. Except now he was also a friend.

She had believed *Günther*'s eyes were truthful, but he'd proved her wrong. She still tasted bitter shame. How could she have trusted him? And truly cared when he did not?

She'd shown poor judgment. Never again. Yet young *Günther* had been different. But when he came with his dad to the Hofer porch ordering Father to war—that showed his true colors.

Now Uncle Johnny introduced her to these beautiful, peaceful scenes. She would live out Father's life here in these surroundings—the part he'd been robbed of living. And do the same for Klaus if he didn't survive. Her stomach spasmed. *Lord, please let him live! Why should I be allowed to have a life of my own in such times? One must live for God and country, not self. That is clear. I will do my best.*

Chapter Twenty-Three

August 1, 1942
Naval Medical Center, San Diego

After a minor back surgery and a month of increasingly difficult physiotherapy routines, Josh waited for his update. He was glad to see Brad walk in smiling

"You came through that corrective surgery fine and are healing fast," Brad said. "Your major muscle groups are starting to release and glide more smoothly into remembered patterns. Those gains are from *muscle memory*," he explained, "Even the best therapist can't make healing happen. Let's measure today's range of motion to update your records."

"You're saying I'm doing well even if I don't feel like it?"

"That's right. You may think your progress is slow, but frankly, you're amazing!" He arranged Josh's legs into figure fours and then folded them further into pretzels. "Tell me when it's all you can stand."

"*Arghh*. I'm there. If I didn't know you were helping, I'd think you were trying to kill me."

"Naw, you're smart enough to know the difference. See this gadget?" Brad held a device that looked like two rulers joined by a circle with degrees printed around its edge. "This goniometer measures range of motion. Incredibly, you've gained four more degrees since last week. Your hard work shows!"

Josh managed a half smile. "Thanks. Glad you noticed."

Brad stretched Josh's legs in new positions. "You're making progress but aren't ready to return to a ship. Our head doc is impressed and wrote a personal note at the bottom of your chart."

"Let's see." Josh craned his neck. "What does he say?"

"To review your progress in a few more weeks to decide your next steps."

"Does he check on all of us?"

"Yes, every individual. That's his job." Brad pointed to scribbled words at the bottom of Josh's chart.

Josh squinted. "I'm glad he's staying abreast of progress. It means a lot."

"He's a fine guy who cares about our patients. For you, the likely choices are a little more therapy here or returning home for out-patient therapy from there."

"I'd like a third choice of having me rejoin *Yorktown* survivors?"

"That's not an option yet. But our head doc is aware of what you've been through and that you're fighting hard for every inch of ground you retake."

"Good to hear."

"Yes, it is. Move to this side. Let's send him new numbers to make him even happier."

"Fine with me." Josh grinned and sat up taller.

Brad recorded the improved numbers before setting the chart aside and rubbing cooling menthol ointment into Josh's muscles. "You're making gains through determination and elbow grease. You're one tough fighting man." Brad's eyes met Josh's. "I'd say you're living up to your last name by chasing recovery with a vengeance."

Josh flexed his muscles. "I'd never thought of that, but I like it."

"Don't blame ya." Brad tapped him on the back. "That's enough for today, but I'm proud of you."

"Thanks." Brad's encouragement soaked into Josh more deeply than the cooling salve. He took a deep breath. "You see that much determination in me?"

"I sure do. Don't you?" Brad's gaze stayed steady. "You're the kind of patient therapists dream of. Let me show you what I mean." He spread two charts on the therapy table. "Here's where you started, in these low troughs. Despite a few low places, you now mostly have peaks and valleys. Your numbers are moving up steadily and rising more." Brad returned his pen to his pocket. "Even if you stopped now, you'd live a good life, but you'll go further. I can't see you settling for anything less than full recovery."

"Great!" Josh pumped a fist. "That's how I feel, and I won't stop. Set higher goals. Push me hard so the doc *has* to return me to active duty with the *Yorktown* crew."

Brad cleared his throat. "Uh, those aren't the two options he wrote down."

"I don't care. Hit me with everything you've got. If my body lines up, he'll change his mind."

"That isn't how it works. Our bodies don't heal that fast."

"Well, that's what I'm aiming for. Don't hold anything back." He stuck out his hand to Brad. "I hope you know how grateful I am for you getting me there."

"You're a pleasure to work with, Josh, but I hope you're listening. People who push too hard sometimes lose ground. What I want to know is, weeks from now if we find we've taken you as far as we can with in-hospital therapy, why are you so against going home to do the rest from there with occasional out-patient visits at your nearest military base? Lots of guys would jump at that chance."

"I'm not most guys." Josh's head hung. "It's not only the

physiotherapy. There are relationships back home I don't know how to mend."

"Uh-oh. Does one involve a girl?" Brad closed the chart.

Josh felt his face burn. "Maybe."

"That happens a lot these days. Last year when I was on a ship in the Pacific, I got a Dear John letter that nearly killed me."

"You did?" Josh winced. "I didn't know you'd been at sea. How are you now?"

"Recovering. It took a while, but hurts less now. San Diego is almost paradise—a fabulous place to heal."

"I'll say. Palm trees, flowers, sunshine." Sitting on the therapy table, Josh studied Brad. "Maybe you understand this part too. My folks are great, but if I'm sent home—I don't want to burden them—or anyone."

"I get it, but I don't see you that way. You're less broken than you think. Anyone who's been through what you have might not feel ready—even when your muscle groups work. Most of us have scars besides those that show on the outside. You know that don't you?"

"I guess." Josh raked a hand through his hair. "I wanted to go home a hero—not damaged goods."

Brad sputtered. "Get over it, Josh. You're far from damaged goods. I wish you could see yourself right." He squeezed Josh's shoulder. "Your hard work is paying off. Your biceps are rocks. Better than most guys. You might out arm-wrestle me."

Josh couldn't hide his smile. "They're stronger. That's from using crutches so much."

"It's all good. We'll give you more time and watch carefully. Our head doc will make recommendations. I'll review and probably add my signature to what he says. Are you okay with that?"

Josh shrugged. "You're a good guy and in charge. I have to be."

Brad tucked Josh's chart under his arm and walked down the hall to his next patient.

Josh sat on the therapy table a while staring at the wall, a dozen scenarios hammering his head. Was he ready for this—facing Mom and Dad? Annie? Ted?

***

Bone weary but on stimulus overload, Erika couldn't relax enough to sleep. She lay awake listening to the night sounds of Vancouver, Washington. When traffic stilled, the surge of the mighty Columbia River rolling nearby echoed through the window. Fewer cars passed outside during nighttime hours. Light, quick steps barely sounded in the hotel hallway. She'd left her bedroom door open a crack so light filtered in when the hallway door opened and someone entered.

Erica rubbed her eyes. A small man dressed in fringed green and brown leather wearing a Robin Hood type cap raised a finger to his lips as he passed, smiling. He entered Uncle Johnny's bedroom and shut the door. She shook herself. She must be seeing things. Or dreaming.

The next morning, Uncle Johnny emerged from his room dressed in a business suit, hair neatly slicked back, and greeted Erika with a hug.

"Good morning. Did you sleep all right?"

She blinked twice trying to reconcile this image with what she'd seen in the night. "I think so, thanks, except—"

"Except?" His dark button eyes shined, innocent and bright.

"Maybe I flew too many miles so I'm imagining things. In the night, I thought someone slipped through this hallway into your room. Did you leave during the night and return?"

"Did you think so?"

"Perhaps—I'm not sure."

"Being over-tired plus traveling so far in a short time is unsettling. Things should stabilize soon. I'll show you more of

Vancouver today. Later, Bob and Sue Vengeance invited us to lunch at their home."

"What shall I wear?"

"What you have on is fine. You couldn't bring much, so I'm sure you need to go shopping."

She glanced at her simple travel outfit—a streamlined brown skirt below a white tucked in blouse beneath a matching fitted brown jacket. Not her usual preferred style, but businesslike.

"You're right, I couldn't bring many clothes. Is there somewhere I can do laundry?"

"Sue will know. She's wonderful. You'll need to buy clothes for your life here too. Vancouver has great shops. She can take you or someone else I'm thinking of could help. I'll give you cash for everything you need."

"You're kind, Uncle, but I don't want to take advantage of you. Once my paperwork is finalized, I'll get work and pay you back. I want to provide for myself."

His face crumpled. "Blast. Another proud Hofer! Sometimes we go too far. Let me be a doting uncle. Your coming gives me joy. I'm blessed and earn well enough, so spending is no problem. I like helping others. Don't take that privilege from me."

"Maybe I didn't say it right. That's not what I meant." Her stomach tightened as she fought tears. "It is nice being cared for, but it's important for me to go forward on my own."

"I see. I hope you'll accept a compromise for now. Let me help you this time, but I'll check with you any time I want to do more."

"Thanks." She nodded. "That will work."

"It's clear you don't want to take anything for granted. Yes, we Hofers are an independent lot."

"That's not bad, is it?"

He guffawed. "No, I should say not. I often wish more of the world were that way. But we also care for our own. Let me claim you for a while at least." A smile crinkled his cheeks. "Who knows? You may support me in my old age."

"You?" Now she laughed. "I'd be willing, but old age won't claim you for a long time."

"You're kind." He patted her shoulder. "Let's go eat breakfast. New friends are waiting downstairs to meet you."

Scrambling as nimbly as a goat in springtime, Johnny rushed down the hotel's stairs instead of using the elevator. Erika clattered after him. A young man and woman stood near a stainless-steel steam table filled with inviting dishes giving delicious aromas. Their faces lit as she and Johnny reached them. The sandy-haired young man had one arm in a sling so used his free arm to embrace her uncle. The smiling young woman hugged him and kissed his cheek.

"Johnny Hofer," the young man said, looking him up and down. "You're a sight for sore eyes and dressed fit to kill. You sure don't look like you did last time. If it weren't for your dark twinkling eyes, you could have walked past us."

Johnny chortled. "That good, huh? Thunderation, whippersnapper." He drew himself to full height. "There are different kinds of disguises, you know. Can't a man wear a business suit to give his niece a good impression and not shock the world to death?"

"Probably a good idea." The young man flipped a lock of hair back from his forehead. "It just takes getting used to."

Johnny snorted. "You're allowed time. Let me introduce you. This is my niece Erika Hofer who has come a very long way. Erika? Meet Ted Vincent and Annie Mettles, recent heroes on the river."

"Josh told me a little." Erika slightly bowed from the waist German style. "It is an honor and privilege. I am glad to meet you and would love to hear your story."

"You will, and we're pleased too." Ted shook Erika's hand. Annie did as well and kissed her on one cheek.

Erika instantly liked the smiling young woman with auburn hair and dark no-nonsense eyes that flashed glints of daring.

"Forget us being heroes." Annie waved in dismissal. "We only did what we had to to save lives to keep our boat from becoming a time bomb. You're the hero, traveling so far from Europe alone!"

Erika ducked her head. "But I had all kinds of help, and, as they say, people do what they must."

Johnny rubbed his hands together. "Bosh. Now that that's over, let's visit over breakfast. Food smells great, and my stomach's shaking hands with my backbone."

During breakfast, Erika couldn't keep her eyes off Ted and Annie. Why hadn't Josh said more about them? They were fabulous! Anyone meeting them would want them as best friends forever. Had Josh's injuries affected his friendship capacity?

"How is Josh doing really?" Annie asked. "Is it true he may come home to do more recovery here?"

"It's one possibility. His top doctor and physiotherapist suggested it, but he'd rather recover enough to rejoin his shipmates in combat. I'm not sure how it will turn out."

"Sounds like Josh—a true-blue patriot." Ted snapped his fingers.

Annie wore no ring, but the loving looks she and Ted exchanged and the way they finished each other's sentences made it clear they were a couple. Strange Josh hadn't mentioned that, unless it happened recently. But no three best friends could stay a threesome forever.

Erika tried to keep up, but Ted and Johnny talked so machine-gun-fast she couldn't follow or understand everything—limpets, and I-25s, and a traitor news reporter attacking Harlan who nearly died but was now wiser and changed.

"He should be." Johnny shivered. "He was knocking on the pearly gates when the Coast Guard snagged him at the last minute. It gives me chills that Sparks or any human could be so coldblooded."

Erika shuddered. Surely Uncle Johnny would tell her those story details soon. Her head whirled trying to put together pieces of that conversation while answering Annie's questions and asking more of her own. She massaged her temples. Speaking English constantly wearied her brain. Worse, if she didn't speak English crisply and clearly, her accent could betray her.

After making a healthy dent in the breakfast servings, Ted said, "Hey, save room for lunch at Bob and Sue's. She won't like it if we don't eat enough of her food to show we like it."

Annie and Erika groaned. "You should have told us sooner."

Ted rose from the table and stretched. "When you two are ready, we'll see more local sights."

"Only show the best parts," Uncle Johnny said. "Do a good job while Smitty and I put our heads together and solve the world's problems."

Erika stared. "Try hard, Uncle. They need solving."

Church bells rang over the town. Automobiles honked in crowded streets while ship horns blasted from the river. Children in leafy parks shouted like children anywhere, except these wore more joyful faces than those back home. Few were happy in Germany these days, but the scenes Erika enjoyed now still brought homesickness.

Erika had recognized Bob Vengeance instantly. Seeing him with his pleasant wife Sue in their cozy home helped her understand Josh better. Such nice parents. No wonder he wanted to please them. Now that they knew Josh was safe, they were relaxed and laughing.

Their easy way together reminded her of Mother and Father's, except Josh's parents were less formal. Their large, older home was cheery and spacious with splashes of bright colors. A partially worked jigsaw puzzle covered a small side table. Another held the cluttered bits of a craft project in progress.

"Sorry." Sue moved loose puzzle pieces to one side. "I always have a project or two going at once."

"This looks like fun." Erika bent down to examine the picture. "I like puzzles. I hope you'll teach me many craft projects."

Josh's mother beamed. "I will if you're interested. Especially if you stay with us. I'll show you your guest room."

Johnny joined them. "Show me too," he said. "It's been a while."

"Charming," Erika said minutes later. "I love handmade quilts and curtained windows with natural views. It reminds me of Grandmother's house in Bavaria."

"Really? That sounds lovely."

"It was." Erika teared up. "I'm sorry, I didn't expect to do that."

She dabbed her eyes with the handkerchief Johnny whipped from his pocket.

"It's understandable," Sue said. "You're far from home. Major transitions are hard."

"But this is also God's blessing. What a perfect room. I'm pleased to stay a while—if I can also see you often, Uncle."

"You will," he reassured. "You'll see me so much, you'll tire of me. I didn't just discover a fine new niece with the idea of letting her go anytime soon." He wiped his watery eyes with the same handkerchief he'd lent her before stuffing it back in his pocket and smiled. "You and I are not very hard-boiled Germans."

"No, I guess not."

They had just come downstairs to get supplies for the guest room when a young man with red hair as wiry and stiff as a rooster's comb and loaded with textbooks nearly sprung the front door from its hinges as he bolted inside.

"Hi-ya," he called, while heading for the stairs.

"Wait. Harlan, it's good to see you again." Ted lightly pounded the college student's back. "So glad you're alive!"

"Me too." Harlan drew a deep breath. "Super close call for all of us. I'm sorry you got shot." Harlan's eyes probed Ted's sling. "How bad's the shoulder?"

"It's taking a while but coming along." Ted moved his sling in a half circle.

Harlan's voice deepened. "Thanks for fighting the bad guys. I'll never forget what happened out there."

"I guess not. You, Char, Annie, and I have everything to thank God for."

"For sure."

Johnny stepped forward. "I'm happy to see you lookin' good, too, Harlan. Who'd have thought we'd face foreign troops on our own river? Good thing we were ready." Johnny put an arm around Erika and drew her forward. "Meet my niece from Switzerland. Erika, this is Harlan, a fine young man studying mechanics."

"Switzerland? Does she—er—speak German?" Harlan's eyes bugged.

"As a matter of fact, she does. It's a neutral country, and over half the people there do." Johnny wrapped an arm around her shoulder. "But nearly all, like Erika, resist Hitler. What's your point?"

"Nothing, but that's good. We should all fight him." Harlan shook Erika's hand before juggling his pile of books and climbing the stairs.

Sue was back with a pile of towels and blankets. Erika took half of the load and followed back up the stairs. "How many rooms does your house have?"

"More than you think. Usually enough to tuck in anyone who comes, but sometimes that means bunk beds and sleeping bags." Sue waved at the back door. "Bob's outside grilling hamburgers. Will you girls help dish up fixings?"

"Glad to," Annie answered. "That gives us time for more girl talk, but first where would you like me to put this dry laundry I bought in from the line?"

"How nice of you. Thanks bunches. Most goes in this linen closet downstairs and the rest in the one upstairs."

The atmosphere around the picnic table reminded Erika of family reunions or fun summer camps in Germany. Although she, Johnny, Ted, and Annie had put away hearty breakfasts several hours before, she was amazed to see everyone lift food from platters to plates and into their mouths like efficient farm combine machines.

"Mmm-mmmm." Ted slowed down and groaned. "Nobody cooks like you, Sue."

"You're hearty eaters but as thin as rails. It's embarrassing—like I can't cook at all."

"Not for long when you feed us like this." Annie began clearing plates.

"Delicious again." Johnny rubbed his stomach. "Did you know hamburgers come from Hamburg, Germany, and frankfurters from Frankfurt, and cologne from—"

"Cologne, Germany!" Annie exclaimed.

Johnny chuckled. "That's right. If our nations shared good ideas instead of war, think how great this planet would be."

"That's true." Annie carried the plates inside and hung up her dish towel. "Are you ready to shop, Erika?"

"I think so. How much time will it take?"

"Not long. I'm efficient. Is there something else you'd like to do? There must be things you thought about seeing once you came here."

Erika studied her shoes. "I can be honest? Please don't laugh."

"I promise. If I visited Europe in peacetime, I'd want to see all kinds of things. What's on your list?"

"Our people love everything about America's old west. Cowboys, Indians, explorers—you name it. I heard this was a fur-trading area and fort before it was a town."

"That's right." Annie rinsed the counter and dried her hands. "Do you want to see Fort Vancouver?"

"Someday. Not today."

"Okay. What then?"

"Well ... wildlife," Erika answered. "My family often hiked the forests to see wildlife, especially beavers."

"Great." Annie snapped her fingers. "Easily done. After

buying the clothes Johnny wants you to have, I'll take you to a place nearby with beavers."

Erika clasped her hands. "Wonderful! I'd love to see their dams and lodges too."

"We will. Up close."

Returning from shopping loaded with packages, Erika and Annie saw Sue in the front yard bending over her rose bushes, watering can in hand.

"How did you two make out?" Sue called.

"Fine. Annie helped me find everything on the list and a few extra things."

"That's what I call a good shopping trip."

"We'll change clothes and be back in a jiffy," Annie said. "We're getting ready for another project."

When they emerged, Sue asked, "Where are you off to now?"

"A wildlife adventure." Annie lifted her camera. "Erika wants to see North American beavers in their habitat."

"Then I know where you're going." Sue pointed. "The slough near the river."

"You're right!" Annie hurried down the steps.

"Wait! I left my camera at the front door," Erika yelped.

By the time she returned, Sue had set up a sprinkler. "Annie's our wildlife expert," she said. "If I had my work caught up, I'd come with you."

"Plan on next time," Annie said.

"I'd love to."

They reached the end of the street and crossed the adjoining park. Beyond that, open fields bordered the tree-fringed slough next to the river. When Annie slowed, taking small steps with the stealth of a North American Indian, Erika did the same.

A field of dry golden stems swayed in a cooling breeze under the hot sun. "I come here often. Keep following. The path is along the edge."

The trail was barely visible, but Erika stayed at Annie's heels. Sweet-smelling grasses swished against their legs and pulled at their feet.

"It's good you know where we're going. A person could get lost here."

"You'd hear the river and find your way."

"Maybe." Heart soaring, Erika placed her feet in the exact places Annie did. Soon they neared the slough and heard the river's splash echo through the trees. Several poplars showed white gashes girdling their trunks as if strong axes had chopped into them. The ground was littered with perfectly shaped sharp-edged triangular wooden pieces.

"Beavers," Annie breathed.

Erika slipped a few wooden chips into her pockets. The animals' front teeth had made precise bites to cut down trees and slide them to the water.

"Beaver slides." Annie pointed. "They're fantastic builders. We have to be quiet. If they're frightened, they'll slap warnings with their tails and leave."

Erika shook with excitement. "Will we see them in action?"

"If we're quiet."

Leaning forward, shoulders hunched, the girls snuck closer to the slough. A round lodge of woven sticks rose above the surface. Soon, a small dark baby beaver kit left its home triggering small waves vee-ing across the water.

Erika's throat clogged. "I'll remember this forever."

Sunshine backlit Annie's hair into a glowing halo.

"See?" Annie suddenly disappeared without a sound. Erika stopped and teetered on the edge of a place where the earth had given way. "Annie?" What had happened? She examined the path. No Annie.

The young woman peered up from a grassy hole she'd fallen into. "I'm fine, but the pesky animals made a deep hole that grass grew over. I slid right in."

Erika smothered a laugh.

Annie clambered up the hole's sloping sides and dusted off her clothes. "That was a surprise, but come on. Let's try this again." They tiptoed forward.

Erika held her breath as a large beaver broke the surface and swam with its kit. She and Annie raised their cameras, took one more step, and while Erika clicked a photo, Annie dropped out of sight again.

Erika stopped, barely avoiding falling into the second pit herself. Hands on knees, bent over and whooping, she collapsed in gales of laughter. As soon as Annie climbed out, she joined in, and their laughter rang loud and free. Startled, the mother beaver slapped her tail in warning before she and her baby dove from sight.

The girls howled louder. "That's hysterical," Annie wheezed. "I'm the local expert showing you special sights and I fall into holes! I promise they weren't there when I came last week."

"I believe you."

They continued laughing and wheezing until they were weak, tears streaming down their faces.

"Funniest thing I've seen in ages," Erika gasped.

Annie rubbed dirt from her face. "We're sneaking up on woodland creatures, like no animal in the woods is safe, and then I'm trapped by them, ho-ho, ha-ha."

"I'm not laughing at you," Erika said, "but any time I think of this the rest of my life, this memory will set me off."

"Me too." Annie wiped her eyes and climbed up and out of the second pit, steadying herself against a tree until she caught her breath. "Instead of us observing beavers, they got a good view of us."

That sent both girls into laughter again.

"My sides hurt, but I can't stop." Annie giggled.

"It's worth it. It's a good hurt." Erika wiped her streaming eyes. "My father would have loved this."

"I give up." Annie hugged her sides. "There's no chance of impressing you now or ever by standing on formality. This is who I am, take me or leave me. What you see is what you get!" She grinned so wide, her eyes shut.

"I'll take it." Erika fanned her burning face. "We're friends forever."

"Forever and always." Annie wiped her cheeks. "I think we've done enough beaver watching today. We'll check for holes next time."

"Next time, I'll lead." Erika's laugh ended with a snort.

They shook hands and retraced their steps, carefully avoiding both holes in the path. Once they reached the open grassy field, they linked arms and returned to Bob and Sue's house. When they tried to share their story, they chortled and collapsed with laughter again. Sue joined them. "I wish I'd seen that. I should have gone with you."

Once they calmed down, Erika asked, "Sue, do you have a sewing machine I could please use? There's something I'd like to sew."

"I sure do. Make yourself at home in my craft room." Sue waved in that direction. "Use anything you see. Call if you need help."

After Sue left, Erika opened the bag of brown and green fabric and leather bits she bought at a fabric store after her clothing purchases. Once she got to work, it didn't take long. When she finished, she tucked the new garment into the fabric bag and gathered her other purchases to take back to the hotel. Her uncle was in for a surprise.

Chapter Twenty-Four

Uncle Johnny peered from beneath shaggy brows. "Sorry, Erika. We need to change our plans and stay in this hotel another day."

"Okay." Erika tried to read his face. Was he upset? Disappointed? She couldn't tell. "Bob and Sue are nice. If it helps you, I'll gladly stay there sometimes."

"It does, thank you."

"Annie invited me to stay with her as well."

"That's good. I hope you'll have many friends here." He carried in her packages from the day's shopping.

She waited for him to put them down. "But I also hope to accompany you sometimes."

"You do?" His eyes clouded. "Maybe. We'll see. So, your shopping went well?"

"Yes. And afterward, Annie and I tracked beavers until she fell into two big holes the animals had dug." Erika laughed again telling it.

"She what?"

"Ah, now you're listening." She couldn't quit smiling.

"I was all along."

"Sort of. The beavers dug deep grass-covered holes and Annie fell in, but I didn't. It was so funny." She chuckled again, remembering. "We laughed ourselves sick, but now we're best friends forever."

"That's good to hear." The pleasant crinkle lines around his eyes deepened. "I'm happy hearing you laugh. That's how it is with Smitty and me. We've done lots of crazy things together that mostly turn out fine and have fun too. Anyone's rich with friends like that. You can never have too many."

"I agree."

Back in their hotel suite, Uncle Johnny's forehead scrunched. "Let me explain why we're staying longer. Governor Langlie needs to see Smitty and me again tonight. When he's in town, he stays here in the executive suite, so that makes meetings easy."

He peered over his bent wire glasses. "He wants time to welcome and visit with you of course, but tonight isn't a time for jawing."

"Jawing?" Her brow furrowed.

"You know. Visiting. Shooting the breeze. Getting to know each other. Oh, pshaw. I need to think carefully about how I talk."

Erika shook her head. "It's okay. I'll catch on."

"There's a situation the Governor wants to talk to Smitty and me about."

"It's good he's here then."

"Yes."

Erika went with her uncle to the executive suite to at least meet the Governor before the men had their meeting. She recognized him the moment he entered by his professional manner. He shook her hand and beamed a warm smile. He was smartly dressed, with his gray hair nicely cut, and smelled like something expensive from the men's fragrance section of a good department store.

"We're pleased you're here, Erika. Welcome. You're a brave young woman to travel so far—but I imagine any relative of Johnny's is brave."

"Thank you, sir. I hope so."

The men exchanged knowing glances.

"We'll find time to get acquainted," the Governor said. "I'm sorry it can't be tonight. Meanwhile, we're grateful for every gain in this war, but they aren't enough yet to allow us days off."

"I understand."

As he shuffled through the manila folders on the executive desk, Erika said, "Thank you for everything you did to help me come here. I will always do my best to be a loyal resident who makes you proud."

"Well, I'm sure you will, Erika. I hope you're very happy here. Your uncle's thrilled to have you."

Johnny reddened. "Don't tell her how much. She might expect me to give her the sun, moon, and stars."

"I'm not like that, Uncle Johnny!"

"Of course not, girl. I'm joshing. But you don't let me do enough for you. My consarned mouth gets me in trouble, I'm sayin' the wrong things 'cause I'm thinking about certain events. Never mind." He stretched his shoulders. "Can you find your way back to our suite by yourself?"

"Yes, I'm sure I can."

"Good. Sleep well then. I'll see you in the morning."

"Goodnight." As she headed for the door, her uncle checked his watch and asked the Governor, "Where's Smitty?"

"Taking Irene to the train station to pick up a telegram they have for us there."

Johnny frowned. "My stars. I could have taken her."

"No need. You can't be everywhere at once, and you deserve time to enjoy your niece. You're usually the one picking up the slack. Let Smitty do more these days."

As Erika closed the door, Uncle Johnny didn't look pleased. Part way back to their suite, she remembered to collect their clean clothes from the hotel's laundry service.

As she folded her blouses and Uncle Johnny's shirts into neat squares, voices filtered into the room. Somehow, the hotel's *L*-shaped corridor paralleled the executive suite. Or the heating system vent carried sounds. She recognized Uncle Johnny's and the Governor's voices but heard two more. One must be Smitty. The other was a woman—Irene maybe?

Erika didn't intend to eavesdrop but overheard key words. "Japanese have taken Guadalcanal, but we're close. They've been sighted in the Aleutians—bad stuff happening. Have to up our game."

She loved geography. Erika recognized most names they mentioned and hoped her uncle would share more. But for now, she needed to rest. After her long day, she fell asleep quickly. Sometime later, she heard a key turn in the lock as her uncle slipped into the suite. Her watch read midnight. Moments later, her uncle left again. His meeting must not be over.

Toward dawn, increasing traffic sounds on the busy roadway outside the hotel made her open her eyes. The door to their suite opened again, and with her door open a crack, she saw Johnny enter wearing his green and brown leather-trimmed garb. Was he only getting back now?

She read her Bible and waited to let him decide their schedule. Whistling snores came from his room. After another hour, shuffling sounds filled his part of the suite. That's when she put on the outfit she had stitched for herself similar to his.

"Good morning," she said entering the living room to greet him. "I'm ready for the day if you are."

He turned from the window and gawked.

"Ready for—where did you get that?"

She twirled in a circle "Most Hofers are resourceful. Mother taught me to sew. After seeing your outfit, I made myself one like it. After all, I am your niece."

He slapped his forehead and chortled. "My stars, you certainly are. What do you plan to do with it?"

"Help you with whatever you do when you wear yours."

"Jumping Jehoshaphat!" His sober expression didn't entirely hide his grin. "You won't need that outfit today, but keep hold of it. It may come in handy." He surveyed her again and shook his head. "Wait 'til I tell Smitty. You're a live one, all right. Every Hofer in history would be proud. But how can I keep you safe and out of trouble?"

From what? she wanted to ask. Instead, she said, "If my outfit isn't right for today, what shall I wear?"

"Let's see." He cranked his neck to check his fancy wristwatch. "Today's the Lord's day, so we'll go to Bob and Sue's church. Next weekend, we're invited to ride along with them when they hold service downriver. I want you to meet residents in that area too."

"Very good." She clasped her hands. "Annie loves the river and says the people there are wonderful."

He gazed at her again, his upper lip quivering. "You may fit in here even better than I hoped."

Her heart warmed as she left to change from the woodland garb into her new green-patterned dress that looked like cool flower gardens. She dabbed gardenia perfume behind each ear.

When she entered the room again, her uncle inhaled deeply. "Very nice. You look as pretty as a flower and smell like one too."

He had also changed clothes. Not as fancy as when he met her at the air base, but he wore a crisp white long sleeved shirt and pleated pants. He added tie-up dress shoes instead of his hand-stitched leather boots. Erika followed as he led the way to church, looking as proud as a peacock.

"I'm thankful to be here," Erika said, as they walked. She would concentrate on thankfulness and not let her heart be torn by heartache over her loved ones back home or the world war raging on three continents.

Lord, as hard as it is, I trust Mother and Klaus to You. Whatever happens, I'll always remember what You and my family taught me and do my best to make You proud.

The church where Josh's parents ministered was everything Erika had hoped for. Nice people, familiar songs that soothed her heart, and an encouraging sermon. Dietrich and many German Christians would have sung some of these same faith-filled songs today. Perhaps Mother in Berlin too. And Klaus? Only the Lord knew where and how he was. What about Josh? Was he growing strong enough to rejoin his crewmates? Or would he be sent home?

Lord, I don't even know how I feel about that. Guard and keep each one.

After church and a fabulous picnic outdoors, Uncle Johnny walked over with his beetled eyebrows raised extra high.

"Erika, I need to level with you. I sold the fancy house I had here in town because I'm gone downriver so much."

"Okay?"

"I mean I haven't replaced it yet. I don't own one here now, but I have money in the bank to buy most anything you like. I've been staying with Smitty some or in my hidey-holes scattered through the woods all over. It's just that none of them are nice enough for a gal like you to stay in."

She jutted one hand to her hip. "Shouldn't you let me decide?"

His face reddened. "Well, I guess—I mean, I never—Anyway, here's a question Smitty and I were jawing over. That means chewing the fat, shooting the breeze."

"I'm learning." She snorted. "Americans have a special way of talking, but it's confusing. How do you chew and shoot at once?"

"We don't." He laughed and blinked like an owl. "What I mean is, what about buying a railroad boxcar and fixin' it fancy or plain, any way you like? If we needed to move it, we could hook it onto a locomotive and park in a rail yard or siding anywhere. Maybe travel at night to arrive somewhere new the next morning. Whaddaya think?"

"I don't know. It's a lot to think about."

"It certainly is." He cupped an ear and leaned closer.

She took a step back. "It sounds brilliant but complicated. I need time to consider."

"That's fine." He risked a laugh. "It's both of those things. I guess there's no great rush."

"Would it help if I narrow my questions down to one?"

"Probably. Try me. I'll answer the best I can."

"Then please tell me where you work and what you do, Uncle Johnny. I still want to help."

"Bless your heart." He scuffed a shoe. "I wish I could tell you. I really do, but I can't yet. I'm retired so can work from anywhere. But I can't tell people what I do."

"People tell me you're a hero. Can you tell me the part that's already happened?"

"I'll try to soon, if you'll trust me."

"I do. Do you trust me?"

"That's a fair question." His smile broadened. He had lost a tooth near the back of his mouth and could use a dentist, but she loved his smile. "So far, I sure do."

"Good. Where is this boxcar?"

"Where do you think? Down the hill in the rail yard where boxcars belong—close to the tracks."

"That makes sense." Her mind churned out questions. "I know you're good at figuring things out, so you've probably got answers. How would we get running water and electricity?"

"I have a plan."

"How would things work when we weren't attached to a train? Or if another train or boxcar needed the same siding at the same time?"

"There are signal lights and ways to switch sidings to solve that. You're a serious thinker." Her uncle stood dumbstruck, like he'd been swarmed by buzzing flies and needed to choose which to swat first. "You're a Hofer all right." He flashed a slow grin. "If you throw me one question at a time, I'll do my best. I know you need answers. A boxcar might work."

His face was so hopeful. She wanted to please him. "I won't know if I don't consider it, will it? It sounds like a huge undertaking, but please don't fix up a new place until I'm here longer. I'll fit into any space you have or stay with Annie or Bob and Sue—but I'd rather come with you."

"I hear ya."

His eyes seemed to follow the buzzing flies. As his eyes darted back and forth, she heard buzzing too.

He cleared his throat. "Even though we don't have the right solution yet, I hope you know how glad I am you're here."

"Thank you. Me too."

"And I do love you." He jammed his hands in his pockets as his face flushed. "But I also have work to do to keep folks safe."

Her face pinched. "Safe from what? Can't you tell me?" Even she heard the pleading in her voice.

"Maybe soon." Kindness lit his face. "I have to ask the governor one more thing."

"Okay. I'll try to be patient. I don't think I can answer about a boxcar until I see one up close."

"Smart girl." He gave an approving look. "You're new here, and there's a lot at stake, but I like what I see. I know God brought you."

"I do too. That's all I need to know for now."

They exchanged grins as he tucked her arm in his. She strolled beside him as they walked downhill toward the river and rail yard when a loud voice rang out.

"Johnny Hofer, stop!" Smitty ran downhill toward them, arms windmilling like a hungry bear was behind him.

"We need you quick." He braked fast on the hill, his work boots raising spirals of dust as he huffed and puffed, catching his breath. "There's trouble on the river." He waved an arm west. "My truck's in the parking lot."

Johnny's head whipped around. "What kind of trouble?"

Smitty eyed Erika. "I'll keep it simple. You know those midget subs at Pearl?"

"Yes. Top secret."

"Right. Our network spotted something similar fifteen miles this side of the river's mouth. I'll tell you more on our way, but we need you now. We'll take my truck and meet our team there."

"Suffering succotash!" Johnny blew out a breath and released Erika's arm. "Sorry, girl, I have to scoot. Stay with Sue or Annie. I'll be back fast as I can. Pray for us."

"I will—but wait!" She stood on tiptoe and pecked his wrinkled cheek. "Come back safe."

"Thanks." He reddened, his hand covering the spot she'd kissed. "Thanks, my dear. Take care of yourself too." His legs ate up the ground to the parking lot while Smitty raced alongside him.

Chapter Twenty-Five

Mid-August, 1942
Naval Medical Center, San Diego

Josh Vengeance expelled all the air in his lungs. He was getting shipped out—but not where he wanted to go. Or when. An open-ended medical leave back home was not progress, but it was where the top medical doctor had assigned him. Josh inhaled and choked. That doctor's decision was enough to make a strong man cry.

I gave physiotherapy my best shot but failed. I'm classed disabled, but there's still a war going on. I could load torpedoes or swab decks—anything to help win this war.

Brad entered the exercise room. "Morning, Josh. Here's your final paperwork. Work hard on these first three pages of exercises especially for your first few months at home, and then reapply for active duty if you want to."

"You know I do." Josh huffed out his breath. "I worked hard to persuade the top doc to keep me here and do harder routines, but couldn't deliver the goods."

"Josh, he noticed and was impressed, but his appraisal is correct. This report means you've gone as far as we can take you with in-patient care." Brad squeezed Josh's bicep. "Your muscles are remembering how to move on their own without you thinking about each step. You've noticed that haven't you?"

"Yeah. I know I'm stronger."

"Your back and leg injuries are taking longer to recover. No surprise there. Your biggest miracle was surviving. Anybody needs time to heal."

"That's what I've heard from day one, but I'm out of time." Josh tossed his medical papers on the chair by the table. "What good is any of this if I don't reach full recovery?"

"What do you mean?" Brad grabbed the papers and tapped the first page. "This evaluation says, 'Further recovery expected.' That's fabulous. Just not in our in-patient hospital program or in time to rejoin your shipmates."

Josh's face twisted. "Then it's all for nothing. I'm nothing."

"Not at all. Where do you get that?" Brad's hand clenched. "I want to grab your shoulders and shake out your goofy thinking. You're no failure unless you decide you are. Many guys on medical leave improve enough to return to active duty. I bet you will too."

Josh met Brad's eyes. "But if I don't?"

"It's not the end of the world. There are other options. Live a day at a time. Be proud of how far you've come. Do you remember the shape you were in when you got here?"

Josh studied the floor. "I'd rather not."

"Maybe you should." Brad gestured to the table. "Lie down face up." He let Josh settle and began kneading his right shoulder. "Here's the scoop. You have good options to discuss with your squad leader or chaplain. Your attitude shows them what your next steps should be more than your physical condition."

"What do you mean?"

"What if you were appraising guys—and you might one day. What would you look for?"

"Inner fire. Motivation."

"Right." Brad squeezed more menthol ointment from a dispenser into his hand. "Don't tense up. I'm going to work this kink out of your lower right leg to get it as loose as your left. It supports weight better then."

"You're right. Hurts less too."

"Maybe I'm meddling, but I think you need to talk to the man upstairs."

"What?" Josh shrugged. "I begged God to return me to full duty, but He hasn't. Even He's given up on me, so I stopped praying."

"Man!" Brad shook his head. "That doesn't make good sense. You make me worry your brain got more trauma than we figured. You've made progress—just not on the timetable *you* want. I'm no theologian, but listen up." Brad's finger stabbed Josh's chest. "When patients bury emotional pain, it slows recovery. That might be your problem. None of us grieves or heals what we can't feel. We have to face pain for healing to come. Face your feelings. Let God work you over like I do your muscles."

"That hard?" Josh sputtered a laugh. "Believe me. I feel plenty."

Brad moved around the table. "Turn over and let me work on your back. Like the rest of us, you have more work to do."

Josh sighed. "Don't you ever quit?"

"Nope. And you don't want me to. Watch me. Massaging your muscles in circular swipes increases your blood flow. The better your circulation, the faster you'll heal. I'm giving you exercises to do anywhere, anytime, and I'll upgrade them to more complicated ones from time to time."

Josh craned his neck to see Brad's face. "Seriously, thanks for what you've invested in me."

"Happy to. My privilege." Brad's hands stopped working. "After you leave here, let me hear from you."

"I'd like that."

"Seeing patients improve is my reward." Brad flipped to a

new page in Josh's chart. "And listen to your body. It knows what you need. Let it recover at its own pace."

"But I wish by the time you discharge me I could walk without looking drunk."

"You're not that far from that." Brad lifted an eyebrow. "There are worse things than limping. Do you figure guys need perfect bodies to be heroes?"

"Maybe not, but it helps."

"Where do you get that? What did you think of your Captain on the *Yorktown*? Turn over to your left side."

"Okay." Josh shifted. "We had two hundred men. He didn't fraternize with us much, but he seemed okay. Ran a tight ship. We respected him."

"Did you notice anything unusual about him physically? How he walked? If he climbed the rigging?"

"He didn't climb the rigging, but that wasn't his job. He walked stiff."

"Do you know why?" Brad tapped his forehead. "He had a great reason. Pull up his pant leg and you'd find a wooden leg from a boyhood farm accident. A tractor rolled over on him. He barely lived, but it hasn't stopped him."

"Seriously? A wooden leg?" Josh gaped. "We couldn't tell. How does he manage all he does?"

"Determination."

"He was all over the place, keeping us calm and focused." Josh scrunched his forehead. "He deserves a medal."

"I hear he may get one." Brad bent and pulled more papers from his briefcase. "I thought you might appreciate the battle report they issued on the *Yorktown* going down."

"Already?"

"Yeah. They made it a priority. Listen to this. 'Skillfully maneuvered by Commander Elliott Buckmaster, the carrier first dodged eight torpedoes. Attacked later by *kamikaze* dive-bombers, the *Yorktown* evaded all but one bomb.'"

"Sheesh. All but one?" Josh shook his head. "We nearly

missed them all?"

"Sounds that way. My point is, don't make having a muscle-bound body your end goal. Work to be a whole person." Brad kneaded again, deeper, until Josh jerked.

"I hear ya, but ouch."

"Is this hurting you?"

"It's probably good hurt." He forced a grin. "You're massaging deep but your words are going deep too."

"Good. You need both."

"Creeps." Josh flinched more. "Ease up a little, or your back compressions will bring me off the table."

"You know, most guys here would jump at a chance to go home. Sometimes being back around strong, healthy personal relationships speeds up recovery too."

"*Humph*." Josh's voice was muffled, face down.

"Are you still torn up about a girl?"

Josh flinched. "I think so. Things have changed, and it's awful. I don't know how to face her and my best friend."

"Gosh. I get it. There, too, the answer is taking a day at a time."

"If you say so."

"I do. And this is experience talking." Brad tapped Josh's back. "You know, if you do go to your folks' place, I have a talented therapist buddy at Portland Air Base. I'd hook you up with Matt."

"Is he as good as you?"

"Close." Brad grinned. "We trained together." As Josh climbed off the table, Brad extended his hand. "Keep it up, Vengeance. And dig deep. I know you have what it takes—all the grit and determination you'll need."

"You think so?" Josh shook Brad's hand. "I like hearing that. I hope you're right."

Brad's words echoed inside him for a long time.

His official discharge happened so fast, Josh didn't have time to tell his folks. Besides, he hadn't fully made up his mind about going home. He could stay in San Diego on his own as an outpatient to heal more. After all, he was a grown man—not someone wanting his parents to care for him.

Packing was easy. He'd brought almost nothing and left with little—two summer uniforms and Red Cross toiletries. He'd lost his Bible and everything else when the *Yorktown* went down. When he flipped open his new Bible from the Gideons, its onionskin pages crisp and clean, he read Psalm 139, and heard Dad reciting it:

"Whither shall I go from thy spirit? Or whither shall I flee from thy presence? If I ascend up into heaven, thou art there. If I make my bed in hell, behold, thou art there. If I take the wings of the morning, and dwell in the uttermost parts of the sea; even there shall thy hand lead me ..."

Josh shut the Bible and tossed it back on the bedside table. Walking across the room, checking he had everything, he glimpsed at his reflection in the wall mirror. His worst scars were fading and less alarming, except when he was tired or cold. Then they showed up blood red against his pale skin. It took less pancake makeup these days to cover them. One day, he'd look less frightening. No one should be a Halloween bogeyman every day of the year!

He opened his tube of Brylcreem and recalled a magazine ad referring to the shortage of the hair dressing. "Some chaps are lucky," the headline read. It continued, "There's such a shortage of Brylcreem, that a chap who does get a bottle is indeed in luck."

The "perfect hair dressing," it was called. Did that mean those who used it had perfect hair? If he were truly a lucky chap, wouldn't he have some pretty gal waiting to run her fingers through his perfect hair?

His face crumpled. His buzz cut wasn't long enough for anyone's fingers to comb. Annie wouldn't explore his hair, that was for sure. And he couldn't picture anyone else wanting to.

Erika? No. She was a no-nonsense young woman who made her patients straighten up and fly right like she had him. He couldn't imagine her finger combing anyone's hair. He traced his fingers through his own. Short. Stubby. He winced as he touched a few dents and the shrapnel scars zigzagging his scalp.

How was Erika? No matter how nice her homeland was, she'd love the Columbia River area. Had she arrived safely? Did her uncle turn out to be all she had dreamed of? Had Mom and Dad met her? They were in for a treat. Letters were taking longer, and there'd been restrictions on teletype traffic with heightened war alerts.

If he went home, what would he do? Limp to the porch, climb the steps, and ring the doorbell without warning? His lips quirked. That would drive his folks nuts but could be fun.

Who was he kidding? He couldn't be fully independent for a while. He needed their support. His shoulders heaved, unable to deny his hunger for home. He pictured the rabbit whose broken leg he'd splinted as a kid. It took six weeks until it healed enough to be set free, but caring for it had been a special time. The animal visited twice later and ate out of his hand. He loved their bonding together more than if he'd observed some perfectly healthy rabbit in the woods that hadn't survived hardship. Josh choked down the lump in his throat. He hoped Mom and Dad felt the same.

Whole or not, he'd go home but try not to lean on them hard. He expelled a ragged sigh. He'd have the transport office schedule his travel. It would be good to see Mom and Dad and the folks back home. Most of them, anyway. He closed the door to his room and limped down the long hall only using two canes and leaving his crutches behind for the next guy. Maybe Brad was right. If Josh stood straight and concentrated on smooth strides, he wouldn't look totally drunk.

Erika glanced at the kitchen clock. She had everything nearly ready. Delectable aromas rose in steamy tendrils from the stove as she ferried filled serving dishes to the table. Just as she finished, Bob rushed through the back door. "Mmm, ladies. I just followed my nose to the best restaurant in town. After you told me what you were planning, I've been craving German food all day."

"I'm sure you were too busy to think of my cooking often, but that's nice to hear." Erika glanced at Sue as she rinsed her hands at the sink and dried them on her apron. "Besides, I had a terrific helper."

"I agree, she's the best." Bob leaned forward and kissed his wife's nose. "She's a tremendous cook, none better, but it's a treat to try new food too." He shrugged out of his jacket and hung it on a peg by the back door.

"My mother's a better seamstress than cook," Erika said, "so this may not win prizes, but I did my best. I'd like Sue to teach me American cooking too."

"Yes, if you like." Sue beamed. "You fit in great here. We'll teach each other."

Bob opened his collar and pushed up his sleeves. "I was afraid the only way Sue and I would gain a daughter was when Josh married, but we didn't want to wait that long. It looks like God has given us a bonus daughter."

Sue laughed. "It's a good thing Josh can't hear you. He'd be embarrassed."

"I doubt it. He's more grown up than that." Bob sat at the table and spread his hands open on either side of the plate, face innocent.

Erika's cheeks grew hotter than from just the heat produced by leaning over a hot stove. "You know him better than I, but I think he embarrasses easily." She placed serving spoons in each bowl.

"It might depend on who he's talking to." Sue removed a milk bottle from the ice box and handed it to Bob. "Erika's such a blessing. Besides all this cooking, do you know what else she did today?"

"Hard telling." Bob filled their glasses and returned the milk bottle to the ice box.

"Shared great activities they do in German Kindergartens that would work well here. And taught me action songs our kids will love."

"Terrific!" Bob grinned. "Those are swell icebreakers. I like them myself."

She poked his side. "That's because you're an overgrown kid yourself, but my very favorite overgrown kid in the neighborhood." She kissed him again.

After sitting and saying the blessing, they dug in. Bob pointed to the bowl of red cabbage with black seeds. "Delicious. What am I eating?"

"*Rotkohl.* Sweet-sour red cabbage with apples and onions. It's not so different from American food really, except for extra spices. The *Sauerbrauten* is roast beef wrapped in bacon and cooked with gingersnaps. It should have marinated longer than two days, but it's almost right. I also made potato dumpling *spaetzle* and apple strudel dessert."

"If enjoying the food is how I compliment the cook, I'm glad I didn't eat much lunch so I have room for seconds. This is fabulous—like Thanksgiving. Thank you."

"You're very welcome. I'm happy you like it."

"I don't like it, I love it! Sue, how did you get roast beef?"

She wiped her mouth with her napkin. "We may have used two weeks of rations."

"It's worth it. Too bad Josh isn't here."

Erika smiled, remembering the first meal she had served him. What would his parents think if Josh tossed any of this?

Bob chewed more slowly. "I spoke with Dr. Brower at the hospital today. His main office gal delivered her baby two weeks early, so he's short staffed and desperate for help. He asked if I knew anyone who could fill in. I mentioned you, Erika."

Erika stopped eating. "You did? What did he say?"

Bob studied her. "I explained you had just come here and told him that your dad was a fine doctor who trained you in his clinic."

"Dr. Brower nearly cheered when I shared that. He'd like to talk with you if you're interested."

"If I'm interested? Of course, I am." Erika clasped her hands together. "I miss medical things so much, but my accent is so strong. Won't that be a problem?"

"You do have an accent," Sue agreed, "but it's pleasant. Perhaps if you just speak more slowly."

"I will try. No license I earned in Germany will be recognized here. Chaplain Merritt helped me find that out in San Diego, but I can study and retest, and I will. What things could I do for the doctor?"

"He's willing to find out. He says you couldn't do actual procedures unless you passed state exams, but you could handle scheduling and medical records fine." Bob mopped up the meat sauce on his plate with a last bite of bread. "You could also set up charts and files for test results. He says no doctor does his best work without a strong support staff."

"That's true." Erika smoothed her apron. "I did those things and more in Father's office. They are not hard."

"They must be similar here."

"I'd love to help. Does he know my final residency papers haven't come yet?"

"Yes, but they're approved and on their way. If you like, I'll introduce you to Dr. Bower at church tomorrow—unless he's delivering a baby. In that case, we'll stop by his office Monday morning. I'm sure you'll like him. He's a great guy."

"I like him already, but everyone here is nice."

"No, not everyone. We have a few bad apples on our local tree. I hope you don't meet them. Dr. Brower is certainly not one of them."

Erika eased her shoulders. "I feel like a new person. Even

though this awful war still rages, I see you both carry burdens but have joy."

"Thank you. What a nice thing to say." Sue brushed Erika's hand.

"But it's true!"

Bob lowered his fork. "Don't give us too much credit. The Lord carries most of the load. None of us can do it alone. We're not meant to and don't have to."

Sue took Bob's arm. "Before we heard Josh was alive, it was unbearable. I thought I would suffocate. Tons of weight lifted when we heard that wonderful news."

Erika nodded. "I can't even imagine. I know how I'd feel if my brother, Klaus, were found. I pray much for that day."

Sue patted her hand. "We'll join you. Let's say *when* he is found."

"Thank you." Erika blinked away the tears that pricked her eyes. She lined up her silverware parallel to her plate as her mother had taught her to show she had finished eating. "How special that I met your son before coming here. And now meet you."

"Yes, that is incredible." Sue brought milk and refilled their glasses.

"The world is small when the Lord's in charge." Bob helped himself to a second serving of beef. "I have to taste a little more. This is so delicious!"

Erika glanced at the flaky golden strudel cooling on the counter. "Are you ready for dessert? Or do you want to wait until part of the meal settles?"

Bob groaned. "Not yet. I'm stuffed. Let's give this perfect meal a little time to rest."

"Fine." Erika tapped her fingernail against her water glass and enjoyed its sound, then stopped. "I just remembered only genuine crystal makes this clear ringing sound."

"Yes. It's a special wedding gift we received years ago from

Germany or Czechoslovakia—I forget which. There's a trademark on the bottom of each piece."

Erika lifted her glass. "You're right. From Bavaria in Germany. My mother owns a set like it." She burst into tears and grabbed her napkin to dab her eyes. "I'm sorry. It makes me miss her."

Sue scooted close and took Erika's hand. "We understand, and it's good for you to remember. You're brave to come so far alone and make all these adjustments. We can't take the place of your home and country, but in time, we hope our area and people begin to feel like a second home for you."

Bob stood and rested a hand on Erika's shoulder. "Sue said that just right. We welcome you here with all our hearts."

"Thank you so much. I feel that. And thank you for praying for my loved ones."

"It's our privilege. Sue and I understand. We only survived the weeks Josh was missing because of all the people praying for us."

Erika folded her napkin. "How did you bear it? You must have nearly gone crazy."

"Yes." Bob gazed at Sue. "I don't want to guess how close we came, but it deepened our faith in God's promises."

"That's right," Sue added. "We're thankful the Lord didn't let that trial last one moment longer. I'll never forget the phone call that ended the hardest time in our lives."

Erika tapped her crystal glass to hear it ring again. Its sound comforted. "It was terrible losing Father. I just want to know if Klaus lives or not." This time she let her smile reach her eyes. "With the Lord bringing me safely all the way here, I know He can do anything."

Bob pushed his chair back from the table. "Who knows? Maybe He will show ways more of your family and friends can escape."

Fighting tears, Erika squeaked, "Thank you. I'd love that."

Chapter Twenty-Six

Bob brought Erika by Dr. Brower's office early Monday since delivering a baby had kept him from attending Sunday morning service. The doctor's thinning gray hair was in disarray. He looked like someone's favorite grandpa, with his lively brown eyes behind wire glasses framed by beetle brows and rosy cheeks.

Erika liked him immediately.

Bob shook Dr. Brower's hand. "You're a busy man."

He laughed. "Always, but it's good for me. Keeps me out of trouble. I've delivered a third of this town's babies and have a few named after me." He chuckled and waved to the wall behind him filled with framed photos of smiling babies. "Many are grown. Now I deliver the kids of kids. You'll see Josh and his friends over there." Brower pointed to the bottom left.

Bob bent to view that row. "I hadn't paid attention when I've been in your office, but what classic shots. Yup! Josh with Ted next to him. Always best friends."

"Where?" Erika scanned the wall. Bob pointed out Josh with wisps of blond hair, green eyes, and dimpled chin crawling on a blue blanket. She laughed. "How cute."

Dr. Brower straightened one picture frame. "Ted's always had that cowlick—fire engine red with a face full of freckles. But it doesn't matter. Delivering them as babies gives me privileges to enjoy them forever. See their tiny footprints underneath?"

"Sure do." Bob stood and came closer. "I'll bring my camera and snap copies next time. Poor Ted—flat feet even then."

"I agree. He didn't let that stop him and still became a hero."

"Incredible," Erika said. "I still have to hear the whole story."

"You must," Bob said, "but it's best if you hear it from Ted or Annie."

Dr. Brower pulled out a chair for her before sitting himself. "Let's discuss my situation before my next patient comes. Bob tells me you have broad experience, and I'm short-staffed. If you're interested, I'd like to call state employment in Olympia to start paperwork."

"Goodness, are you that sure I can help?" Medical paraphernalia overflowed shelves and bookcases. Just like home, she smelled the pungent aromas of medicines and antiseptics.

"From what my friend Bob tells me, I'm sure you can help. Even if it's only part time."

"Then yes, please." Excitement rippled through her like a racehorse at the Berlin racetrack. "I would enjoy helping you very much."

"That's great to hear." Dr. Brower slapped open a clipboard and wrote furiously. "How do you spell your name?"

"Erika Hofer. H-O-F-E-R."

"That's right, same as Johnny."

"He'll be glad knowing you can help here. He and Doc and I have been friends a long time."

"I'm happy to meet the people he's friends with."

"And we like meeting you—but don't tell her too many stories of our shenanigans." The doctor moved his glasses to the top of his head. "Let her form her own opinions about us."

"But I want to hear more stories about my Uncle. I don't know him well yet but like him very much. I'm interested."

"Of course, but I'll only tell you the best stories. He's a brilliant, fascinating character. We're great friends."

"Excuse me. I must ask. I hope this wouldn't happen often, and I haven't even started work yet, but if my uncle needed me, could I get time off to help with his special projects?"

Bob and Dr. Brower locked eyes.

"The answer is yes," the doctor said. "He would only ask if it was important."

"If it's urgent, you might find us there helping as well," Bob chimed in.

That evening, as if to prove Bob's statements true, Erika watched Johnny, Smitty, and Bob quickly gather extra clothes and supplies and disappear again in Smitty's sputtering pickup.

"I'm afraid life is like this on the river in wartime," Sue said. "Make yourself comfortable. We'll have a good time even without them."

"Yes," Erika said, "but I'd like to help also."

"Possibly later—I'm not sure. But not tonight." As Sue placed dinner leftovers in the ice box, the kitchen wall phone rang. "Hello? Yes, she's here." Sue passed the receiver to Erika.

"Erika, this is Dr. Brower. I'm pleased to say I have temporary approval for you to start work even before your permanent paperwork arrives. This is short notice, but is there any chance you could start tomorrow morning? We'll provide uniforms for you."

"Yes, thank you, s-sir." She stammered and swallowed against the lump in her throat. "I'm delighted. What time?"

"Is seven o'clock too early?"

"No. I'll be there."

As soon as Erika hung up, Sue hugged her. "How wonderful.

Your life here is moving forward fast, and I suspect the Lord will open even more doors."

Erika found the illnesses in America were similar to those in Germany. Fevers needed cooling, broken bones needed setting, pregnant women wanted safe deliveries and healthy babies, and older patients craved encouragement. Partly retired farmer Henry Becker came in for his arthritis checkup and smiled hearing Erika's accent in the exam room.

"My folks came from the old country," he said. "Hearing you makes me think you did too."

"That's right." She filled out his name on the exam record.

"Mom learned English well after coming here, but since Dad passed away she's forgetting more of it. Now she mostly talks German. Sometimes she imagines she's there again."

"Many people experience that as they age," Dr. Brower said. "They lose short-term memory, while childhood things stay in clearer focus."

"My brothers and sisters didn't learn German well," Henry said. "I'm rusty, but as the oldest, I talk with her more than the others do."

"That's good for her." Dr. Brower tapped Henry's knees, checking his reflexes. "I'm sure that's a comfort. It makes her feel less alone."

"I worry about her. She's overdue for a physical, but it's hard for her to get around. She still has basic energy, but there's a rasp in her lungs. Coming to town seems to confuse her." He sat up straighter. "Do you ever make house calls, Doctor?"

Dr. Brower removed his stethoscope from his ears. "Not as a rule, but in your case I'd consider it." He turned to Erika. "Especially if my new assistant came along."

"I'm willing," Erika said.

Two days later, Dr. Brower joined Erika in the lunchroom. "I can go to the Becker's tonight or tomorrow. Is there a chance one of those evenings could work for you?"

"I'm free tonight."

"Then let's go. I'll drive my car from here and take you home afterward."

The Becker Farm was past the beaver slough but near the river. When they pulled in the driveway, Henry greeted them with a wave.

"You're hard workers. That's an impressive earthen dike.

"You're hard workers," Dr. Brower said. "That's an impressive earthen dike.

"Dad insisted on it. It's similar to dikes they use in northwestern Europe to save their lowlands. Dad brought that idea when he came."

"Smart. It works."

Built from beautiful, peeled logs tightly fitted together, their home and barn reminded Erika of quaint places in Bavaria. Sturdy rail fences surrounded thriving fields of crops. "Your place is lovely. Wonderful craftsmanship."

"Thank you. We've worked hard and are pleased. Father learned good work habits in the old country and brought them here," Henry said. "Everything he built is strong and lasts forever."

"I see that."

Henry's mother, Elsa, sat in a maple rocker, her gaze distant, while her hands held knitting needles that flew back and forth. "*Ja, ja,*" she muttered, answering no one in particular from time to time.

"She wins ribbons at our county fair every year for all kinds of useful items," Henry said. "She knits as fast as most knitting machines, with few mistakes."

Erika stood back, guessing that Elsa was knitting a warm cap from the shape of the wool in her lap. "I believe you."

"Is *gut*." Elsa cast off a final row of stitches and bound the edge.

"*Wunderbar. Es ist sehr gut.*" Erika held the soft blue and lavender cap against her cheek before returning it to Mrs. Becker's hands.

The old woman's eyes focused on Erika. And then she studied the cap she'd just made. She smiled until her gums were visible and loosed a flood of German. When Erika answered, Elsa rose and embraced her, her eyes misty. "*Wunderschöner Engel.*"

Dr. Brower watched them. "What did she say?"

"She called me a beautiful angel." Erika patted the woman's hand.

"Well, that's true. Now, help me ask a few more health questions as I check some things." He placed his stethoscope against the old woman's chest to listen to her lungs. "Have her breathe in deeply."

"*Tief einatmen bitte,*" Elsa requested.

"That's good. Now have her inhale and exhale slowly several times."

Erika gave instructions, and the woman obeyed.

After a few more moments, Dr. Brower slipped his stethoscope back into a pocket of his long white coat. "Henry, she's doing well and may outlast us all."

"That's good to hear. How much she still manages to do pleases and surprises me." He turned to Erika. "And Miss Hofer, you made this process much easier for us. Thank you."

"Yes. She certainly helped me too," Dr. Brower said.

"You're welcome. It was my pleasure to come."

"*Danke, danke.*" The old woman grasped Erika's hand. She nodded as Henry brought two parcels of fresh honeycomb.

"This is for you to take home," Henry said.

The doctor touched his finger from the comb to his mouth. "Delicious. Thanks so much. This is truly *wunderbar.*"

Erika slipped her hand from Henry's mother's grasp to accept her parcel. "Bob and Sue will love this. *Auf Wiedersehen.*

Goodbye." Erika rested her cheek against Elsa's, and the woman pressed her newest knitted hat into Erika's hands.

"Take." Henry's mother said in German.

"For me? Are you sure?"

"*Ja.*" The woman repeated her words.

"How lovely. *Danke*," Erika spoke in German. "I would like to come again."

"Yes, please." Henry walked them to Dr. Brower's car. "That was wonderful. You made Mother very happy."

"I was glad to." Erika hugged her gifts. "She made me happy too."

When Erika got home, she found Sue as chirpy as a spring robin. "Before you got here, Bob came briefly for supplies but left without knowing how much longer they'll be away."

"I'm sorry I missed him." She handed Sue the honeycomb. "This is fresh from the Becker's farm. And the old grandmother gave me this hat she knitted." She modeled it before dropping into a chair.

"Both are very nice. The honeycomb's a treat."

"I would like to know what's happening down the river. Can't you tell me anything more about what the men are doing?"

"I really can't. It's their story to tell." Sue sat down near her. "You've probably heard about the Japanese submarine entering our river?"

"A little. Annie has to tell me more."

"Yes, it's best coming from her. For years, she wanted to take books with residents up and down the river who didn't have library access. The governor approved her idea for state funding, but then Pearl Harbor changed budget fundings. But the military had funds for undercover volunteers to do river surveillance, and she jumped at the chance. Ted signed on as her mechanic, and Smitty's sister-in-law was their river pilot. A Japanese sub invaded, and they were betrayed." Sue blew out a breath. "It was a scary close call."

Erika gulped. "That sounds even worse than I thought."

"I believe Annie or Ted are free to share the story now, although the public can't know the full story. Ted found a way to trigger the Japanese explosive to blow up early. It sank *Books Afloat,* and he got shot. Smitty and Johnny rescued Ted, Annie, and Char just in time."

Erika rubbed her arms. "That gives me chills. My uncle and these people I've just met did all that? They are the real heroes."

"Yes, that's true. The absolute best."

"I want to show courage like that. I had the Lord's help many times coming here."

"Yes—and He watched over Ted, Annie, and Char. We don't want more attacks to come, but if they do, we'll be ready. That's why the men dashed off so fast. Bob said they hope to be back tomorrow or the next day."

"Can we ask them what they're doing?"

"Yes, and if they can tell us, they will. Right now, the Japanese did something terrible, far north on an Alaskan island. Our men are stopping them from coming closer."

Erika sighed. "I didn't know so much was happening here on American soil. I thought this was simply a quiet place of natural beauty with great people. No wonder the Japanese would like to own it."

Sue picked up a notepad and pencil from the side table. "Erika, I'm changing topics. Do you think we can cook another German dinner sometime when the men are home? I'd like to include Johnny and Smitty."

Erika scooted her chair closer. "Of course. That would please me. I have ideas for many good dishes I think you'll love."

"Perfect. Let's see what ingredients I can gather in the next few days. I believe you could turn anything into a feast."

"I would try. And thanks for explaining about the men."

"Pray for them to stay alert and for Josh to heal enough to come home, if he's supposed to, or return to his fleet."

"It's hard for him. I'm praying God shows him the right choice."

Later that night, Erika pulled out her diary. Her entries in Germany and brief notes during her trip to this land already seemed like a lifetime ago. Tonight she added highlights of her welcome to America and the door opening for medical work. She missed her family and homeland, but the Lord was also busy here giving her more family and blessings in this promised land.

Thank you, Lord. Please care for my loved ones as well as you are me.

Chapter Twenty-Seven

Late August, 1942
Naval Medical Center, San Diego

Josh wrestled with the official terms. *Medical leave. Not approved for active duty.* With each passing day, reality settled more. He would leave San Diego and return home. He couldn't explain all the reasons why. It's just what he needed to do.

His legs were still wobbly but getting stronger. The crowded streets and sidewalks were a strenuous obstacle course that delayed him as he searched for the train station. He lurched drunkenly, his duffle on one shoulder, pulling him off center as he plowed forward. Short of breath and wiping sweat from his brow, he finally held the baggage receipt stub confirming his duffle was checked through to Vancouver, Washington. He limped even faster to catch the train heading north. It belched smoke, already building a head of steam.

Grabbing the vertical metal bar by the passenger car steps, he swung himself onboard and hobbled to an empty rear seat. For now, he was done riding ocean waves. The train chugged away from San Diego until there was no water in sight, not even raindrops outside the windows. The train's wheels *clickety-clacked*, but couldn't roll fast enough for Josh. Each revolution on the tracks sang, *Going home, going home, going home*. Less than a year ago he'd enjoyed riding south on another train to enlist. He didn't expect to return to his hometown and parents' house this soon, much less needy and broken.

But this decision was right.

At intervals, the train pulled onto sidings between towns. It stopped in small stations where locals climbed onboard selling sandwiches, fruit, cookies, or small pies. His pocket held a one-dollar bill, two dimes, and a nickel. He should have gotten cash before he left town, but it was too late now.

He motioned to the sandwich maker. "How much for the egg salad?"

"Today's special—four for a dollar."

"Sounds good. Give me four."

Josh noted the scarred man in the seat ahead hadn't eaten since San Diego—yesterday morning. The man's scars showed he'd been badly wounded, but there was no way to know how many more scars he bore inside.

Josh tapped his fellow passenger's shoulder and offered the sandwiches. "Buddy, do me a favor. I wanted to give that fellow business, and egg salad was on sale. I've got four but can only eat two."

The man's Adam's Apple bobbed. "You sure?"

"I'd count it a favor."

"Thanks." His hand reached out and grasped two sandwiches.

At the next stop, Josh bought a Golden Delicious apple for a nickel, the freshest he'd eaten since leaving Washington state. Hours later, he craved cookies, remembering how the sugar crystals melted on his tongue when Mom baked.

"How much?" he asked the housewife bringing them warm and fresh from her oven, the sweet cinnamon smell making his mouth water.

"Thirty cents for six. Guaranteed the best you'll find anywhere."

"Except for what my mom bakes." He fingered his two dimes. "I'm sorry I'm short."

"You're not. That's just right, sailor." She swept his dimes into her pocket and wrapped six large cookies in wax paper. He and the man ahead each devoured three.

The train rolled through the Willamette Valley, blowing its whistle loud and long at crossings each time white barricade arms came down, and he glimpsed orchards in some of America's best farmlands. Then the rolling hills evened out and they reached the Columbia River separating Oregon from Washington.

The train wheels braked and shrieked as they crossed the Interstate railroad bridge to enter his hometown. On the river below, boats blasted their horns. Bells rang from the church next to Esther Short Park, named for a pioneer mother who'd reached this end of the Oregon Trail with two children. The church where Dad preached. Their house stood next door.

Josh checked his watch. Early evening. His parents should be home. Leaving the train, he slouched down the street and slid his pack behind the holly hedge at the yard's corner. He smoothed the wrinkles from his uniform and stood as straight as he could. He plastered a grin on his face and ordered the butterflies in his stomach to still. His boots and twin canes thundered on the hollow wooden porch steps. He paused at the front door, hearing more than just Mom and Dad's voices inside. Mealtime. He could use one.

Should he ring the bell? Knock? No, he turned the knob. The dining room voices stilled at the door's opening squeak. A chair scraped the floor. Then heavy footsteps.

"Hello?" Dad called.

"It's me," Josh answered, "Can you put another plate on the table?"

"Josh!" Dad reached him in long strides, a groan tearing loose from deep inside. "Son! Thank God!" Dad's arms crushed him so tight Josh winced. "Sorry, son." He eased up but didn't let go. He wept. So did Josh.

Mom came hollering. And hugging. "I won't let go in case you're not really here."

Her words made no sense, but then again, they did. She squeezed with a strength Josh didn't know she had. She touched his damaged cheek, sadness in her eyes. But she did not scream.

A second person ran to the porch and plowed into him with a big hug before Mom grabbed him again.

Wait! Erika?

Then Dad and Mom corralled him in a three-way hug tighter than the plaster cast he'd worn for six weeks. Their hugs and joyful voices cocooned him.

Mom wept and laughed in turns. Josh brushed the tears from her cheeks. "It's okay, Mom. I'll be home a while."

"You'd better be, but I'm holding on just in case." She smiled through the last tears still glimmering in her lashes. "Look at you." She pushed him to arms' length. "Skinny. You need meat on those bones."

"Is that all you think of? Fattening me up?" He glanced at Erika and laughed. "It's not this young woman's fault. She did her best to feed me."

"That's good, but it's my job now." Mom's smile beamed brighter than the biggest lighthouse on the Pacific coast.

Josh scrubbed his eyes to keep from sobbing like Mom.

"Are you surprised to see Erika?" Mom pulled her forward. "She's staying here while her uncle handles some business."

He grasped her hand. "Small world. I figured he would claim all your time once you got here. It's nice to see you."

She flushed and pulled her hand back. "I delivered your letter to your parents like you asked. Welcome home. You're looking better than when I left."

"You think so?" Josh scanned his legs and feet.

"Yes. Stronger. And moving faster and more smoothly."

"Good. I'm trying hard."

Her smile was brighter than when she was in San Diego. Something was going right.

"You need time with your parents. I'll go take care of kitchen tasks. Do you want to eat first?"

"Yes. No. I don't know what I want to do." He laughed. "Give me a plate, and I'll grab time with my folks first but save me time too. It's been a while. I want to hear how you like our town and everything." Her eyes seemed bluer than before. "We need to catch up."

"Just tell me when."

Dad hovered. "How are you, Josh?"

Mom already had a plate piled high. "Thanks for clearing up, Erika. Josh? Let's go in the study. You can stretch out on the couch while you eat. We want to hear everything.

Lying in his own bed that night, Josh's body molded deep into his mattress more comfortably than anything the Navy had provided. Some aches and pains eased, and he slept soundly. But just before sunrise, he was startled awake.

He was home, near enough to the river to hear its song and morning sounds. But different men's voices mingled with Dad's in the kitchen. Josh's watch read 4:55 a.m. What was going on this early?

"We need to include Josh. He's been through a lot, but he's a fighter."

Josh didn't recognize that voice.

"He's not healed yet," Dad warned.

"He doesn't have to be perfect to do the job. He's got the know-how." That speaker had a slight accent. "Let's ask him straight up. He'll know if he's ready or not. It might do him good. The pulley system Smitty and I rigged up should help him."

That must be Erika's Uncle Johnny.

Now their neighbor, Smitty, jumped in. "If he says no, we'll leave him alone. But if I were him—I'd beg for a chance to fight on the home front."

"But if it's too soon, he'll hurt himself." Dad again. "I'll wake him and see what he says."

When the bedroom door creaked open and Dad slipped in, Josh already had his eyes open.

"It's all right, Dad. I'm awake. You can turn on the light."

Dad did. "It's so good to have you home. You're barely back and not all the way healed, but there's a problem my friends are wondering if you'd want to help with—*if* you're up to it."

"Try me. I think I'm up to quite a bit. I want to hear more." He sat up and ran one hand over his short crewcut. "Besides, I'll bet it's interesting because my hair feels tingly electric like on the *Yorktown* before the torpedoes hit."

Dad gripped Josh's shoulder. "We don't want that much excitement, but there is trouble."

"Tell me. Let me help." Josh swung his feet over the side of the bed and winced.

"You're hurting."

"No worse than usual. Whatever's happening, I'm your man." He grabbed both canes and stood, balancing himself.

"Slip on your robe and come to the kitchen."

Mom was already there toasting a stack of sliced bread and had her coffeepot billowing out its bracing smell. Seeing Erika stand at the stove scrambling eggs, like she belonged there, made Josh smile. She beamed as Josh limped in and turned to a small wiry man nearby with a thatch of gray hair and eyes shaped like hers but darker. It had to be her uncle. His clothing was ordinary enough, despite Dad's warnings he might look bizarre.

"Uncle Johnny? I've told you about Josh, and here he is." Erika laughed as her uncle jumped from the table and gave Josh a handshake as crippling as the grip of any channel lock.

"Pleased to meet you, sailor." His accent was slight. "Happy you're home from that awful *var*."

"Me too. That's quite a grip you have. "Johnny released his hand and Josh massaged it until his blood began to circulate again.

Instead of a handshake, Smitty pulled Josh into a hug. "Proud of you, youngster. And I'm thanking God you're back. We've heard of your exploits from when the *Yorktown* went down. Strong stuff."

"Exploits?" Josh's stomach lurched. "There weren't any. I washed up near dead on some small unnamed island. Natives there saved me from the Japanese, or I wouldn't be here—end of story."

"Wow." Smitty and Dad exchanged glances. "Maybe he doesn't remember," Smitty mused.

"Guess not." Dad looked proud. "But this isn't the time to set him straight."

"Right." Smitty tipped back his captain's hat. "Here's our situation. We're only hearing details now, but about the time the Japanese attacked Midway, they also invaded Alaska's Aleutian Islands—as a diversion."

"The old divide and conquer trick," Dad said.

"It worked." Smitty angled his hat further back. "By invading Attu, they showed what yellow-bellied stinkers they are."

"Stinkers?" Mom raised an eyebrow. "I think you want to use a stronger word there."

"I do ..." Smitty grinned. "But I'm a gentleman, and there are ladies present."

"Thanks for noticing." Mom carried homemade blackberry preserves to the table.

"We could call the Japs devils and not exaggerate," Dad said.

"Stinkers? Devils." Smitty checked the note in his hand. "Anyway, here's the report of what they did on Attu. It's the farthest west of the Aleutians—closer to Japan than most of Alaska, so taking it was like picking ripe fruit from a tree."

"Too bad it's not a thorn tree," Josh said.

"Or the tree Judas hung himself from." Bob rubbed the back of his neck.

"We'll make it thorny for them," Erika's uncle's eyes glittered.

Josh laid his canes on the floor and pushed them under his chair. "What's Attu's economic value?"

"Very little. A pretty wild climate. It's hard to grow anything. There's fishing but no mining we know of." Smitty hooked his thumbs in his belt. "It is a vital location for ocean transport routes."

Josh's head bobbed. "That makes sense."

"Breakfast is ready." Mom dusted her hands on her apron. "I hope you fellas can eat while you talk."

"Hasn't stopped us yet," Smitty said.

"Sorry, I didn't have enough rations for bacon this month."

"What you fix is always fine, Sue," Smitty said. "No complaints ever."

"Thanks."

"Hold on." Johnny pulled a can of Spam from a vest pocket. "A family downriver gave me this for helping them. There's a good slice in here for each of us." He handed the tin to Sue. "Here you go. Fry her up."

"Glad to, Johnny. Thanks for sharing." She sliced the Spam into her hot pan where it sizzled. "Help yourselves to toast and jam while I fry this." She turned the slices when they browned and then served them on a plate. "Here you go. A feast fit for kings. Bob, ask the blessing so we can eat and start your meeting."

"Sure thing, but I'd like you and Erika to sit first."

They joined hands while Dad committed the food, the day, and each one around the table to God's care. Josh sat between Mom and Erika, their hands joined. It was too good to be true, being home again, eating Mom's food, sitting next to this brave girl who'd escaped the Nazis, but who still had loved ones in danger.

"Better than hospital food, right Josh?" Erika's eyes sparkled.

His eyes pleaded with her not to tell. He noticed she liked teasing him. "No comparison." He took a bite. "Delicious! He chewed briskly, hoping Erika would stay quiet and get busy with her own food.

Smitty leaned on the table. "Last night, Johnny and I met with volunteers part way downriver. Based on their reports, we're tightening and increasing our network."

Erika's eyes widened. "Does that mean you need more helpers?"

"Pretty much. If we get the right ones. We have good people in place, but more would be better."

Johnny dipped the corner of his toast in egg yolk and chewed and swallowed it down with a sigh. "Good cooking!"

Each one at the table polished off their food. Most ate seconds, relishing real coffee with cream.

Smitty forked in a last mouthful of cheesy eggs and then pulled folded papers from his shirt pocket. He glanced at Erika. "This part's not sensitive, so I'm free to share. One of our guys gave me these notes and a map. The U.S. Navy figured Attu would be a target. They'd been given orders to evacuate the forty-five native Aleuts there and an older American couple helping them. The Navy was within a day of getting there, but the Japs came sooner than expected."

Josh stopped eating. "I don't like the sounds of that."

"Yup. Over eleven hundred soldiers swarmed the island and captured the Aleuts plus the American couple, Foster and Etta Jones. She ran the school. He radioed weather reports. Smashed the radio when he saw the Japs coming so they couldn't use it. When he wouldn't fix it, they killed him."

Josh poked his fork in the air. "What about the others?"

"Some Aleuts were killed. A bunch of kids died from trauma. Forty-some adults got shipped to Japan to work in mines. They sent Jones's widow to Yokohama as a prisoner of war. We've had no reliable reports since. We think she's alive and hope for the best."

"That's terrible." Erika cradled her head in her hands. "What do you expect the Japanese to do next?"

"That's anybody's guess," her uncle said. "We hear they're setting up death camps like Hitler's, but we don't know much."

Erika shook her head. "We didn't want to believe the rumors we heard about what Hitler was doing. Maybe if we'd had more courage to find out and resist him."

"Erika, that wouldn't have stopped him." Her uncle's eyes warmed. "He'd just put you and those opposing him in the same camps. Recent events make that clear. It's better you're here."

"I know. But at least now the world has to believe the evidence. It's so hard to imagine human beings doing such things to one another."

"Maybe they're not human. None of this sounds good, whether they're Japanese, Germans, or plain devils." Dad took out his own paper and pencil. "The Japs may offer the Attu prisoners for exchange or ransom. We're not sure. The whole situation needs constant prayer for wisdom."

"Yes," Mom said. "Unceasing prayer."

Those who hadn't finished pushed their food around their plates for a few moments until they laid down their silverware.

Smitty eyed Sue. "We don't aim to waste your good cooking. I'll finish mine later, but we must hear and understand what's happening now to face it and stop it."

"Exactly right. Tell the rest, Smitty." Dad laid his crumpled napkin on the table.

"Intelligence says the Japs are occupying Attu and building outposts on other islands. It's a dot-to-dot pattern heading this way."

"Not surprising." Josh heard the tension laced in his mother's words. "How close?"

"They're making steady progress." Johnny unfolded a paper. "Show them this map, Smitty."

Smitty cleared a space in the middle of the table. "Thank God the tide's turning in the South Pacific, but they're pushing back for footholds on our northern coasts. Bob, you've updated us on those attacks. Besides where they already are on Alaskan islands—" He tapped the map. "They're here, here, and here. Plus moving south to Vancouver Island in Canada. They'll probably hit Port Angeles soon, and if we don't stop them, move on to the Olympic Peninsula."

"That close?" Josh sat up straighter. "They obviously have a plan. So, you chased away the Japanese sub that entered the Columbia, but they haven't given up."

"As far as we know, that's right." Johnny turned to Smitty. "What's the most recent sighting around here?"

"After the attacks on our river failed, they've been scarce, but their radio traffic is up. Can you fill us in on that?"

"Okay." Johnny cleared his throat and swallowed. "They're using complicated codes but we're cracking 'em nearly as fast as they invent them." He beamed a radiant smile. "Our Navajo code talkers drive them nuts."

"Wonderful!" Josh's head buzzed. He swiped a hand over his forehead to drive away the suddenly recurring sounds of Jap zeroes diving, exploding torpedoes, ships sinking, and men screaming. He had screamed then and bit his lips so he wouldn't do it again now.

Don't let me make a scene.

Smitty took over. "Some recent messages encourage Germans around here to rise up and help the Japanese and Italians. They want more uprisings happening in our country to defeat us from within."

"That's pretty standard strategy," Josh said.

Erika groaned. "I hate hearing that happening in this beautiful place. Or anywhere."

"We do too." Josh didn't realize he'd closed both hands into tight claws until muscle aches traveled up his arms. He unclenched his hands and flexed his fingers. "Do you seriously think any Japanese or German-American residents among us would sabotage?"

"None I know," Johnny said. "But of course, it's a real threat. If people get panicked enough, there's talk of a presidential order to lock up people of Japanese or German heritage."

Erika paled. "I guess that's to be expected. Hitler would do the same. He *is* doing it."

Josh saw Smitty's eyes on him.

"If you're ready, that's where you come in, Josh. We need trained and savvy volunteers to beef up our network."

"You see my limited physical condition."

"That has little to do with your training and courage. We consider you an asset."

His heart surged. "What do you need from those of us around this table?"

"We're still brainstorming. Most of us here are already deeply involved." Smitty's eyes shined. "As far as we're concerned, you came home at just the right time. You've been through incredible battle action and survived."

"So far, but not on my own." His face heated. "I told you, I got hurt and was lucky to have help."

"Luck? I think it was more than that." Johnny's eyes flashed. "You're not seeing the picture correctly. After the *Yorktown* went down, you also saved other men. Maybe you don't even know it, but it sounds like you did lots of things right."

Josh quit breathing. "Don't you listen? As far as I know, against all odds, I floated ashore—as crazy as that sounds."

"Apparently a report with more details got delayed," Smitty said. "The War Office is finalizing eye-witness accounts now. You should receive a copy soon."

Josh opened his mouth but shut it again. Warmth spread from the pit of his stomach through his limbs. "Sounds good. I'll take a look at it if that happens. I'd like that to be true but don't see how ..."

"Never mind. Truth comes out like cream rising to the top.

We hope to keep you close to home to allow you more time to heal, but some events on the river are at crisis stage. You'd be a big help. Like the recruitment posters say, 'Uncle Sam needs you!'" Smitty pointed at Josh with such a broad smile on his face, it made his captain's hat angle down.

Josh smiled back. "Thanks. I hear ya."

Warmth lit Dad's eyes. "Josh, even if you haven't done any of the amazing things they say, we're mighty proud."

He expelled a breath. "Like I said, I hope I am who you think I am. Anything I did was unintentional—sheer survival instinct. I was wounded, barely alive. I still can't figure out how I made it, or why the natives risked their lives to help me."

"God's plan." Erika spoke softly.

"You're the kind of help we want," Smitty said. "We send out teams two by two. At first, new members stick with volunteers who've done lots of surveillance. Tough times mean tough calls. Our teams work together to sharpen each other's skills. Erika, there are things you can do. You'll be with me."

"That would be my pleasure, Captain Smith." She nodded to the retired captain.

"Smitty to you, young lady. Josh, we're putting you with Johnny. You each have strengths that complement each other."

The two men sized each other up.

"Sounds good," Josh said.

"Yup. I'm all for learning new tricks. I might teach you some too." Johnny laughed so hard his whole body shook.

"During emergencies," Smitty said, "sometimes we do assignments like Chinese fire drills and all scramble into action together."

"Sounds better yet," Josh said. "Sometimes we did things like that on the *Yorktown*."

"Chinese fire drill?" Erika echoed. "Are the Chinese fighting this war too?" Confusion tightened her face and those around the table laughed until Sue explained.

"In the circus or sometimes in traffic, passengers in two cars stop, all climb out to circle around the vehicles, take new seats, and drive off. The stunt is called a Chinese fire drill."

Erika blinked. "They really do that?"

"Not often, but sometimes. It's fun to watch"

"What that means for us," Smitty said, "is that we try to learn each other's jobs well enough to fill in and help each other when there's a problem."

"Oh." Erika beamed. "Why didn't you say so? Now I understand."

Chapter Twenty-Eight

Mid-August, 1942
Vancouver, Washington

Erica stared as Dr. Brower's receptionist, Maxine Smythe fussed, "I've fallen behind and need help. Can't anyone see that?"

Erika shook her head and turned her attention to the waiting patients. One kind-looking older woman had brought in her husband whose speech became confused after several strokes. He gazed into space, while his wife and the nurse spoke English. His occasional responses were so low-pitched and guttural, the nurse wrote in Karl Miller's chart, "gibberish, the result of strokes."

Mrs. Smythe glared. "Whatever the cause, he's speaking German, our enemy's language. That's dangerous. We should check patient records to find all suspicious foreign connections." Adjusting her glasses, she opened a file drawer and rifled through their contents.

"Karl grew up speaking German," Mrs. Miller told Erika. "Their family name, *Müller*, means Miller. They milled flour in the Old Country but simplified it when they came here. He's forgetting more English these days but remembering childhood German."

Nurse Nalley nodded. "That's common among stroke victims."

Mrs. Smythe stood and snatched the Miller chart from Nurse Nalley's hand. "Let me look at that a minute. Since we're fighting Japan and Germany, I don't trust foreign speakers. They shouldn't live here. We didn't dream Japan would invade our river, but they did. Now that they're partners with Germany and Italy, can you imagine what could happen if local sympathizers backed our enemies?"

"Maxine!" Nurse Nalley's hands dropped to her hips. "That hasn't happened, and I can't picture local residents aiding the enemy." She snatched the chart back. "I need this now."

"Authorities are checking that traitor news reporter's contacts. They'll find something."

The nurse huffed. "They might if they dig deep enough. If not, they might invent something. German-Americans have lived here for generations and helped build up this area. So have Hawaiians, Scandinavians, and other hardworking immigrants. They've shaped our life here."

"And brought danger. You're too trusting." Maxine waved away the nurse's words. "Until President Roosevelt's Executive Order, we thought our Japanese-American citizens were fine. Now they're being locked up. Frankly, authorities should investigate all citizens with foreign roots. They should all be locked up as far as I'm concerned.'

Nurse Nalley turned deep red. "Maxine, that's rude. You're going too far." She glanced at Erika. "This kind of conversation should only happen in our lunchroom with Dr. Brower present."

"No. You're wrong." Mrs. Smythe scribbled more words in the small tablet next to her scheduling book.

If only Erika could see what the receptionist had written in her tablet. Heat burned in her cheeks. She wished they'd give her a chance to prove not all Germans were like Hitler.

The nurse turned to her patients. "Mr. and Mrs. Miller? I'll prepare the exam room now and be right back for you."

Did Maxine believe what she was saying? Mr. Miller's mind was failing—that was all. He was old and ill, needing help—not dangerous. If speaking German helped him calm, they'd get more accurate results in today's medical tests. Erika sat in the empty chair next to him. *"Guten tag, mein herr. Sprechen sie Deutsch?"*

He snapped alert, his smile growing. *"Guten tag. Fraulein. Danke."*

Mrs. Miller melted. "Oh, thank you. He gets confused and locked in the past. I hope Dr. Brower has answers."

"I think he will. He's a wonderful man."

The woman's smile grew. "That's comforting, exactly what we need." But then her face crumpled. "It's terrible. Karl loses more English with each mini-stroke."

Erika clasped her hand. "Don't give up hope. My father was a good doctor and sometimes saw stroke victims regain their language ability. Some even fully regained clear speech again, like broken bones that heal so well you can hardly tell where they were broken."

"I would be so thankful!" The woman's eyes filled with tears. "We don't know anyone else locally who speaks German. Would you consider giving me your name and a phone number so I can call you if Karl has a problem?" She pulled a blank index card from her purse and held it out to Erika. "I'd only contact you in an emergency."

Erika hesitated. "I guess that would be all right—if it didn't happen often. I haven't been here long. Here is the phone number of the friends I'm staying with. Or you can reach me here at this clinic."

"I'm grateful." The woman read what Erika had written "Thank you, Erika. Would you be willing to say a bit more to Karl now?"

"For the next minute or two." In German she said, "God

bless you, sir. How are you today? Are you enjoying this weather? Dr. Brower is a good doctor who will help you."

After each response, she asked another question. "How old are you? When is your birthday?"

He answered clearly and plainly, becoming more confident. The longer they talked, the calmer he became.

"It's wonderful what you're doing," one young mother said while juggling her toddler.

But a large, disheveled man in the corner glowered as if in pain. Maybe it was concern for the grandmotherly woman sitting next to him. Must be his wife. Laugh lines edged her eyes, but deeper blue shadows tinged underneath. One of her hands shook with slight palsy. Each time her husband spoke in her ear, her hand shook more and she pulled further away. She held her hand steady in her lap and soon weighed it down with her other hand.

Anytime Erika kept spoke German, the disheveled man grew more perturbed. "Stop! Now! We don't allow foreign stuff since President Roosevelt rounded up the Japs. We don't know what you're saying, and our receptionist is smart. It's time to lock up all Germans and Italians, too, and anyone who threatens our freedom!"

Erika blanched. If only Dr. Brower were here. The man stood and hovered over the receptionist, who was busy on the phone. When she didn't acknowledge him, he grabbed a wooden pencil from her desk and snapped it in two. He dropped the pieces in front of her.

"Don't let foreigners talk in here," he roared. "We don't know what they're saying. It's dangerous! They're taking our freedom away."

Who did he think he was—an Old Testament prophet?

She reddened. "Mr. Gibson? Please take your seat."

"No." He glared. "I won't. Make Dr. Brower see my wife now! We came clear from past Pioneer Grange and have waited over forty minutes already. It's not fair." He tapped his watch. "No excuses. You owe us good care, or I'll tell the town folks you're no good."

Mrs. Smythe shrank in her chair and covered the phone's mouthpiece with her hand. "Dr. Brower can't see her yet. H-he's still at the hospital across the street delivering a baby."

He thumped her desk with each word. "He. Should. Be. Here! Every patient deserves equal treatment. And why do you have foreigners here? That's awful. What if they're traitors like that reporter who helped the Japs? Or the doctor in Kelso arrested for sending messages to Germany? He's in the hoosegow somewhere now. Serves him right." The man whirled and shook a fist in Erika's face before muttering something to his wife and storming outside. The door slammed so hard it rattled, making the slanted blind covering the glass fall to the floor.

Other patients in the waiting area sat stunned. Mrs. Gibson cried quietly into a tissue.

Erika asked the man's wife, "Is he all right? Is there anything I can do?"

She trembled. "I—I'm not sure. I haven't seen him this bad before. He's impatient and suspicious of everything lately. It's better for all of us that he waits outside." She found a dry part of her tissue and dabbed her eyes again.

"He's right about one thing!" Mrs. Smythe waved a hand like a military officer giving orders. "Things are out of control in our country these days. We should stay on guard and suspect everyone until they prove trustworthy." Unsmiling, she scribbled more words in her small tablet, and then her voice shrilled higher. "Having an unexpected baby arrive didn't help, but it's not our fault. Fitting in missed patients is more than anyone can do!"

Erika's stomach sickened. The doctor had encouraged her to speak German to help Elsa Becker during her exam at their farm. Should things be different inside the clinic? Earlier today when he'd rushed past her from Exam Room A to B, he'd waved and said, "Thanks for helping out so well, Erika. You're a life saver."

He'd dashed past before she could reply.

Lord, I know during wartime people don't know who to trust. That Corporal in San Diego was suspicious of me. Lord, help me do so well that Mrs. Smythe and others see my heart more than my accent or actions. Help me change the atmosphere and make the right difference here.

"Erika, are you all right? You look drained." Sue greeted her as soon as she walked into the house.

"Yes." Erika rubbed her hand over her face. "Today was difficult. Have you met Mrs. Smythe, the clinic receptionist?"

"I've seen her there. I believe she and her husband moved here recently from Portland."

"That's right." Erika filled her in. "And then a baby decided to be born mid-morning so Dr. Brower rushed to the hospital. Mrs. Smythe skipped lunch to reschedule patients and crowd in the missed appointments, but one patient's husband got upset and became nasty."

"Really?" Sue frowned. "Of course, all parents want Dr. Brower to deliver their kids. I've heard he has a long waiting list of new people wanting appointments."

"It's true, I've seen it. In fact, he's not taking new patients right now. That partly caused what happened today. People kept phoning to sign up with him or patients wanting their appointments moved up. Mrs. Smythe did her best to keep up until it just got to be too much for her, and she snapped. The man I mentioned was hateful."

"That's strange." Sue raised her eyebrows. "People don't usually act hateful around here.

"He sure did. He said people from Japan and Germany and maybe all foreign countries should be locked up and not allowed in." Erika rubbed her breastbone, hoping to ease the ache that had lodged there all day.

"That's extreme. "Do you know his name?"

"Yes. We're supposed to keep names confidential. But since you're a pastor's wife, I think you'll pray. It's Gibbon or Gibson."

Sue froze. "From Pioneer Grange?"

"Yes. He said that. Where is it?"

"Downriver a ways. I'm sorry you ran into him. He's been having a hard time and can be really unpleasant."

"Do you know what made him that way?"

"I don't know all the reasons. Bob knows more, but his only son, Charles Jr., was a pilot over Europe and got shot down. No one's heard if he's dead or in a prison camp."

"That's awful."

"Even worse, that son's pregnant wife hemorrhaged when their baby started coming early. They couldn't get her to the hospital in time, and they lost her and the baby. Mr. and Mrs. Gibson are raising their older grandson, Charlie." Sue hesitated. "Annie had a run-in with Mr. Gibson about the grandson using her floating library. She thinks Mr. Gibson makes young Charlie's life miserable."

"I can picture that. So, he hates everything German or anyone foreign because he's ... heartbroken?"

"Pretty much. He's one of those people who blames his pain and problems on others."

"I've met people like that too. If I could tell him how things really are in Germany, he'd understand that I hate Hitler and this war as much as he does."

"I don't recommend trying. It's too dangerous. Bob visited him several times and says he's talking wild lately—making crazy threats."

"He got so out of control in the clinic today and turned so red, I thought he might have a stroke. It started when he heard me speak German to another patient—said we should be locked up like the Japanese."

Sue hung her head. "I'm sorry to say he's not the only one saying that. It's not typical, but I've heard a few others." She filled her watering can and moved from house plant to house plant through her living room.

"These are beautiful," Erika followed as Sue watered each one.

Sue moved on to a hanging basket. "See this? It's a maidenhair fern."

"It's lovely, like living green lace."

"Yes. Actually, Mrs. Gibson helped me start this plant from a cutting, but it's drooping." Sue touched the soil. "It seems to have enough water. Maybe it needs more sunlight." She moved the hanging basket closer to the window.

"If I see Mr. Gibson again, I wish I could tell him how sympathetic German Christians feel."

"I understand, but that isn't a good idea. He threatened Bob."

"He did?" Erika's eyes widened. "That's awful."

"Bob said Gibson almost hit him. When someone hurts that much, we can pray and be available, but be cautious about approaching them." Sue paused in the doorway. "There's one other thing I should tell you."

"What's that?"

"West of here, in Kelso-Longview, a nice, retired local doctor has relatives in Germany—his mother's sister and kids we think. He'd heard of heavy bombings there and worried that they suffered food and medicine shortages."

"That's true. There are severe shortages."

"He's also a ham radio operator, part of an international communications club. Before the war, he often talked with relatives in Germany. That mostly stopped once war broke out but he got worried when he didn't hear from his family there. He connected with them recently to see how they were and to ask if they needed help."

Erika frowned. "Did he get through?"

"He did. He knew the risks but did it anyway. Other radio club members overheard him speaking German. One of them turned him in. They confiscated his radio and put him in custody while they do an investigation. He admits speaking German to relatives, but says it was innocent and only concerned humanitarian needs."

Erika nodded. "Even if that's true, it's likely hard to prove. What will happen?"

"We don't know. Our state doesn't have prisoner of war camps yet. He's being held in an Army brig at Fort Lewis near Tacoma."

"A *brig*? Mrs. Smythe said he was in a *hoosegow*. Do you know those words?"

"They're really the same thing—just different ways of saying a *jail*."

"Will he face treason? I know that's very serious." Erika's voice trembled.

"We hope not. He's a good man. Many of us have spoken on his behalf, including Bob and me. He's done so much good through the years. Radioing family in Germany was unwise, but we're praying the espionage charge will be dropped."

Erika sank into a chair. "Dietrich warned us that in wartime people yield to hysteria. I understand why the doctor contacted his relatives. I worry about mine. But he had little chance of accomplishing much good and a high risk of causing his relatives' arrest."

"After you shared your clinic experience today, I thought you should know." Sue turned toward the kitchen. "I hope it never happens, but someone could think the same of you."

"Oh, dear." Erika bowed her head. "I understand. Thank you."

Chapter Twenty-Nine

Early September, 1942
Portland Air Base and Vancouver, Washington

"Josh, I'm impressed. Tell me more about the exercise system that produced these results." Brad's therapist friend, Matt, said. "Who designed these pulleys and contraptions? Has the public seen them? These are great! According to your numbers, you've advanced a long way since your treatments in San Diego."

Josh grinned. "It seems that way to me. I'm pretty happy with being able to do more things again."

"I'll say." Matt flipped through records and then checked Josh over thoroughly in the physio department at Portland Air Base. He double checked recorded numbers and took second and third measurements of Josh's improvement. "Brad will be jealous. I like that a lot."

Josh chuckled. "It's a program put together by friends of my dad along the Columbia River. They're old guys retired from some kind of science jobs."

"I want to know them. Could you work that out?"

"I'm not sure. They stay very busy."

"Please try. They're seriously brilliant—not amateurs. It looks like they're using simple materials but know what they're doing to get results like this. They should patent the system." Matt's fingers traced the apparatus shown in one photo, His eyes riveted to the page. "I think I could almost make a blueprint. It looks like they have you up to speed with one cane most of the time now, and sometimes you're not using that. Amazing!" He shook his head, today laying the photos down next to the X-rays Brad had sent. "They're taking you forward faster than Brad or I could. I'd like them working for us."

"I appreciate you confirming my progress. I can tell I'm stronger."

"I'll update your records, but frankly, I can't do better." Matt tugged an ear. "Do you know if they're military or ex-military?"

"I don't, but I've wondered. Smitty's a retired tugboat captain. I'm not sure about his buddy, Johnny Hofer."

"Hofer?" Matt gave a sharp look. "Are they that incredible pair that rescued folks from that floating library after they managed to sink the Japanese sub?"

"They might be, but they don't want too much said."

"It's hard not to admire those guys—local heroes!"

"So I've heard."

"Gotcha. Well, you're in great hands. If you can wrangle me an invitation, I want to meet them." He handed Josh a small card. "For now, I'll only have you come in monthly to satisfy Navy records. If anything comes up, here's my card and contact information."

Josh palmed the stiff printed card and slid it into his shirt pocket.

"It's a pleasure to meet you, Josh, and confirm you're doing this great. I can't wait to tell Brad."

Josh returned to his dad's car walking faster and straighter than when he'd come home weeks ago, and only using one cane for climbing steps. At the top, he twirled it like a baton. His smile stretched from ear to ear. After today's evaluation, he would draw Navy disability pay for the next six months at least and still help the river volunteers.

That afternoon, Johnny led Josh to his dented, camo-painted pickup. "This time, it's you and me, son. We'll drive this rattletrap as far as we can and finish up on foot. Are you up for that?"

"I'll do my best, but after a busy morning, a ride sounds good." Josh swung into the cab easily without challenging his arm muscles at all. "I like the sound of your engine. She runs fine."

Johnny patted the hood. "She should. Ted gives Clarabelle a good going over once a month."

Josh swallowed "Figures. I haven't seen Ted yet since I've been home. How's he doing?"

"Dandy. He's at his dad's place mending fences. You know—relationships, not cow pastures. Ted's dad should be highly pleased with his son. Just because Ted isn't an athlete doesn't mean he isn't an outstanding young man. He's made of strong stuff. It's time his dad acknowledges that."

"All I know is, Ted's dad is super demanding. I'm thankful for my dad. I don't know how Ted stands it. I'm glad he's always been my best friend."

"Yeah, lucky you. He and Annie will get hitched soon. They'll be great together."

Josh's neck burned. "I'm still getting used to the idea. It was always the three of us."

Johnny searched Josh's face. "I wondered about that, but things change. Are you up for walking a ways past the end of this road?"

"I'll manage." His face relaxed. "I got a good physio report today. The specialist really likes your gadgets."

Johnny's smile broadened. "That's good to hear." As he turned his truck steering wheel sharply, his very well-developed arm muscles strained his shirt sleeves. That's when Josh noticed his hands.

"You're missing your trigger finger."

"Yup. Funny thing about that. I went into the woods one day and came back without it. It kept me from being drafted, which is best. My background's German, so I wouldn't want to fight Germans and shoot relatives by accident, but I'd give my life to keep this country safe."

"You've proven that. Let's hope more isn't necessary."

"I hope the same." Johnny expelled a slow breath. "In early days, I started out working at Boeing."

"Dad told me. I'd like to hear more. Was Smitty there too?"

"He was. On the ground floor in Research and Development. Before he went tugboat captaining. We did terrific projects. The rest is history. That submarine model we built saved Annie and crew when they needed rescuing."

"Fabulous. Can I see it? Will you give me a ride?"

Johnny slanted his eyes. "After you've sailed on big ships? Not sure. She's cramped. But we're creating a dream machine that might win this war once we get the bugs out."

"Then that's worth doing! Speed things up!"

"We're trying. You know those amphibious ducks that are great on land or water?"

"Yeah. A friend's buying one to log his swampy woods."

"They're perfect for that. Ours is a composite water-air ship with hollow metal pontoons on top and a matching pair beneath with motors and passenger space in between. It'll churn through water or fly above at a good clip."

"That's awesome, like an angry goose rising from water to attack its enemies."

"Ha-ha. What a good comparison. We don't have the design nailed down, but we'll get there. We're researching compressed-air vehicles too. There's talk of flying aircraft carriers."

"That's a stretch, but as a Navy man, I like it. Can I see your models or mockups?" Josh flexed his fingers. "I'm itching to get involved!"

"I see that. Hold your horses. I'll talk to Smitty."

"Good." Josh grinned. "He's been my friend a long time."

Johnny steered the truck away from the main road paralleling the Columbia to bounce down a gravel lane. Josh clutched the door handle to avoid slamming his head on the truck's roof. "This is like a rodeo bronco. I could yodel."

"That could make life interesting, but we need to keep quiet." Johnny held the steering wheel in a vise grip. "Smitty and I drew straws to test our last prototype. He won, but crash-landed and got banged up, so maybe didn't win in the long run." Johnny swallowed a laugh. "Poor fella. That's when we designed the pulley system."

"It works fine." Josh bounced again. "How bad did he get hurt?"

"Nothing broken, mostly serious sprains."

"How long ago? He seems good now."

"Pretty much. It hasn't been that long, but those pulleys work wonders." Johnny cranked his head to scrutinize Josh. "You do look better."

"That's what the therapy guy said. I'm happy to be this good, Johnny. Huge thanks to you guys. I can tell my back is stronger. My neck and legs need more work, but they're coming."

Josh braced his hands against the truck's dashboard before they hit the next big bump. "Oomph."

"Yeah. It's hardly a road. When do you think they'll release you to go back to your shipmates?"

"I don't know, but the head therapist at the air base raved about my progress. I told him you invented the system. He wants to meet you guys."

"Shucks. Anyone can do what we did. We rigged up weights, pulleys, and other paraphernalia to get Smitty strong. It worked. To see him now, you wouldn't know he'd crashed, except for the stiff, achy joints old guys get."

Josh laughed. "Sometimes young guys do too. You two will never get old."

"That's the plan. And we want you to make a full recovery."

Johnny rubbed his chin. "Smitty and I've been talkin'. We're glad you gave our contraptions a workout."

"Me too." Josh scrutinized Johnny. Kindness radiated from the small-but-powerful man. "I'd be stupid not to. Look at the results they've already brought. I've known Smitty forever. If you hadn't told me he had a crash, I wouldn't believe you. You should patent them."

"We might. Our gadgets may not work for everyone, but they got you limbered up."

"That's for sure." Josh's smile spread wide.

Now Johnny turned the truck from the gravel road to bump along a dirt track that finally became flattened grass. He pulled over and took a compass from his pocket to read coordinates. "This is it." He rolled behind a stand of evergreen trees and cut his engine. "Step out and take a look. If I do this right, this truck won't be visible from ten feet away. And then I'll disappear." He stood near a tree and pulled a green and brown leather patchwork shirt over his head and slipped on mottled leggings.

Josh had never seen anything like these garments. They were crisscrossed pieces of sewn leather patched so many times, it was hard to name the original colors or identify where one started and the other ended. They made perfect camouflage.

Johnny donned a Robin Hood style hat and stepped near a cluster of spruce trees. He disappeared and quietly called, "Can you see me now?"

"Holy smoke, no. I know you're there," Josh said, "but you're invisible."

Johnny waved a hand. "What about now?"

"Same thing. I see a little movement—that's all."

"Good. Stay farther back since you're in city duds or you'll stick out like a sore thumb. Next time we'll make you special boots, too, instead of your clonkers."

"These are Dad's, but I'll try whatever you've got." Josh tried to picture himself in woodland garb but couldn't. Still, he wanted to learn from Johnny. He stretched his legs to size up Dad's heavy boots compared to Johnny's feet clad in light-weight, handcrafted leather moccasins that curled at the toe like leprechaun boots. His mouth dropped open. A man might want to dance in them.

"Where did you get those? They're fabulous."

"Should be. I made them. They're light and comfy. I tanned a deer hide like my friends at the Cowlitz Reserve showed me. Doubled it under for thick soles. I can walk across sharp rocks without hurtin', and if they get wet they dry easy, no shrinking." Johnny made a circle with his thumb and forefinger and drew it to his eye. He sized up Josh's feet through the opening. "I can measure your feet and whip you up a pair fast, even for feet your size."

"Honest?"

"Sure. I have what I need—leather, needles, thread. It would be my pleasure."

"That's super nice."

"*Pshaw.* It's nothin'. I'll get you woodland garb, too, so you can be invisible. Except you have to wear what I give you." He flashed a grin.

"That sounds fair. I'm willing."

"Yeah. I think you are."

Josh eased his shoulders. Laughter bubbled inside.

"For now, walk behind me and be my lookout. We're tracking a mean old coot who stirs things up with wild threats like sticks in a hornets' nest."

"Who is he?"

"Name's Gibson. His pilot son is missing or dead in Germany, and it made him crazy. They live near Pioneer Grange, but no road goes all the way there except a narrow lane along the river that's too visible for us to use. C'mon." He motioned forward. "We'll go quiet from here."

Johnny picked his way through ferns, evergreens, maple, alders, and elderberry on what might have been a deer trail as stealthily as any James Fenimore Cooper hero in *Leatherstocking*

Tales—Natty Bumppo come to life. Josh glided behind Johnny, not daring to blink lest he lose sight of the man.

"Careful where you put your feet. Even making the tall grass wave can give us away."

The foliage around them formed a green living cathedral with a singing choir of songbirds.

Clanking sounded ahead, and Johnny motioned him to stop.

"What *is* that?" Josh breathed.

"Not sure. But I hear it too." Johnny held a finger to his lips. "This is the back of Gibson's land. Let's see what's happening." Josh followed Johnny's careful steps, determined not to rattle a bush or crack a branch. And then through the foliage he glimpsed Gibson standing by an outbuilding. They crept nearer as his hammer rang out striking iron nails.

"It's some kind of log shed," Johnny whispered. "Their home is next to the Grange Hall closer to the river." He shaded his eyes. "He's nailing wooden covers over the windows."

"I wonder why." Josh pitched his voice low. "It'll make it dark inside. Is he a photographer?"

"Not that I know of. Around here, folks use root cellars or basements for such needs, not darkened windows."

Johnny pointed. "His grandson's helping. He's also *Charlie* after his dad. His grandpa is *Old Charlie.*" Johnny craned his neck. "He's up to something."

The lanky, unsmiling twelve-year-old handed his grandfather plywood squares or insulation or nails whenever he asked. The boy jerked his head back occasionally to flip his blond hair out of his eyes.

"You bring enough nails?" Gibson's voice was gruff.

"Yessir. Brought the full can like you said." The boy lowered the can to the ground and hoisted the next plywood square for his grandfather. "What are we fixin' this place for?"

"Didn't say and don't want you askin'. I might not use it but need it ready in case."

"Okay." The boy bent and put more nails in his grandfather's hand.

"Don't ask Grandma either 'cause she don't know. Isn't supposed to know. Sometimes a man does what he has to, to keep his family safe, and they don't even know." He waved a hand. "Come this way. It's time for the windows on this side."

As Gibson and his grandson rounded the shed's corner, Johnny and Josh ghosted through trees to the opposite side.

"Phew, that was a mite close," Johnny whispered. "Good thing Old Charlie's hard of hearing, but the boy isn't. Annie says he's a good kid who deserves a fair shake, but his grandpa rides him hard." Johnny raised a hand. "While they're busy, let's scout the house and Grange Hall."

The home's exterior was decent—two stories of fitted logs with a large garden to the side. Mrs. Gibson bent weeding a flowerbed near the river.

"Some say she's as nice as he is mean." Johnny dropped to his knees and crawled forward combat style. "He's worse since their son went missing."

"That might do it," Josh answered. "Erika's in torment not knowing if her brother's alive or not."

"Your poor folks." Johnny clucked in sympathy. "It's amazing they didn't crater when no one knew zilch about you."

Josh followed, putting his knees in exactly the same places. "I hate what they went through. I can't repay that or make it up to them." His throat closed.

"You don't have to!" Johnny growled a whisper. "But they don't want you feelin' bad. They just gave you over to God. Give them credit for releasing you to grow into the man you're meant to be. I think you're almost there."

"I doubt that. Not yet. I joined the Navy to serve but got sent home hardly able to walk. Ted stayed home and became a hero."

"Funny about that." Johnny tapped Josh's arm. "God gives us free will, but He works things together for good for those who seek Him. Believing different is balderdash. Being a hero just means the real person inside finally shows up. Ted did. You did too." Johnny laid a finger aside his nose. "Rumor says you've got an award coming you don't know about."

Josh shook his head. "I don't see how."

"Wait and see." Johnny moved forward. "C'mon. Let's finish surveillance before Gibson and the boy head back."

The Pioneer Grange Hall stood at the river's edge. The wooden dock out front was big enough for a good-sized boat to tie up to. The narrow winding road along the river appeared to get little traffic. A large white sign with bold black and red lettering covered the Grange Hall's front door.

"Let's read it." Johnny slipped through the underbrush to creep closer. He peered, blinked, and blinked again. "Does that say what I think it does?"

"Let's see." Josh wriggled forward and squinted. "Home Defense League here Saturday, seven p.m. Do you hate weak government? And foreigners endangering our country? Join and rise up. Do your part. Drive them out. Lock them up! Save America for Americans!'"

Johnny squirmed. "It says that?"

"Yes, sir."

"He's stirring up folks along the river. A few agree, but Jumpin' Jehoshaphat, I didn't think he'd start sedition." Johnny rubbed dirt from his face. "He's more dangerous than I thought. I hurt for his wife and the kid."

"I'll say. How do we proceed?"

"Take my camera." Johnny pulled a black box from his vest. "Get shots we can show the others, and let's skedaddle."

Back at the truck, Johnny changed from woodland garb into ordinary clothes. "Forget what you did out here. We took a fall stroll in the woods is all. We had a nice time. Nothing major."

"Right." Josh snapped a salute. "As far as I'm concerned, we weren't even here."

"Better yet. Smart man."

Chapter Thirty

Early September, 1942
Vancouver, Washington

As the sun set and streetlights flashed on, Josh and Johnny reached the Vengeance home. Johnny turned his truck into Mom and Dad's driveway, following its curve behind the house. He parked in the extra garage stall and lowered the door. "Your folks are good to let me park here. Most people know Smitty owns a beat-up pickup but don't know I have one. I like to avoid notice."

Josh smiled. *Good luck with that.*

They trudged into the house. Dinner had ended and the dishes were cleared, but Mom hopped up.

"Here you two are! You must be starved. I'll heat the leftovers."

"Thanks, Mom."

"No, don't bother." Johnny waved a hand. "We need to start tonight's meeting."

Josh's stomach rumbled. Why had Johnny turned down dinner so fast? This was like the military. Getting something in their stomachs waited 'til after the crisis.

Josh surveyed the room. Erika sat head down at the table. What was wrong? She looked as upset as the night fireworks terrified her. He'd talk to her later.

She wasn't the only one. Smitty slumped nearby. He didn't even look up when Josh and Johnny entered.

Johnny nudged Smitty. "What's up?"

He swung his head like a wounded bull in a bullfight ring. "Plenty."

"What the dickens, friend?" Johnny gripped his friend's shoulder. "Spill it."

Smitty swallowed hard. "It's awful—tears my guts. Erika and I stopped to visit the Mitchells. You remember them? Live halfway between Elsie, Oregon, and the river? His brother, Jim, and wife lived there with them until six months back when they moved to southern Oregon—did a church plant."

"Kind of." Johnny nodded.

Face ashen, Smitty exhaled a shaky breath. "The Japs have reached a low point the whole world should condemn. They don't respect modern rules of war. They should be strung up and roasted over a slow fire." His hands clenched and unclenched. "I'd like to do it myself."

"I see that, but you're not usually that riled up." Johnny waited. "C'mon, Smitty. Tell us."

"Remember those fire balloons we read about in the Tillamook paper last year?"

"Yeah."

"The Japs are making them but can't control them. Wherever they land, they burn up everything."

"I figure." Johnny raked his hair. "Last year they were experimenting. Did they find how to make them?"

"Sure did—made thousands. Three hundred crossed the Pacific. One killed some of my friends."

"Around here?" Josh asked. "Why aren't their reports? I didn't expect our homeland to become a combat zone."

"No. None of us did." Smitty met his gaze. "They'll release more news soon. The government's investigating but keeping the lid on to avoid hysteria—just like they haven't said much about *Books Afloat* sinking the Japanese sub. People could panic, thinking that Jap sailors might knock on their back door."

"Or not knock—just barge in." Erika shuddered.

Smitty licked his dry lips and guzzled the glass of water in front of him. "You can be sure there will be total hysteria if the public hears much, so Governor Langlie says absolutely no leaks. If people slip up, it could mean jail time. And it should."

"Loose lips still sink ships," Josh said.

Just then, Bob swept through the door, kissed his wife hello, and sat by her. "I got here as fast as I could—visited lots of sick folks today." He looked around. "Hey, what's with the sober expressions? It's like a funeral in here."

"Nearly." Smitty turned. "I'm telling them about the fire balloon that killed my friends."

"I just heard about that." Bob sobered. "Terrible. You knew the people?"

"I did." Smitty fisted his hands. "Jim, the husband, is brother to the Mitchells who come here sometimes. He and his wife took teenagers on a picnic near Klamath Falls. Halfway there, they took a break. Jim asked a road construction guy for fishing tips while his wife and the teens went into the woods. They found a giant balloon up in a tree with a rope dangling. Elyse hollered they found a rope, but before Jim could get there, one of the teens must have pulled it."

"Oh no." Josh gulped. "They always say to investigate first."

"Right." Smitty breathed deeply. "It blew sky high, blasted a huge hole, and threw logs every which way. Elyse and four kids died instantly. Another girl caught fire but died just as Jim and the construction guy got there."

"That's awful," Sue said.

Smitty's face crumpled. "Jim and Elyse had only been married a year. Great couple. She was expecting their first kid." He lowered his face into his hands. His shoulders shook. "N-nobody deserves that!"

Bob scooted back his chair. "You're sure it was the Japs?"

"As sure as I know my name. They bragged they were researching them last year, plus now they gave details on how they're made—balloons seventy-foot tall by thirty-three-feet in diameter. Filled with lighter-than-air gas, jet stream winds carry them here with flammable magnesium to ignite on contact. They can't steer them—just turn them loose to explode where they land."

"That's horrific," Josh said.

"I'm so sorry." Tears streaked Sue's face. "How can humans do that to each other? I don't understand."

Smitty shook his head. "It's good we don't understand. Maybe they're not human—don't have consciences. They have more nasty schemes too. A seaplane dropped a bomb on Oregon's coast that started a forest fire, but men on the ground put it out. They launched a plane from a sub to drop bombs on forests, but rainstorms drenched those fires. Nobody got hurt."

Josh made a fist. "People will get hurt if Japan keeps it up."

"Exactly." Smitty rubbed the back of his neck like it ached. "So we have to stop them every time. Or what happened to the Mitchells will keep repeating."

"We'll track them down." Johnny ground his teeth. "They'll meet red-blooded Americans who won't quit."

Josh sat taller. "I'm with you, Johnny. Sign me up. I'll pay any price to beat them."

"Me too," Erika said. "No matter the cost."

"Good." Smitty gazed around the room. "We're all agreed. Let's plan strategies to stop fire balloons plus pay attention to our other troubles along the river."

Bob's face darkened. "There's also an ugly new problem in town."

Conversations erupted around the table.

"In Vancouver? What's that?" Smitty asked.

"I'll let Erika tell you."

At that moment, Josh startled as two soft, cool hands slipped over his eyes. Hands that were soothing and healing. That smelled like spring lilies in mountain valleys. And rain. And the river. His world spun. Only one person in the world had hands like that.

"Annie!" He pushed his chair back and wobbled up before she threw herself into his arms, laughing and crying, kissing his cheek. Happiness lit her eyes as she tapped his arm. "It's really you, big guy. We're so glad you're home where you belong."

He kissed her cheek lightly and released her. "You look wonderful."

"Thanks. Compared to the alternative, it's great to be alive." Tears washed her face. "We prayed so hard—never quit. And here you are, like old times!" She hugged him again.

"I needed those prayers." Josh turned to gesture Erika's forward to introduce her when Ted stepped in and pulled Josh into his strong arms. Laughed and hugged him tighter. Josh squeezed back, his breath in gasps as the joy of seeing his best friends refilled him. "Ted. Annie."

"Yeah, buddy. We're here." Ted barely whispered, "God saved you too. We'll talk soon."

"Yes." Josh squeezed him longer. "Look at you—bigger, stronger. A true hero."

"You're another." Ted mussed Josh's hair. They gripped their forearms and laughed again.

Johnny pushed to his feet and threw his arms around them. Others stood in line. And then Josh introduced Erika.

"Surprise, Josh. Thanks to Johnny, we've already met and are friends." Ted and Annie pulled up chairs to join the table.

"Whatever you're doing, count us in," Ted said. "We're ready."

"So great you're here," Smitty said. "Even better than old times."

"Yes." Johnny cleared his throat. "Josh and I also have news. We were downriver. I don't know if the man is crazy, or pure evil, but something's bad wrong with a guy there. He's dangerous. We have to act fast."

All eyes turned to Johnny.

Chapter Thirty-One

Mid-September, 1942
Vancouver, Washington

Erika loved working in Dr. Brower's clinic. It was larger than her dad's practice and saw more patients daily, but the treatment given and gratitude received were the same. The doctor and most staff praised Erika's efforts, but after the nasty incident with Mr. Gibson, she walked on eggshells around Mrs. Smythe. After that, she noted some conversations stopped and eyes followed her when she entered the lunchroom or reception lobby. She began doing more of her tasks in the back room.

Instead of troubling Dr. Brower, Erika waited until she got home and asked Sue, "Why are people so suspicious of people from foreign countries? Europeans admire the words written on your Statue of Liberty, 'Give me your tired, your poor, your huddled masses yearning to breathe free.' Don't Americans know we're here because we love that freedom and are grateful?"

Sue met her eyes. "Sad, but true. Besides the teachings of Jesus, I don't know a finer statement. Please don't take it personally. I doubt the problem you're noticing is tied to anything you're doing or not doing. People get squirrelly during wartime, afraid and suspicious of everyone."

"That's what my father said." Erika's throat thickened. "I miss him so much, but I didn't want him to be right."

"I'm sure." Sue pulled her into a hug. "Try not to worry about occasional silly people."

When she got to bed, Erika tossed and turned. Eventually, fitful sleep took her to Germany where *Günther* pounded on the front door.

"Come now," he hollered. "Your mother has fled. You must come to Berlin and take her place, or they will kill her when they find her. It's your duty."

Erika's heart thudded so rapidly she couldn't breathe—could barely answer. "Did someone take Mother? Or did she go on her own? How can I take her place?"

Günther scowled. "The *Gestapo* sent word she escaped but won't get far. All borders are closed. Unless you return, consider her dead."

Dead? His words echoed inside Erika until she screamed. She heard footsteps thunder down the hall. Sue ran into the room and switched on the bedside lamp. "Erika? You were dreaming. You're safe." Sue sat on the bed and brushed her forehead.

Erika struggled to open her eyes and wildly scanned the room. "I'm not in Germany?"

"Far from it. What frightened you so?"

"I couldn't breathe." She couldn't stop trembling. "*Günther* came with awful news."

"*Günther?*"

"Someone I cared for but who lost his way. It seemed so real." She sat up and swung her feet over the bed's side. "I cannot let her die."

"Who?"

"Mother fled the Berlin office, which brings a death sentence. They pursued her. I have to know if it's true. It's dangerous, but

I must find a way to help, maybe to go. If I'm hearing the Lord, He will keep me safe."

Sue handed Erika a tissue. "But you have friends much closer. Didn't you say Chaplain Merritt knows your friend in Switzerland? Could they help?"

Erika rested her head on Sue's shoulder. "I can't think, but yes. Perhaps Oskar can learn something, maybe even contact Dietrich."

"Bob has Chaplain Merritt's phone number."

"That's good. And he has a way to reach Oskar."

Sue patted Erika's back. "Are you okay if Bob makes that call? He knows the phone system better."

"Yes. I'd be grateful."

"Can you try to sleep again now?"

"I don't know." Erika checked her bedside alarm clock. "It's 3:30? I'll read a while." She reached for her Bible.

"That's good. If you're okay then, I'll have Bob start a phone call but crawl back in bed a while."

"Yes, please. And thank you." After reading for an hour, Erika got up to make a special breakfast. She'd nearly finished when Bob entered the kitchen and rattled the coffee pot.

"Something smells delicious. I'll make coffee."

"Thank you. You do it better. Did you reach Chaplain Merritt?"

"Not yet. It's still early. I left his twenty-four-hour answering service a message. He'll be in the office later, and they'll ask him to call Oskar."

Erika sighed. "At least it's a start."

Sue came to the table. Once Bob asked the blessing, all three dug in.

"What do you think of these?" Erika looked at them anxiously. "These are *Flensjes*, Dutch Pancakes. In Europe, we like them with lemon juice and powdered sugar, but does it taste sour to you?"

"Not at all. It's one of the best things I ever put in my

mouth." Bob took a second small helping. "Make this anytime. Give Sue the recipe."

"Yes, This is a keeper."

"I'll be glad to." Erika needed to remain busy as she awaited news, so she worked as usual at Dr. Brower's office. Time passed slowly but at least helping patients was better than being a nervous wreck at home.

By the time she came home from work, Bob said, "Chaplain Merritt reached Oskar, but there are problems connecting with Dietrich. The usual methods aren't working. Oskar says not to worry—he'll keep trying until he gets through."

She gulped. "Thank you, but I do worry. It's not a good sign. It means Dietrich or his communications people may have been arrested." She twisted her hands.

"I know, but remember, God's in charge." Bob covered her hands with his. "And we're praying."

More phone calls over the next two days also failed.

Erika had Sue teach her to knit. Soon her needles clacked back and forth making mittens and hats nearly as fast as Elsa Becker.

"This is fun," she said. "And relaxing."

Sue laughed. "They say it's effective craft therapy for mental patients."

"I'm not surprised. Worrying about Dietrich and my family might be why I love it right now."

Steps pounded on the porch, and Josh breezed in.

"Nice to see you," his Mom said.

When Erika jumped up to say hello, she dropped her ball of yellow yard and it unrolled to Josh's feet. "Well, look at you," he said. "A regular knitting machine."

"Practically, thanks to your Mom." Why did her cheeks heat.

She removed the extra sweater she'd been wearing. "If you need anything made, let me know."

"I might. I'll think about it and let you know." He picked up the ball of yarn and tossed it back to her.

"Are you home for a while or just stopping in?"

"I'm gathering a few supplies for another special project with Johnny."

"In that case, I'll bet you need food packed up," Mom said.

"Music to our ears," he said. We've been on the run all day and didn't have time to stop for anything."

"Then I'll fix you right up. You can take it with you if that's better."

"It is. Thanks."

Erika put the ball of yarn away in her knitting basket. "Are you and my uncle still getting along fine?"

"We sure are. What a great guy. He may do more to make a strong man of me than the whole US Navy."

"Don't tell him that." She laughed. "He might get, how do you say, a swelled head?"

Josh chuckled.

She waited as he continued his reconnaissance mission through the house. He didn't know how handsome he was when he smiled. His fading scars added more character. Erika climbed the stairs to her room, but hearing his voice float up made her pause.

"How is she doing really? Erika isn't quite herself."

"Be patient," Sue said. "She's been shaken to the core. The war news is horrible. Newsreels are worse. No wonder she's having nightmares. Of course, she's worried about her mother, and her usual contacts aren't getting answers."

Erika finished climbing the stairs. She hoped Sue wouldn't reveal how she dreaded going to sleep now after dreaming Mother had fled. How she pictured her dead, tortured body and was told to plan her funeral. She wanted Josh to think she was strong. She shuddered and prayed for peace and answers instead of more nightmares.

The ringing telephone woke her early the next morning. She rushed downstairs, but Bob had already hung up.

"Anything?"

"Sorry, not yet. Merritt says another communications expert friend will try to reach Bonhoeffer tomorrow by ham radio. It's dangerous, but if Dietrich's in Munich, it works sometimes."

Erika folded her hands. "Dear Lord, help him. Protect Mother too."

That next night the phone rang again. It was daytime in Europe. Erika reached the bottom of the stairs in time to see Bob grab the paper and pen near the phone and scribble. "Thanks, that helps." He turned with a smile. "Oskar's ham radio friend did reach Dietrich. It's true your mother has fled. He believes she's safe, because she mailed him a postcard showing Dutch scenery that reached him yesterday."

Erika gripped Bob's sleeve. "What does it say?"

"Oskar wasn't completely sure. See if it means something to you."

Our Aunt T. suffers a bad cold. I'm fixing her chicken soup. We may visit the sea. Will write more soon.

Erika couldn't hold back tears. "That's wonderful. In our family's code, Aunt T. means *Trentje* in the Netherlands. She has gone there! They're Nazi occupied but safer."

"I hear they have a strong resistance movement."

"Yes." Erika wrung her hands. "Mother. What are you doing? How will you live? I can't lose you too."

"She may be safe. We'll try to learn more."

Josh turned to Johnny as they left their meeting with several new volunteers downriver. "That went well. They're great guys."

"Yes. Happy to have them connected." They reached Johnny's truck and climbed in. "So, what do you think, youngster? Was that enough for one night?" Johnny reached the street leading to Josh's house.

"I don't know. What do you think?"

"I'm wondering if you have energy for one more task."

Josh breathed deeply. "If you do, I do."

"Fair enough. Smitty suggested we check the sluice gates at Bonneville Dam for their water flow records. That power grid is a tempting Japanese target."

"For sure—if they manage to get that far, but we won't let them. Let me run inside and grab better boots first."

"Sure thing." Johnny swatted Josh's arm. "While you're at it, grab a swimsuit too. Did the Navy teach you frogman skills? Secret diving techniques? We could use them."

"As a matter of fact, I know a few. I'm still crab-like on land but a fish in the water."

"Good man!"

Josh slid out of Johnny's truck. Even after long days, he limped less than a few weeks ago. The fresh air and sunshine helped. His face was healing more than he hoped, the scars fading. His chest expanded. *Time to write Brad.* He looked up as rain drops hit his face. "Shucks, Johnny. Rain's coming. I'll also grab rain slickers and raid Mom's ice box."

"Now you're talkin'. Everything she cooks is good."

Josh entered the house with stealth tactics and sidled into the kitchen and boot room to grab rain gear. His heart nearly stopped as a ghostlike figure descended the stairs and breezed past. He gulped and stuck out an arm.

"Ouch," a young woman's voice said as she backed into the coats and jackets hanging on pegs behind her.

"Erika. What are you doing? Are you all right?" He switched on the dim hall light and found her pale and shaking.

"I didn't think you were home."

"I wasn't." He shrugged. "Doing missions with your uncle sometimes means stopping home to grab supplies at strange times. Why are you up?"

"I couldn't sleep, so I came downstairs."

"But why are you wearing a coat? And carrying a suitcase." He stepped closer. "Are you leaving?"

"Don't hate me. I have to." Her hand shook so hard, she dropped the note she was holding. She bent to retrieve it, but Josh dove faster.

Dear Bob, Sue, and Josh,

Forgive me for not facing you. You are a wonderful family. I will never forget you. Please understand I'm responsible for Mother. I may be all she has left. I'm not sure I can reach Germany or the Netherlands to help, but I must try. When this war ends, perhaps we can return for a new life here. Thank you for your love and prayers. God bless you.

I will always love you, Erika.

"What is this?" Josh demanded, thumping the paper and not bothering to keep his voice low.

"Shhhhh. Please be quiet. I think you know."

"You know God brought you here. What do you think you're doing? Even if you find a way to travel there, it's certain death. Does Johnny know?"

"No." She thrust her face into his. "And you must not tell him."

"Do you have money for airplane tickets? Germany isn't letting passengers in or out."

"Then I would travel as close as I could, even if it's dangerous." When her eyes filled, she looked away.

"The *Gestapo* probably posted alerts to watch for at border crossings."

"Yes, I know. But if she were your mother, wouldn't you try?" When her shoulders slumped, Josh gripped them.

"Erika, don't do this. You'd be throwing your life away."

"I know I'd probably fail, but I have to try." She jerked to shake free of his grip but he held too tight. Her eyes blazed.

"Each day I wait means Mother could die. I can't stand it anymore." Now she cried and slumped into him.

"Erica, please." He still gripped her shoulders, shook them a little. "You know God's in charge—not you. Let people there help. You could die!" His voice quivered. "What good would that do?"

"Probably none." She searched his face. "But what is it to you?"

"Plenty. I-I—" He held her face in his hands and kissed her. She yielded for a moment, her lips soft, but then pushed away and slapped him so hard his head jerked.

"In my family men only kiss the girls who are special to them."

"Who says you're not?" He folded his arms across his chest to keep from kissing her again. "I would only kiss a girl who is very special."

"But you—" Her eyes startled.

"Don't go." He caressed her cheek and rested his hands on both of her shoulders. "Dad and your friends are trying to find your mom to help her. If we don't get answers soon, we may smuggle someone into Germany or the Netherlands. Maybe Johnny. Maybe me. But not you!"

"Why? And how soon?" She pulled free. "She's my mother, my responsibility."

"Because I—"

She studied him. "You feel strongly."

"I do. But tonight, our concern is your mom. You'll help her most by staying safe. That's what she would want. Trust us to find contacts. Turn over every stone. Don't do anything foolish. Promise you'll wait."

"Maybe. If you want. But for how long?" A slight smile lit her face.

"At least two or three days. Until we hear something. Where were you going anyway?"

"I don't know." She shook her head. "I just had to do *something*."

"But it needs to be the *right* thing. Not a terrible risk. Let us share your load."

A door opened upstairs. Dad came to the head of the steps. "I hear voices. Is everything all right?"

Josh motioned her back farther between the coats and jackets.

"It's me, Dad." Josh stepped into the light. "I'm home getting gear for a late run to Bonneville. And raiding the ice box. I should be back around noon."

"Okay, then. Stay safe."

"You too."

After Dad left, Josh placed a gentle kiss on Erika's forehead. This time she didn't slap him.

"I'll find a time to tell you how I feel about you," he said. "But for now, go back to bed. Try to sleep. Let us carry this."

"Thank you. I'll try." She squeezed his hand.

Chapter Thirty-Two

Mid-September, 1942
Vancouver, Washington

Three days later, Erika was busy filing updated test results in patient folders when she was called forward to the lobby. Two men in dark suits holding fedora hats by the brim and carrying briefcases stood by Mrs. Smythe's desk. They didn't look like patients.

Erika turned to the receptionist. "You called me?"

"Yes, these gentlemen are here to see you." Mrs. Smythe's eyes flickered.

"Erika Hofer?" The taller man pulled a document from his briefcase. "Don't be alarmed, but in wartime we investigate foreign nationals, especially those from countries with whom we're at war. Is there a private room where we can talk?"

Her head whirled until she remembered the empty boardroom. "Yes. Come this way." As she led them down the hall, she glimpsed the receptionist gloating. Erika's stomach clenched. In the boardroom, Erika invited the men to sit in the handsome chairs matching the solid wooden table.

"Thank you," the taller one said, and showed his name

badge. "I'm Special Agent Hughes. This is my partner, Jones. We're with the US National Immigration and Naturalization Service. This shouldn't take long. Just show us the paperwork you carry to support your residency claim in the United States."

"Of course." She reached for her clinic I.D. clipped to the lanyard hanging from her neck. "I carry my Red Cross Refugee card at all times tucked behind my clinic employee card." She tugged it out and held it between two fingers for Hughes and his partner to view. "I keep more registration paperwork in my clinic locker if you need it."

"Yes."

She rose and brought back various cards which the agents reviewed and photographed.

Hughes tented his fingers. "This helps but not enough."

Erika's head pounded. "I have more documents where I'm staying."

"Where? You don't have a permanent address yet?" Jones stabbed his pencil in the air.

"Not yet. My uncle, John Hofer, is arranging one. He's respected in government circles. You may have heard of him."

Hughes and Jones shook their heads. "Not us personally, but he may be known to those higher up. Our work is compartmentalized. No matter who your uncle is, we need the documents you used to get out of Germany and into the US."

Heat climbed Erika's neck. "But I don't have them all."

"Why not?" Jones edged closer.

"Hitler closed the borders to prevent people leaving. Fortunately, I have a Swiss passport."

"Fortunate indeed. I hear those bring a fortune on the black market." Jones extended his hand. "Show me."

"I don't bring it to work. Few people carry their passport every day."

"True. Where is it?"

"At the home where I'm staying. It brought me here to find

my blood relative who is American by birth. He is sponsoring me for residency."

"Fair enough," Jones said. "Give us the house address. We'll take you there, and everything will be fine. We just need to know more about your travel here."

Erika's shoulders dropped. "I can't list every step. Red Cross authorities brought me to America where I volunteered at the Naval Medical Center, San Diego. Their head chaplain helped me reach my uncle."

"That sounds pretty slick," Hughes said.

"Too good to be true," Jones answered.

"But it *is* true." She shrank inside herself. "I had a long, hard journey and am thankful to be here. I will always conduct myself for the good of this nation."

"Impressive sentiments."

Hughes jotted her words in his notebook with one eyebrow raised. "You've done a lot of travel during wartime." He tapped his pen against his teeth. "If you supply the documents confirming these steps, you're fine. Otherwise ..." he barked a short laugh, "When it sounds too good to be true, it usually is. Does it sound fishy to you, Jones?"

"Like a mackerel. Too many unanswered questions. More like award-winning fiction." He snickered.

The agents partnered like a doubles tennis team swatting balls back and forth in a fast-moving match. Hughes smiled and swung his racket, his teeth gleaming white. When he smiled, Erika glimpsed a gold crown in his lower jaw, but his eyes stayed cold. He reminded her of a hungry wolf she'd seen cresting a ridge in the Bavarian Alps. That memory always made her shiver.

Hughes swung his tennis racket harder. "How do we know your *Führer* didn't sneak a pretty, blonde, blue-eyed young woman into this country by plane or boat for high-level espionage?"

"You must believe me. Nothing I've done suggests that!"

"But it's your job to prove it." Jones spread his hands on the table. "You look like a nice enough girl, but that's the kind our enemy would send." He winked. "Don't worry. Everything will be fine once we see your passport, and the paperwork that confirms your story."

She shook her head like a cow being herded into a slaughterhouse. "That's what I'm saying. I can't show the paperwork for every door God opened. He worked miracles to get me here. I'll provide the documents I have, but they may not be enough."

"You'd better hope they are. Show us what you have, and we'll decide." Jones snapped his briefcase shut.

Hughes drummed on the table. "Miss Hofer, we're meeting talented forgers these days. We hope you're not one of them. With modern technology, documents are easily duplicated. Impressive counterfeit currency is being printed. Germans are among the most skilled."

"Gentlemen, that has nothing to do with me!" She swallowed hysteria and blinked rapidly. "Ask anyone I've worked with in San Diego or here. They'll tell you."

"We will, but tell us why we should believe anyone German?" Agent Hughes asked.

Her voice rose. "Because Hitler is my enemy as much as yours. Ask the head of the International Red Cross in Geneva. Or the lead chaplain in San Diego. They know my heart." She twisted her hands together. "Give me time to prove my innocence. And talk to my uncle. Even if you don't know him well, someone in your bureau must. He's a trusted citizen who will confirm my story."

Hughes tipped his chair back. "If you have such a relative, you'd be wise to phone him."

"Of course, I will." Her voice broke. "But he's gone on field assignment for—for Governor Langlie."

"That sounds impressively vague and mysterious." Hughes tapped his pen against his teeth. "You say you have documents where you're staying? Whose home is that?"

"Pastor Bob Vengeance and his wife, Sue."

"I hear they're good people." Hughes jotted down their names.

"They are. The best!"

When Nurse Nalley stuck her head into the boardroom, Erika's teary eyes locked with hers. The nurse whirled and disappeared. Moments later, Dr. Brower rushed into the room, his white coat flying.

"Gentlemen, what's going on?"

"Just routine investigation of foreign nationals, doctor." Hughes stood and showed his badge. "I'm Special Agent Hughes. This is Jones from our National Immigration and Naturalization Service. In accordance with President Roosevelt's First War Powers Act, we investigate suspicious contact or communications between the US and all foreign nations."

Dr. Brower huffed out his breath. "What does that have to do with this young woman? She's a legally registered refugee who's made a hazardous journey to join her respected relative here."

Jones stretched to full height. "She was heard speaking German to American citizens in public."

"What of it? She helped me with a patient who lost their ability to remember English."

"Unwise. You'd think your medical colleague in Kelso getting arrested would be enough to show our agency is serious about investigating subversives," Hughes added.

Dr. Brower jammed his hands into his pockets. "My medical practice is understaffed. Erika is highly qualified and her work is exemplary. She has top references from our Naval hospital in San Diego. I secured her temporary employment status with our state's Department of Labor in Olympia. Her permanent papers are expected to arrive any day."

"We know that." Jones spoke again. "We're monitoring her closely. It's just that despite good reports, we can't ignore the fact that she speaks the language of enemy combatants in public during wartime."

"Good grief." Dr. Brower breathed in so much air, he appeared to double in size. "That's what this is about? Comforting a patient in a medical crisis by speaking his birth language? Unbelievable!" He hissed out his words, turning so red Erika feared he might have a stroke.

"Wartime makes us examine everything," Hughes said.

"But surely you judge the merits of each situation." Dr. Brower stepped closer and both Hughes and Jones stood and took steps back.

"I'm not through. Is it a crime to help patients in crisis communicate in the language most comfortable to them?"

"Not criminal." Jones cleared his throat. "But suspicious. We must investigate all complaints."

"Complaints? I'm about to make one."

"She has two lodged against her, but all Miss Hofer has to do to be pardoned is provide adequate documents."

"And if she can't?" The doctor squared his shoulders. "What then?"

Erika thought he must have played football in his youth.

Hughes took over. "It's more complicated." The papers here in her locker are not enough. We'll drive her to where she's staying, examine what she has, and report to our superiors. They'll give further instruction."

"Fine. I'll expect updates at all stages." Dr. Brower's grandfatherly face took on a fierceness Erika had not seen. His twinkly blue eyes darkened to steel.

Jones gulped. "If you insist."

"I do. Complications like this make it hard for me to practice good medicine."

Hughes sighed. "That's not our intention. We're simply following government directives. For now, please excuse Miss Hofer while we pursue our next steps."

The doctor rested a comforting hand on Erika's shoulder.

"Don't worry, we'll straighten this mess out." He turned to the agents. "Who lodged the complaints?"

"That's privileged information, sir. We're not at liberty to say."

"I'm at liberty to find out. They had no cause." Dr. Brower's face hardened to a profile that belonged on Mount Rushmore. "I'll add to your workload, gentlemen, by insisting that you investigate my other employees equally. I won't have one treated differently than the rest. Start with me. I have nothing to hide." He thrust out his chest. "Investigate everyone in our organization down to the janitors and delivery men."

Hughes and Jones blanched. "That may prove difficult."

"How unfortunate. I'll expect results by Friday afternoon, or do serious inquiry myself. Follow your next steps if you must, but I'll expect to hear from you soon."

"Yes, sir." Both men backed against the boardroom wall. "Get what you need from your locker, Miss Hofer. We'll go now." Hughes clapped his fedora on his head. Jones did the same. They turned and left the room.

"Don't worry." Dr. Brower patted her shoulder. "We will get to the bottom of this, and they will apologize."

"Thank you, Doctor." She blinked through wet lashes. "Could you also try to reach Uncle Johnny to make sure he knows."

"Of course, I will. Guaranteed."

She followed the agents down the hall past Mrs. Smythe at the receptionist desk, and onto the sidewalk. The men opened the back passenger door of a black government car and radioed their status to headquarters. Hughes slid into the driver's seat.

"Miss Hofer, direct us to the Vengeance home."

On a spacious green corner lot surrounded by gardens and flowerbeds, Bob and Sue's home looked inviting. Tensing her muscles to stop trembling, Erika led the men up the steps and knocked on the front door instead of entering.

When Sue opened the door, her eyes widened. "Goodness, is something wrong?" She took a step back.

Jones explained while Erika slipped past Sue and climbed the stairs to her room to retrieve the documents zipped into her suitcase lining. Her German birth passport was buried in the metal box behind the big tree in her family's backyard. She pocketed the Swiss passport to show Jones and Hughes. It was top quality, the best Oskar could arrange.

Lord, let this satisfy the agents. Her sinking stomach warned her it might not.

Hughes opened it first. "Impressive. That's the best fake passport I've seen. My compliments to the artist." He handed it to Jones.

He whistled. "Yes, outstanding, but forged. We'll send photos to our superiors to show them the quality of the work being done. They'll be impressed. This moves your case forward immediately. Pack enough belongings to come with us for an inquiry to determine your circumstances. We'll drive you to our facility. With luck, you may convince our authorities that your case has merit and return here in a day or two."

"Gentlemen, wait." Sue gripped Erika's arm. "Where are you taking her?"

"To a facility near Fort Lewis."

Sue blinked. "May I come along?"

Jones exhaled. "Only blood relatives are allowed. We'll notify you when we reach a verdict."

Sue tightened her hold on Erika. Her eyebrows nearly joined. "A verdict concerning what?"

"Whether she can remain in the US or be deported back to Germany."

"Gentlemen. Wouldn't that be a death sentence?"

"That's her nation of origin. She's their responsibility, not ours."

Sue released Erika's arm and dropped her hands to her hips. "Can't this wait until my husband comes home? He'll want to talk with you. If her Uncle Johnny doesn't return in time, let us be her guarantors."

Jones shook his head. "Thank you for offering, but no. National security comes first. Thank you, Mrs. Vengeance." They opened the front door and stepped out. "Erika, come with us."

She refused to cry. "Goodbye for now, Sue." Erika dragged her feet. *Dear Mutter. Stay safe. It's good you can't see the trouble I'm in.*

Chapter Thirty-Three

Late September, 1942
Vancouver, Washington

Josh observed and listened as two other team members corrected detailed maps.

Smitty pinched his nose while sliding a window open. "*Ooo-eee*. For pity's sake, leave these windows open a crack when we leave this place so it doesn't smell like a wolf's den."

"Smitty, you're picky. Natural earth smells don't hurt a soul." Johnny slanted an eye. "Leave even a tiny space and raccoons and other critters will squeeze right in. Do you want them for company?"

"Not especially. Or a bear barging in if we're dumb enough to leave food around. Fresh air helps, though." He eyed the ceiling. "Maybe I'll cut an air vent into the attic."

"Might not hurt." Johnny's eyes lit. "The smell will improve in a jiffy if you'll let me brew my coffee. Boiling it all day gives it my distinctive flavor. By day's end, it's solid in the pot." He lifted the dented blue enamel coffeepot from the stove's surface, rattled it, and lifted the lid. "See Josh? I break off a piece of dried coffee, any size I want, add water, and stir." He pulled a knife from his pocket and carved off a wedge. "It's good to chew on. It gives a man a boost even if it does darken his teeth. But plants in these woods brighten them up again." He held the pot out to Josh. "Want some?"

Josh's stomach rebelled. He held up his hands. "No—No thanks. I'm not quite ready." *I want to learn all I can from this guy, but maybe not in every area.* He turned to Smitty. "How much of what he said should I believe?"

"Most of it," Smitty said. "Best stay away from his brew, or you won't get shut eye for a week."

"Not just coffee." Johnny grinned. "I whipped up a trench cake for us that soldiers invented during the last war." He lifted a clean towel from a round brown cake and sliced it into wedges. "Mmmm, smell that? Flour and sugar, and eggs, if we can find them. Soda and vinegar to make it rise."

Josh accepted a piece and waved it near his nose. "Smells good."

"Of course. And tastes better. Nice and moist. Try it. I added some currents growing out back for fruit. Make vinegar from them or fallen apples. A fella can live in these woods if he knows what he's doing."

"I'm convinced." Josh broke off a piece. "Nice texture. Mom would like it." He bit, chewed, swallowed, and ate some more. "Fabulous, Johnny."

"Did you doubt? Stick with me, and I'll treat you right."

"That's another true statement," Smitty said while making short work of his cake and getting more. "Johnny, what were you telling me about old Charlie Gibson's causing problems again?"

"Yeah. We want to tell all of you. Worse than before. Spreading hate all up and down this river. Josh and I did a reconnaissance of his place. Copied the words he posted on a sign at the Grange." He passed notes around.

Smitty propped an elbow on the table. "Someone told me he's gone off his rocker, but he must have skidded clear off."

"Looks that way," Johnny agreed. "I heard he's spouting about starting a Pacific Northwest version of the Ku Klux Klan."

"In the Pacific Northwest?" Josh's voice deepened. "He'll never get away with it, because we'll stop him."

Johnny's eyes narrowed to slits. "Good man."

Josh's dad pulled a notepad and pencil from his shirt pocket. "We don't want anything like that around here. I say arrest him or send him to the state hospital for mental evaluation."

"But we need a clear-cut charge—catch him red-handed." Smitty pushed up his shirt sleeves.

Johnny nodded. "Shouldn't be hard based on what we've seen lately."

"For sure." Josh studied these men around him. Seasoned faces etched with wisdom and experience. Not military, but brave non-military lieutenants and generals. He drew a deep breath. "What made Gibson so extreme? Do you men have a strategy?" He recalled the reconnaissance scenes of Gibson's place again. What else did they show about the man?

Bob sighed. "Not sure. We think a big part of his problem is that his son is missing overseas. I know having Josh gone so long without word almost drove us crazy."

Josh's face fell. "Sorry, Dad."

"You couldn't help it." Bob gripped Josh's arm. "Thank God you're home. Because I knew how that felt, I stopped to talk to Gibson twice but got nowhere. He called me a sympathizer and collaborator. Said I should resign as a pastor. Warned what he'd do if I came back."

"He did?" Johnny scowled. "Threatened you? Was he serious or blowing wind?"

"Hard to say. He may not know himself. He might be so heartsick he's crazy. But whatever the cause, if he's that deranged, he's plumb dangerous."

"Sounds that way." Smitty leaned back. "For sure a loose cannon, but I've known him a few years. I'd like a chance to stop by and try to talk sense into him. See if I can calm him down."

"You think you can make a difference?" Johnny asked. "He needs to smarten up fast."

"Not sure, but I'd like to try. 'Innocent until proven guilty' is still our American way."

Bob wrote Gibson's name after Smitty's in his notes. "It's worth trying but do it soon. Can you update us later this week and tell us if you make progress?"

"Should be able to."

"What else is on our agenda?"

Just then the hand crank phone on the wall blared three shrill rings and made them all jump.

Smitty was the closest. "Good, I actually fixed it." He untangled his long legs from the bench and grabbed the receiver. "Sue? You want Bob but Johnny first? Yup." He held out the phone to his friend. "Here, Johnny."

"Who took Erika?" Johnny stiffened. "Where? Darn right I will. The phone didn't work because squirrels ate the wires. Smitty just fixed it." His face pinched. "Poor girl. I'll get there by tomorrow morning somehow. You better believe I'll file a complaint. Thanks, Sue. Here's your hubby." He passed the receiver and rubbed a hand over his grizzled face. "Can someone lend me a razor? I've got a job to do."

"What's up?" Josh leaned forward.

"Bad stuff. Men from US Immigration and Naturalization took Erika from Brower's office, demanded paperwork for every part of her travel. She doesn't have it because of Red Cross planes and rides. It doesn't look good."

Josh's knuckles whitened. "Where did they take her?"

"Up north near Fort Lewis. They're labeling her a dangerous alien."

"Of all the—" Josh's voice became gravel. "How stupid. No one who knows her thinks that. It's just suspicions or jealousy from someone at the clinic. She mentioned a receptionist. I'll go there and talk to Mrs. Smythe now." He pushed himself up from the bench.

"Hold your horses. Not yet." Johnny gently tapped Josh's chest. "I'll take care of it another way. I'll bet the agents are taking her to the same place they're holding Dr. Krossner while they judge his radio messages."

"They haven't solved that yet?" Josh clamped his hands to his head. "Erika told me she's helped calm several of Dr. Brower's patients by speaking their childhood language. We've always had good folks around here with German heritage."

"That's true, but war makes people crazy." Bob pulled his eyeglasses from his face and polished the lenses on his shirt. "There's no accounting for how some people think or act."

"Or they don't think at all." Josh slammed a fist into his hand.

"Right." Smitty watched Johnny gather gear from around the room. "What's your plan?"

"Only blood relatives can be with her. I'm going to Fort Lewis."

"How for heaven's sake?" Smitty's eyebrows rose. "There's no road, just the river. Our boat and driver don't come back until tomorrow."

"Doesn't matter." Johnny stopped and tugged his hair. "I should've planned better. Phoned her more. Once I get to Kelso, there's a road."

"But how can you get there? Our air machine isn't ready."

"I'll think of a way if I can calm down." Johnny shrugged into his jacket and plopped his Robin Hood hat on his head. "Actually, a friend of mine from the Cowlitz Reserve keeps an old canoe hidden near here. It's in bad shape but should get me to Kelso. From there, I'll figure out the next step."

"You always do," Smitty said.

Bob grabbed Johnny's shoulder. "We'll pray up a storm."

"No, not a storm." Johnny grinned. "Pray up good weather. Walk me to the river, Preacher. See ya later, fellas."

"Wait up." Josh pulled a letter from his backpack. He tugged off the outer envelope and scribbled words inside it before resealing the flap. "Take this to her."

Johnny slid it into his pocket.

"Phone us when ya get there," Smitty called, and then blinked at Johnny's woodland garb. "You're going dressed like that?"

Johnny peered down. "I guess I'd better figure that out. Where shall I phone? Will you be here tomorrow?"

"Not sure. Doubtful." Smitty surveyed the men around the table. "Try here first and then Bob's place, or mine. Keep tryin' 'til you reach one of us."

"Okay. Wish me luck." Johnny shifted his pack, opened the cabin door, and blended into the night.

"There goes my buddy on another adventure." Smitty threw his bedroll onto a bunk. "Tomorrow I'll stop by two places to thank volunteers. I'll also try to see Gibson."

"I do wish you luck," Bob said, "and I'll pray."

Heart racing, Josh walked along the riverbank with his dad. "How much trouble is Erika in?"

"Plenty if she's detained in the same place as Dr. Krossner and undergoing the same process. But if anyone can help her, it's Johnny."

Josh leaned on one cane. "I just wish there was something I could do. I'll at least ask Chaplain Merritt to vouch for her, but I'd like to do more. She's a good friend."

Dad stopped walking. "Is that all she is? I think I see more."

Josh also stopped. "Are you kidding? After getting it so wrong with Annie, I'd be smart to leave girls alone. I've got major issues to figure out."

"Those will come, son. Life delivers growing pains on many fronts."

"That's a good way of putting it." Josh pitched a rock into the river. It skipped twice before it dropped into the current. "Meanwhile, I admire these volunteers I'm meeting. Most aren't military, but they're resourceful and mean business. Nothing sneaks past them."

"You're right about that." Dad choked up. "I can't tell you how thankful we are that you're home. Meanwhile, it's great to have your help on the river. We never know what's going to happen next."

"I see that. I'm glad to be involved."

"And I still think there's more to your Midway story."

"But I've told you all I remember." Josh rolled his shoulders.

"Navy officials are still piecing together information. Some survivors insist you saved them."

Josh pitched another rock. "They have big imaginations."

"Maybe not."

The relief boat and driver were late coming the next morning. He dropped them off where Dad had left his car, and Josh and Dad barely reached home and sat down to Mom's beef stew and biscuits when the doorbell rang.

"I'll get it," Mom stood. "You two keep eating." She returned followed by two Naval officers in full uniform.

Josh scrambled to his feet, saluting. "What's happening?"

"Seaman Apprentice Joshua Gideon Vengeance?" asked the tall one with the most scrambled egg braid on his shoulder.

"Yes, sir. That's me."

"We're sorry it's taken us this long to compile a report and find you."

Josh glanced from one man to the other.

"While debriefing Midway survivors," the senior officer said, "four relayed the same incredible information. Then we realized no one had interviewed you."

"What kind of report are you talking about?"

The junior officer stepped forward. "Your outstanding heroism following Midway keeps coming up. Do you recall rescuing wounded men after the *Yorktown* went down? Or staying afloat in the water for several days?"

"Are you kidding? All I remember is the stuff seen in nightmares."

"But in your case, from all we're hearing, we believe the events are true." The taller man's eyes softened.

Josh wobbled but remained at attention. "I was caved in, badly wounded. I couldn't help myself let alone anyone else. If you're looking for a hero, I doubt I'm your guy."

"Apparently, in critical circumstances you rose to the occasion." The junior officer stood straighter. "Our reports are consistent. We're not sure why you surrendered your dog tags, but one survivor had them."

"He what?" Josh's head jerked. 'I have no idea how or when I lost mine. I just know they're gone. The Defense Department is issuing new ones, but I'd rather have my originals." He grinned. "If you have mine, they have dents."

"These do. Take a look." The senior officer fished in his pocket and withdrew two stainless steel ovals dangling from a chain. They were inscribed with Josh's name, serial number, blood type, start-up date, and service branch. The bottom edges were as chewed as if they'd met up with a meat grinder. The senior officer dropped the chain and tags into Josh's hand.

Josh stared and slid his thumb over the dog tags. His stomach dropped. "I never thought I'd see these again. I remember a bit—a guy's burned face."

"That's right. They led us to you. Four wounded men tell us you bravely rescued them after the *Yorktown* went down—at your own peril and with no regard for your own safety. They say there were others, but not everyone made it. Still, saving four shipmates is incredible. You have our utmost respect."

"This is crazy." Josh shook his head. "Of course, I'd like it to be true, but how could I? I only remember washing up on a tiny island. Locals risked their lives to hide me from the Japs. They're the heroes."

"They saved you for sure, but that's all you remember?"

"Honestly, yes." Josh hesitated. "But in nightmares, I swim through burning oily water, breathing in nasty smoke and swallowing stuff ..."

The younger officer flipped open a notebook. "From what we hear, that was real. You don't remember your actions?"

"Nope. I can't tell what's real or hallucinations."

"Maybe this will help. The men you saved gave details, but we heard most from the fellow who had your dog tags. Most of his clothes had burned off and he had two broken arms so he couldn't keep himself afloat. He claims you weren't in much better shape but swatted out the flames and held him up with your own body by swimming underneath him. Later, you floated him on debris and towed him with your belt. Others say you helped them in similar ways and made an improvised raft after you swallowed so much water you nearly drowned and couldn't swim anymore."

"Sounds impressive, but it wasn't me."

"Don't be so sure. None of them would be alive without your help."

Josh wobbled again.

"At ease!" the shorter officer said. "Sit down."

"Yes, sir!"

"The first man wanted to know your name. He says you gave him your chain and dog tags when he asked for them to remember you. After he was rescued, he found your name listed among men missing in action and presumed dead. He figured your loved ones deserved your tags and should know what you did. Once he contacted us, we sent out a tracer telling us you'd been found. We tracked you here. We like honoring living men instead of awarding posthumous medals."

'Yes." Josh leaned back in his chair and eased his shoulders.

When the tall officer reached forward and shook his hand, Josh said, "I'm telling you again, I'm nothing special. If I did anything, it was instinct. Anyone would have done the same."

"You're wrong. Other men there didn't act as courageously. You saved lives. Heroes do the impossible. That's the difference between ordinary and outstanding seamen."

Dad's chest swelled. "That's great, Josh. We were already proud, but this is fantastic!"

Josh spread his hands. "I don't know what to say. I keep telling you, I don't deserve it."

Mom stood and slipped an arm around Dad's waist. "Josh, the evidence seems to say the contrary. Maybe you should listen."

The senior officer took a breath. "The seaman with your dog tags wants to thank you in person. So do several others."

"That's unnecessary." Josh ducked his head, blinking away a sheen of tears.

"Try telling them that," the junior officer said. "Their matching stories helped us piece your conduct together. Your dog tags were the crucial evidence. Our research brought us here. We wrote up a citation based on your heroism."

The younger man opened the black attaché case at his feet and removed a stiff envelope with Josh's name. The senior officer opened it and cleared his throat.

"On the night of June 7, 1942, and through the next several days, Seaman Apprentice Joshua Gideon Vengeance, though severely wounded, repeatedly risked his life to save seriously injured men. He upheld individuals and later lashed debris together for a raft. He towed it with a belt looped around his stomach and kicked and towed it through shark-infested waters.

"After many hours, Vengeance passed out, and the current swept him out of sight. As the others neared a small island, their raft stuck in sand, and they were rescued. Search and Rescue did not locate Vengeance there. He was declared MIA (missing in action) and this citation written." The senior officer handed a second paper to his partner.

"Seaman Apprentice Joshua Vengeance? Two weeks from tonight you will join several Portland-Vancouver area servicemen being honored for incredible valor and courage. You will receive the Asiatic-Pacific Campaign Medal and American Combat Medal as well as the Purple Heart and Navy Cross."

Josh's mouth dropped open.

"It's an honor you will accept, Vengeance." The senior officer cracked a smile. "The hardware you'll receive will fill considerable space on your service blouse."

Josh lost his composure and laughed until he was out of breath. "Thank you, gentlemen. You've given me the most amazing and confusing day of my life."

Chapter Thirty-Four

Mid-September, 1942
Fort Lewis, Washington

Sitting behind two federal agents in the back seat of the black government car, Erika fought panic. Leaving town, some scenery initially looked familiar, but they were soon whizzing past places she had never seen.

Hughes stared straight ahead, busy driving. Jones, in the passenger seat, turned to face her. "We'll be at Fort Lewis in time for dinner."

Did he want to set her at ease now after terrifying her earlier? Should she trust them? No. They had men of his kind in Germany. She wrung her hands.

"You seem smart," Jones continued. "Please understand it's nothing personal. We have to follow procedures. If you try hard, you might recall the names of more travel connections people and places. Then things will go better for you."

"And if I can't? I already gave you everything I have, and you're not satisfied." She sank back against the car seat and closed her eyes. *Uncle Johnny, do you know where I am? Did you get word that I need your help by tomorrow morning?*

Her heart raced. Chances were slim her uncle could save her now. She was a prisoner of the U.S. Government.

Lord. Help!

As they drove north, graceful corridors of evergreens, like the majestic trees in Germany's Black Forest, lined both sides of the highway and made her homesick. The lump in her throat thickened. Thanks to Hitler, the homeland she recalled didn't exist now. Locked in the back of this government car, perhaps the America she had respected and believed in didn't exist either.

She held her breath to keep from crying.

The dormitory structure they took her to on the base was adequate. The clean, good-sized first-floor room had a single bed, desk, and small bathroom. Its best feature was the large window with a breathtaking view of a tall cone-shaped mountain.

"That's Mt. Rainier," Jones, the shorter agent explained, waving that direction. "Get settled, and we'll be here in twenty minutes to take you to dinner."

He made the meal sound special. Festive. But once her door clicked shut, she found it couldn't be opened from the inside and took stock. The wall phone had no dial tone. The scenic window didn't open. As it grew dark, no light spilled from the other rooms near her. All was dark. *I'm a prisoner.* She threw herself face down on the bed. Numb. *Lord, please help me.*

She was confined on a major American military base awaiting the possible charge of being a dangerous alien suspected of espionage. Had she left Europe and survived a grueling journey to be imprisoned now? Locked up tight instead of using her medical skills to assist others? Surely they wouldn't return her to imprisonment or death in Germany. She was willing to go there if it meant rescuing Mother, but she might be free in the Netherlands. *I still believe You're saying my life is to count here, that You will protect Mother.*

If I'm imprisoned here, my life is wasted. If they return me to

Germany, my life will probably end. And likely Mother's and Klaus's, if he still lives.

Again, she softly heard her Savior say, "Trust."

She lowered her head. *Forgive me. Many Bible heroes spent time in prison. You endured undeserved death to redeem us. I trust You whether I ever understand the reason for these hardships—or not.*

Still. It was hard to be sure.

Calm came slowly. *Only You can bring good out of evil. You've guided my steps this far. Nothing happens without Your permission. Please help these officers believe me. Please bring Uncle Johnny in time.*

She thought again of the mountain scene beyond the window. It soothed her heart.

I wish Mother and Klaus could see this beauty. If only I knew they are alive. Yet the same God who builds mountains can remove them! Yes! She would picture the Lord doing that.

She stood, splashed water on her face, and patted her hair. Twenty minutes later, true to their word, the agents knocked on the door to escort her to dinner. She held her head high. *These men will not break my spirit.*

At a table across the dining room, a gray-haired, stoop-shouldered man sat eating alone.

"That's Dr. Krossner, another German," Jones said scornfully. He studied Erika. "I'm not sure whether to introduce you or not —perhaps you're already acquainted."

She bristled. "We are not. I know few people in America." Impressive in his wool tweed suit and green knitted vest, the man looked more like the owner of a hunting lodge than a physician.

Hughes stood and crossed the room. "Good evening, Dr. Krossner."

"Hello, sir." The older man tilted his head, eyes hopeful. "Do you have news regarding my case?"

"I'm sorry, not yet. We're still researching. So far, your financial records confirm your story. You sent only humanitarian aid."

"As I told you from the beginning."

"But your radio contacts with Germany are troubling—highly unwise during wartime."

"I'm paying for that. My only crime is worrying too much about family and friends. Your research will find I've caused no harm." The doctor's eyebrows met. "I did nothing political. Patient care has always been the heart of my practice."

"Your patients praise your care whether they paid you or not."

"Yes. I take my physician's oath seriously." Weariness lined his face like the cracks in a sidewalk. His eyes turned to Erika. "And who is this?"

"Erika Hofer," Hughes answered, "a young woman who recently traveled here from Switzerland. Her father practiced medicine in Germany. Have you met?"

Erika interrupted. "I told you we have not."

"I'm asking him."

"We've not had the pleasure." The doctor studied her. "Where do you live, Erika?"

She stood to approach him. "Recently in Vancouver, Washington. My uncle is John Hofer. Do you know him?"

"I've heard his name associated with heroism."

"That's right," Erika said.

His eyes examined her again. "Why are you in this facility?"

"A misunderstanding. I helped two older distressed patients by speaking their native tongue—German. And I lack some of the travel documents these gentlemen require."

"Then perhaps your uncle will help."

"He would if we could reach him." She lowered her head. "He doesn't know I'm here."

"We've left messages," Hughes explained. "He's out of pocket but may get them. Enjoy your meal, Doctor." The waiter delivered their delicious-smelling entrées and Hughes returned to the table.

The doctor gave Erika an encouraging smile as she followed.

Later, back in her room, the stressful day plus the good meal made her groggy, yet she couldn't sleep. She stretched across the bed praying. She left the drapes open to view Mt. Rainier every moment, even in moonlight. She repeatedly committed Mother, Klaus, and her own situation to God.

At dawn, pulsing pastel colors painted the mountain pink and pearl, chasing shadows away. As the light increased, new hope surged within her. She turned on the bedside lamp and read her Bible, and then quick taps at her window startled her. A dear figure waved.

"Uncle Johnny!" She rushed to the glass. He was dressed even more fashionably and dapper than when he'd met her at the airport. His eyes twinkled. Every hair was combed in place.

He put a hand to his mouth. "Sorry it took me this long. It was exciting getting here. Now, let me rouse those agents and straighten things out."

When he left, Erika collapsed on her bed, weak with relief. A powerful song they sang at Dietrich's camp flooded her soul.

Lord, You did it! I'm sorry I doubted.

Minutes later, seated in the dining room for breakfast, Erika sat next to her uncle, enjoying his presence. Dr. Krossner was nowhere in sight.

Johnny spread a linen napkin across his lap., "Thank you for meeting us early, gentlemen. I tried coming sooner, but had several obstacles to overcome."

"We tried contacting you and failed, Mr. Hofer. We heard you were downriver—somewhere in the bush. How did you find us?"

"So it's true. You knew where I was and didn't wait for me concerning Erika?" Johnny narrowed his eyes.

"More or less." Hughes shrugged. "She was our focus. We didn't think you could join us. There aren't actual roads where you were."

"That's true too." Johnny laughed. "But riding rail cars works. I only reached Olympia at midnight, but Governor Langlie met me. He's interested in Erika's case. He also appreciates my help so has pulled strings for us. His experts gave me your location."

"But we didn't—" Hughes and Jones locked at each other.

Jones wiped his upper lip. "We didn't tell them."

"You didn't need to. They know things." Johnny held his silverware elegantly, cutting a delectable ham slice into small square bites. He chewed each one carefully and blotted his lips with his napkin. "Excellent cuisine." He narrowed his eyes further. "But now, down to business. Washington state currently has two Japanese-American POW camps, but you are not legally set up to detail other ethnicities yet. Bear that in mind regarding Erika. Yes, Dr. Krossner's radio contacts were unwise, but as of 8:30 p.m. last night, a federal judge ruled him innocent of international harm."

"He did?" Hughes' fingers drummed the table. "What are you saying?"

"Without federal approval, it's presently illegal to detain anyone of German extraction under Washington state's POW guidelines. We hope you've kept thorough notes explaining your actions, because you'll be required to give account to a higher agency. You may have been following orders, but they appear flawed."

Jones grabbed papers from the black attaché case at his feet. "What you're saying doesn't match the instructions from our superiors."

"That's unfortunate. It's old information now. Last night's ruling takes precedence. The authorities above them are not pleased. It's very important to have the right documents."

Jones's face swelled like a horned lizard.

"Careful, Jones," Hughes warned. "Don't say anything more. We have to contact headquarters."

John Hofer nodded. "Good advice." He took another bite. "Once I finish eating, I'll deliver you the telegram from the White House."

"From the—?" After choking on his toast, Hughes clutched his glass of water and drank.

Erika patted Johnny's sleeve. Her heart soared.

He swallowed coffee from the fine porcelain cup before returning it to its saucer. He smacked his lips. "Ah. Someone here knows how to brew a proper cup of coffee." He refilled his cup and drank again. "Gentlemen? Would you like more?"

"Not me, thanks." Jones turned his cup over. So did Hughes.

"I value the governor's support," her uncle said, "and any man who recognizes good work and rewards it." His eyes became hawk-like. "I hope you don't mind him bypassing your agency. In fact, he went above the House Un-American Activities Committee. After midnight last night, Governor Langlie woke a White House aide. After hearing our river team's recommendations, the president dictated a directive regarding Erika, which the governor's top assistant, Irene Pruitt, transcribed for us. I brought it here." He looked them in the eye. "I'm sure you regret the unpleasantness my niece has endured as much as I do." He plucked an envelope from his breast pocket and placed it in Agent Hughes's hand.

Hughes slit it open with his table knife. He read its contents and blanched. "Jones, listen up. 'This message is your Cease and Desist Order concerning charges against Erika Hofer regarding subversion and Un-American activities. Her voluntary service in our Naval Medical Center, San Diego, and her conduct since is exemplary. She represents the good-hearted loyalty of American citizens better than many who are native-born. We endorse her resident status request and encourage her to pursue citizenship. We're aware of a discrepancy concerning her travel documents and are moving to correct that matter at the highest government level. We entrust her to the care of her paternal uncle, John Hofer, who has earned the grateful thanks of this office and our nation.'"

The paper fluttered in Hughes' shaking hand. He turned to

Erika. "Thank you for your cooperation, Miss Hofer. You're free to accompany your uncle."

John Hofer smiled. "Where would you like to go, Erika?"

She drew a deep breath, inhaling freedom. "Dr. Brower's clinic is shorthanded. I'd like to return to work to help."

"Why am I not surprised?" Her uncle chuckled and glanced back and forth between the two agents. "I understand your co-workers are busy doing background checks on the clinic's other employees."

"Yes." Hughes glanced at a notebook. "They haven't finished, but they've found one concerning problem."

"Good investigators usually find more buried beneath the surface." John Hofer laid down his napkin and pushed back from the table. "Erika, if you're ready, we should reach Vancouver around noon. Dr. Brower will be pleased."

"So will I." She smiled so wide her cheeks hurt.

Her uncle stood, straightened his tie, and smoothed the lapel of his well-cut suit. "I came with no vehicle, but the Governor kindly assigned Miss Pruitt to help us. She's outside waiting in a government car." He lifted three fingers to his head in salute. "Goodbye for now, gentlemen."

"Goodbye, Mr. Hofer," Hughes echoed and stood. "Miss Hofer? Thank you for your gracious attitude."

"Please understand we were just doing our job," Jones stammered. "No harm intended."

She looked him in his eye. "None taken."

It only took a moment to gather the things from her room. She hoped to see the German doctor, but he was nowhere in sight. *Lord, thanks for helping him too.*

As Erika and Uncle Johnny walked to the waiting government car, Johnny reached into his pocket and withdrew another envelope.

"Josh didn't like you being detained. He sent this."

"Thanks." Blood warmed her cheeks. She loosened the envelope's flap, fingers shaking as she read his note. As her lips curved in a smile, she nearly stumbled into the car except for her uncle taking her elbow.

"Careful, dear." He opened the rear passenger door to hand her in and climbed into the front passenger seat. "We're ready, Irene."

"Good." Miss Pruitt's smile dazzled. "I'm happy that you're free, Erika."

A tender look passed between the Governor's aide and Erika's uncle. Her uncle and Irene Pruitt might be closer friends than she'd imagined. Miss Pruitt had described herself as a dedicated career woman without time for a family. One day Erika would ask Uncle Johnny why he had not married.

"Thanks for all you've done." Erika smiled and relaxed against the leather seat.

"I'm always pleased to help." Miss Pruitt's voice was as sweet and rich as dark chocolate. "Hopefully, your hardship is past. I'll drive the scenic route back to show you more of our sparkling lakes and evergreen forests."

"Wonderful. Difficult times aren't so bad when they end like this."

"Spoken like a true Hofer." Her uncle leaned over the seat to pat her hand.

As the car purred down the roadway, Erika's last view of the mountain glowed in a cloudless sky.

"Yes. Some things are turning out very well." Erika brushed Josh's letter safely tucked into her pocket. She released her breath with a sigh and leaned against the luxury car's window. There was no comparison to her terror of the previous afternoon.

Despite breathtaking scenery and lakes that sparkled like those in Germany, she dozed a bit. When she next opened her eyes, Uncle Johnny sat closer to Miss Pruitt than before, his arm reaching across the driver's seat behind her head. They talked in low tones and shared a laugh.

"Thank you, Irene."

"You're welcome, John."

"I appreciate the impressive suit you found me. It came in handy. I'll get it dry cleaned and returned for others to use."

"No need, John. I bought it to have on hand for you for situations like this."

"You did?" He moved nearer still. "What do you mean?"

"I respect the ways you help so many. I guessed your measurements and bought quality clothing I found on sale. I wanted to do it for you. I'm glad it worked."

"It certainly did. That was so nice. I—don't know what to say."

"John Hofer doesn't know what to say?"

"Not this time. I—Thank you isn't enough!"

"Yes, it surely is. And you're most welcome."

Erika kept her eyes open. She loved seeing Uncle Johnny fussed over. When he glanced back, his cheeks were apple bright. Miss Pruitt also glowed.

The awe-inspiring scenery was a bonus as they neared Vancouver. Erika sat up straight and patted her hair. "Thank you for this special trip, Miss Pruitt."

"My pleasure, Erika. Let's plan another visit soon. Perhaps dinner in my home or a picnic in a special spot?" She turned to Johnny. "Of course, you're invited too."

"We accept." Gleaming like a Christmas tree, Uncle Johnny answered before Erika could speak. She covered her mouth with one hand to keep from immediately commenting on what seemed like romance in the air. "I love picnics," she finally said.

"Good." Miss Pruitt said. "Soon."

Chapter Thirty-Five

Erika's heart sang as they reentered Vancouver. Already the scenic river town seemed like another home. She pressed her face against the window glass recognizing familiar streets. "Can we go straight to the clinic? Their afternoons are so busy." She wanted to be there, she really did. Yet facing Mrs. Smythe ...

"Yes, we can," Uncle Johnny said. "They'll be so pleased to see you, they'll probably form a welcoming committee or start a parade."

Erika's face heated. "Goodness, there's no need to do that. Many of them have already made me feel very welcome." Her foot bumped the suitcase at her feet. "Could you drop my suitcase by Bob and Sue's so I don't have to carry it? I'd appreciate it."

"Glad to," Johnny said. "Their house is on our way after dropping you."

Irene parked in front of the clinic, but her eyes stayed on Johnny. Their gazes locked.

"Thanks again," Erika called as she hurried to the clinic entrance. She opened the door and stopped. Annie Mettles sat at the receptionist desk beaming. What had changed in under twenty-four hours?

"Welcome, stranger. The governor's office said you'd arrive about now. Thanks for coming straight here."

"You're welcome. I didn't realize the governor kept such close track of things."

"Let me assure you, he does. Not much gets past him and his staff."

"That's good, isn't it?" Erika slid out of her coat and grabbed a set of scrubs. "It's great seeing you, Annie, but what are you doing here?"

"I used to fill in here sometimes. Dr. Brower asked me to take Mrs. Smythe's place since she had to leave."

"Something came up?"

"You could say that."

Erika scanned the nearly empty waiting room "Are there more changes?"

"Some. Once you're settled, Nurse Nalley will cover this desk while we have a few minutes to catch up in the lunchroom."

"Sounds great."

"Welcome back!" Nurse Nalley wrapped Erika in a hug.

Dr. Brower came right behind. "I can't believe those spooks kept you this long. At least their inquiry forced rats and mice out of our woodwork."

Erika's eyes raced to the walls' baseboards. "You have mice and rats in here?"

"No, no." Nurse Nalley spouted a hearty laugh. "Don't take us literally. That just means the investigation helped us identify some people who've caused trouble."

"That's good." Erika propped her head in one hand. "But you're still confusing me. Americans talk funny." She slipped her employee lanyard over her head and headed down the hall to patient records with a spring in her step. Soon, Nurse Nalley changed places with Annie, and Annie found Erika.

"Follow me. You'll like what I get to tell you."

"If it's about Mrs. Smythe not being here, I already do."

"Smarty!" Annie winked.

They sat at a lunch table munching peanut butter cookies.

"You made these?" Erika asked.

"I sure did."

"They're wonderful. Thank you!"

"Of course. After the tension Dr. Brower said was here yesterday, I thought maybe the staff needed cheering up."

"What a good way to do it."

"It turns out Maxine Smythe has good receptionist skills but didn't tell the whole truth about her own background."

"Oh?" Erika took another bite.

"Her last name isn't really Smythe. It's Schmitt. I mean, it is if it got translated."

"You're kidding!" Erika stopped chewing. "That's very German. Do you know why she changed it?"

"Why do you think?"

"She was hiding something."

"Bingo. Schmitt is their legal family name for a few generations, but they were afraid of anti-German sentiment during wartime. Especially after their son got into trouble. They were so afraid, they unofficially changed their name and moved to our smaller town from Portland."

"That's a major change all right. I didn't know they had a son, did you? She had no family photos on her desk. We wouldn't have known she was married except she wore a ring and was Mrs. Smythe. But she didn't talk about her husband."

"No one knew. She kept all family details private."

"How old is their son? What kind of trouble was he into?" Erika took another bite. "These cookies are terrific. The best peanut butter cookies I ever had!"

Annie grinned. "After graduating high school, their son Benson joined the Navy but got off on the wrong foot."

Erika glanced at her feet, and Annie poked her. "Not literally. That means he didn't behave wisely in the service. He decided his drill instructors were too tough. When he had night janitor duty in the officers' club, he drew Hitler mustaches on every officer's photo."

Erika shivered. "That wasn't smart."

"Nope. He said it was a joke, but the officers didn't laugh. He got a disciplinary write-up, and double kitchen duty, but didn't learn."

"There's more?"

"Sure is."

"He sounds immature. Doesn't he know that the military expects good conduct?"

"Maybe not. He told his barracks mates Germany was smart to kill Jews to build a super race."

Erika gasped. "Are you serious?"

"I'm afraid so. Even worse, he didn't realize one man in his squad was Jewish and was horribly insulted. A chaplain had to get involved."

Erika slapped her forehead. "Is he crazy? Or stupid?"

"Maybe both? He bragged he'd be treated better in Hitler's Army. When Dr. Brower heard what he'd said, he insisted the kid have a mental health evaluation."

"I'm sure. His ideas about Hitler's Army aren't true." Erika's finished her cookie and twisted her hands. "He'd be jailed for his comments or worse. Do you know what his father is like?"

"No, but we can guess. Dr. Brower says the dad has a hard time keeping a job. That's why Maxine was desperate to look good and keep hers. Now her husband is threatening Dr. Brower for laying her off. He's even threatening you if she isn't hired back."

"Me?" Erika rocked her head back. "How am I involved?"

"You're not, but he's one of those nutty people who blames everyone else."

"Maybe the dad's attitudes have shaped the son."

"We're sure of it. Maxine is frantic. Right now, Benson is in the brig while authorities decide if he should get a non-judicial punishment or regular court martial."

Erika shuddered. "Those both sound serious."

"They are. Maxine's complaints about you made Dr. Brower so mad he wanted everyone investigated. Having a healthy working relationship in our clinic is very important to him—not conflict."

"I can tell. My father believed that a healthy atmosphere made patients heal faster. Will Maxine be back?"

"I doubt it. After the upset she caused, Dr. Brower doesn't want her here. She claims she was being a good citizen by turning you in, but instead she pulled the roof down on her own head."

"She what?" Erika glanced at the ceiling. "Wait. You're not talking about a real roof. You mean her plan fell on her."

"Yes." Annie poked her again. "Good for you. You're learning."

"It's about time. Are things calming down in the clinic? Or is there more trouble?"

"Improving some, but Maxine often talked to the deliveryman who collects our lab samples. He agrees with her that foreigners shouldn't visit America during wartime, let alone stay. He says it endangers our way of life and his children. He doesn't favor violence, but he has friends who do."

"That's not good. I don't want people upset that I'm here."

"Most aren't. I hope you don't mind, but I encouraged the delivery man to talk to you. Get to know you. Then he'll calm down. Especially when he hears you have a presidential pardon."

Erika wrapped an extra cookie in a napkin. "But for now, I'm not supposed to talk about that, at least about the government's involvement."

"You're good on your feet." Annie laid a hand on Erika's shoulder.

Erika looked at her feet and laughed. "No, you don't mean that."

"Right. It just means you think quickly and figure things out. I find the people who are the most afraid are the ones with the highest prejudice levels. Maybe Dr. Brower should talk with the delivery man."

"No, I'll try." Erika pursed her lips. "I'll fight my own battles. The man acts professional when he's here. What's his name? Rogers? Robbins?"

"Something like that."

"I hope I'll act relaxed and confident when I see him."

"You will. We know God brought you here. More will recognize it soon."

"Thanks." They stood and exchanged a quick hug. "Talking helps."

"Good." Annie checked her watch. "There's one more thing. You know I ran *Books Afloat* as a floating library on the river before we had to blow her up to stop a Japanese attack."

"Yes."

"There isn't time to tell you the whole story now. I still love taking books to folks along the river. A terrific man near Kelso gave me his grandfather's fabulous book collection. It's stored at church in boxes until I get a boat. Smitty has good connections with other tugboat captains. One will let us use his boat once a week. Ted will be the mechanic, but I need someone to help organize and catalog books. I was wondering if—"

"If you're asking me, my answer's yes! Don't even think of asking anyone else. I want to do it."

"Super. I hoped you'd say that. And who knows?" Annie grinned. "We may see more beavers along the way!"

"Ha ha." Erika swatted her. "Next time I'll lead to keep you out of holes."

"No, I'll manage. But I'm glad you'll be involved."

"Happily!"

They brushed cookie crumbs from their hands and rinsed under the lunchroom faucet. "I'll give you details later. We'd better get back to work."

Chapter Thirty-Six

Late September, 1942
Vancouver, Washington

"Johnny, the whole thing's nuts. They're awarding me medals and a new pay grade—it's unbelievable."

"Horsefeathers!" Johnny tapped Josh's shoulder. "Uncle Sam may be slow, but he's not stupid. He does his homework. You're the right man, or I'll eat my hat."

Josh laughed. "Can I watch?"

"Maybe. But I'm speaking the truth, and I'm a good judge of character. I can easily picture you saving lives while risking yours."

"But so many guys died … Why did God spare me?. It feels selfish. I hope He shows me what He'd like from me so I don't let Him down." Josh turned away.

"Ask Him what He has in mind. He's not shy. I'll bet He has amazing things to say."

"You're right. It's time."

"Meanwhile, here's what our team needs from you You're stronger than you were. There are two new situations we need your help with. Are you ready?"

"I am." Josh lifted his clasped hands like a winning prizefighter. "Put me to work."

"Will do. Start by looking over this map. I marked two new concerns ..."

For Erika, the Saturday boat trips on the Columbia were as wonderful as when Mother and Father took her cruising on the Rhine as a child. Now she spent most Saturdays traveling with Annie, bringing books to the same families they'd supplied before *Books Afloat* got blown up.

Erika stood on deck, the wind ruffling her hair. "Thanks for bringing me, you two! My heart might burst."

"Don't let it, but we love bringing you." Annie snapped photos. "Miss Clark and her school families are hosting a yummy picnic today to celebrate our renewed library service."

Erika craned her neck looking everywhere at once. "I feel guilty being so happy with much of the world suffering in war."

"God gives us days like this to store up for the harder times. All moments, good or bad, weave life's tapestry." Annie flung her arms wide to embrace the scenery around her. "Enjoy today. Tomorrow may be darker."

Erika spread her arms as well. "I wish my family and friends could see this. It's hard to imagine evil in a world this beautiful."

"Yet it's there."

Whistling a cheerful tune, Ted checked engine speeds and fluid levels before bringing boxes forward to the book room. An hour later, he snugged *The River Queen* against the Mile 93 dock and extended the gang plank.

Annie hoisted her blue and yellow library flag high enough to flutter in the breeze. "Welcome, Miss Clark, students, and parents. We're thrilled to come again with a floating library, even if we can't guarantee regular service yet." She beckoned. "Please come aboard!"

Erika finished her last displays and stepped aside. "This is heartwarming."

"A glorious repeat of last year, minus some disasters." Annie welcomed the joyful children who surrounded the book tables.

"Glorious with two exceptions," Miss Clark said. "We found the owner of last year's escaped bunny and persuaded her to leave it home this time. Also, Mr. Gibson still won't let his grandson visit your library. He lets Charlie attend school more now but says reading anything besides textbooks is a waste, and he's not sure about some of those."

"That's sad." Annie turned to Erika. "Let me introduce my new helper."

Erika extended her hand. "The pleasure is mine. It's hard to think any adult could see these children so excited and not know this library is a very good thing."

Annie's head bobbed. "I know. Let's pray he changes his mind."

Chapter Thirty-Seven

End of September, 1942
Vancouver, Washington

As much as Erika loved her days in Dr. Brower's clinic, trips on the river were even better. Chugging down the Columbia taking books to children and families who didn't have them thrilled her. Some days, Annie took the boat as far as Jeb and Janey Jarvis's at River Mile 75 in Kalama or even farther to the lively Reynolds family at Mile 69 on the Oregon side.

Erika joined Annie at the prow watching the wind whip the river into small waves. "Have I told you the news?" Annie's voice broke the silence. "Governor Langlie officially started a *Books Afloat* donation fund to help us buy a replacement?"

"No. That's wonderful."

"Meanwhile, Smitty arranged for us to use this tug each Saturday through the rest of the year. So far, that fits his friend's schedule because he wants to take weekends off."

"Terrific." Erika spread her arms like wings. "As much as I love Dr. Brower's' clinic, it would be a dream to be here doing this on more days."

Annie snapped her fingers. "I'm glad to hear you say that because I have an idea. You learn super-fast and do so well helping kids and grownups. If there's a weekend when I can't do this, I'd like you to handle the library part of a run."

"Me?" Erika squealed. "Do you think I could?"

"I'm sure."

"That would be heaven."

End of October, 1942

Vancouver, Washington, and Columbia River

One month later, after four more boat trips, Annie greeted Erika as she boarded the tug.

"I'm glad you're here. Remember when I said I'd ask you to lead a library run if I couldn't be there?"

"Yes." Erika flashed a smile.

"Well, that will happen soon. Next weekend Governor Langlie's hosting an event in Olympia and says Ted and I have to go. We don't know the details. He'll send us the write-up he's putting in the paper, but he insists we must be there."

"You know I'm happy to help."

"Thatta girl, I knew I could count on you." Annie waved a hand. "Like I said, Ted will train Josh on the engine. Smitty will pilot and be your boat expert, but you're the librarian."

"Thank you." Erika grabbed Annie's hand. "I'll do my best and make you proud."

"I'm already proud. I'll send this week's book order your way so you have a record of who gets what."

"Perfect." Erika's smile grew bigger.

"I'll want to hear all about it when we're back, but also have fun. When we finish today, Ted and I have to see if we have clothes decent enough for the Governor's event or if we need to go buy something."

Hours later, Annie hugged Erika goodbye before dashing to climb into Ted's snazzy roadster, *Henrietta Ford*, where her grinning fiancé raced the engine.

"Have a good time," Erika called.

"Thanks." Ted gave a jaunty wave, his arm now in a smaller sling. Henrietta backfired and lurched once before smoothly rolling forward.

Early the next Saturday, Erika was ready long before Smitty arrived in his dented pickup to drive her to the boat. She breathed in the river's freshness as well as the fragrance of spicy evergreen trees growing along its banks. "The *River Queen* isn't much to look at," Smitty said, "but she purrs like a kitten. Well, lookee there. Josh is already at work loading boxes. Good man!"

"Yes, he is. He said he wanted to come extra early to check everything out."

"He's probably also happy to be on a boat again. I would be."

"Morning," Josh propped his cane against the tug's cabin and kept working.

Erika lifted the food bag Sue had sent. "Hey, Josh. Here's the giant lunch your mom sent. Are you free to come get this?"

"Yes, ma'am. On my way!" He crossed the gang plank fast and with only a slight limp. His skin glowed from days outside with Uncle Johnny. "I requested cherry pie! I hope she remembered." He opened the food bag and let out a whoop. "She *did* remember." He lifted the bag in triumph.

Erika laughed. "Don't sound surprised. You know she can't refuse you."

"There are some privileges to being an only child. I'll share, but for now I'm taking this to the galley."

"Afterward, stand by to free our anchor line." Smitty checked off his list. "We're almost ready. And Erika, don't worry about how low we're sitting in the water. *The River Queen's* got good ballast."

"You call that ballast?" Josh smirked. "It makes her look more like *The River Drudge* than *The River Queen*, but you're a good skipper."

"You'd better believe it. I've sailed more years than you've lived." Smitty straightened his back.

"Josh, be nice!" Erika swatted at him but he moved away. "Consider the important work she's doing."

"If you say so. Now that you mention it."

She cocked her head. "I do, and you'd better agree, or I'll decide there's no hope for you."

"Don't do that!" His eyes twinkled. "There's always hope for a nice guy like me."

"Then this might be a good day to prove it."

Smitty said, "Whenever you two are through chin-wagging, we'll get underway."

"Right." Erika checked Annie's clipboard. "We have a schedule to keep. Josh, please pray for us."

He jerked upright. "Uh—is this a pop quiz?"

"Pop fizz?" Erika frowned. "Are you thirsty?"

"Never mind." He paused half a minute and bowed his head. "Lord, You know what today holds. We're grateful You're in charge. Make today exactly what you want. Make us a blessing everywhere we go and bring us back again in safety. In Your name, Amen."

"That was good." Erika smiled. "You're closer to the Lord than you think."

"Uh—" He wiped his brow and faced Smitty. "Ready for me to cast lines?"

"After I start the engine. It looks like our first stop is Ridgefield again for Miss Clark and her school youngsters."

Erika checked the list. "Correction. It would be except for this note Annie left. Mrs. Gibson says her husband is away and asks us to stop at Pioneer Grange with the books for her grandson."

"Really? Is that safe?" Josh looked at Smitty. "That man's caused some trouble lately."

"Hard to say." Smitty scratched his head. "If Gibson's gone, it should be okay. Let's see the note."

"Sure." Erika handed him the paper. "Maybe he's had a change of heart."

"He needs a heart change." Smitty's forehead wrinkled. "It's typed but sounds all right. Mrs. Gibson's a nice woman who's endured plenty. I'd like to help her. Let's do it."

Josh saluted. "Aye, aye." He started the engine, and they churned downriver. One hour later, they cut speed to coast up to the Pioneer Grange. Josh looked to shore. "You remember Johnny and I came here last month to check this place out?"

"Yup. How do things look now?" Smitty dropped the engine to its lowest setting.

"Fine, near as I can tell."

"Let's hope," Erika said. "I don't want to run into him again. When he exploded in the clinic, I wanted to run away."

"Don't blame you. In the long run, he hurts himself most of all." Smitty glanced at his watch and then across the river. "You know, Mrs. Hodges at Mile Eighty-six there in St. Helens phoned last night. She was hoping we could drop off the box of books Erika put together for her, but she's not on today's schedule. We're committed to Miss Clark and her school kids. But if you're okay here, Erika, Mr. Hodges has a hand-held radio transceiver. If I can raise him, and he can meet us fast on the pier, we can cross quickly and take care of that without even stopping our engine. Then she'd have what she needs. What do you think?"

"I think you should do it," Erika said. "It's fine with me and a good use of time."

"Let's see if I can raise him." Smitty adjusted his radio's antenna before speaking into it.

"Is that a walkie-talkie," Josh asked.

"Similar. A Canadian invented this—it's a great help to servicemen."

"That's what I heard. Our officers had a couple, but I haven't seen one up close."

"I'll hand you this when I'm through." The signal crackled and screamed until Hodges answered.

"Hodges—St. Helens."

"Smitty here. We have books your wife wants and could be there in eight minutes, right after we make the Pioneer Grange drop-off. Can you meet us at the pier? Great. She'll be happy. Over and out."

"Well, that sounds good." Erika said.

"Yes, it's working out. Josh, help Erika to the porch before we go."

"Sure thing." He took several steps.

"No." Erika hoisted the books. "That isn't necessary. It's only a few, and the front door's right there. If you leave now, you can finish, and we'll still reach Woodland on time."

Smitty took another look around. "We'll watch from here until you're inside."

Josh folded his arms. "Are we that pressed for time that we can't wait?"

"It's just that Hodges expects us, and we need to reach Miss Clark on time or she might leave and take the kids with her. I'd let you stay, but I need you for the turnaround." Smitty lifted his captain's hat and fanned his face.

"Really, you two. Go do what you need to. I'll be ready by the time you're back."

Erika climbed the wooden steps to the Grange Hall and knocked on the front door. When there was no answer, she freed a hand by balancing the books on one hip and turned the knob. As the door opened, she saw light shining in the back room. "Mrs. Gibson?" she called. "It's Erika, bringing library books."

"Back here," a hoarse voice croaked. "Come in."

"Sounds like you're catching a cold," Erika said. "I'll be right there." She shifted the books again to wave to Smitty and Josh.

Smitty craned his neck in all directions. "The coast looks clear. I guess we're good."

"I'm fine." Erika waved again as Smitty descended the stairs to open up the engine and Josh reversed the tug.

Arms loaded, Erika stepped inside and closed the Grange Hall door. "Coming."

She was halfway to the back room when the overhead light switched off. She inhaled something sweet but bitter that made her choke. A rough fabric hood dropped over her head and tightened.

She dropped the books and clawed the hood, gagging on the pungent-smelling cloth. The hood wouldn't come loose. She couldn't breathe.

She gasped as someone slung her over their shoulder and half-carried and half-dragged her. She fought the encroaching blackness. "Let me go!"

"No!" Gibson's harsh voice boomed in her ear. "For a German from the Master Race, you're a trusting fool."

His evil laugh sent chills through her.

"What are you doing?"

"Teaching you a lesson." He jerked the hood tighter. "I said you weren't wanted here, told you to leave, but you didn't listen. I know you're helping Hitler and the Japs beat us. Well, I'm stopping you. And you'll pay for shootin' down my son!"

She *oomphed* as he threw her to the rough floor, knocking the rest of the breath out of her. When she tried to struggle away, he caught her. "You won't help them again. If it weren't for people like you, my son would be alive."

She fought for breath. "Are you sure he's not? And why blame me for what happened to him? I hate Hitler. He killed my father. Are you sure your son's even in Germany?"

"Where else could he be?" he snarled. "They shot down his plane. I figure he's dead, and you'll pay. The Bible says an eye for an eye, a tooth for a tooth, and a life for a life. I'm taking yours."

He pressed her against the rough boards and bound her hands and feet tight.

"Hurting me won't help." Erika twisted her head aside to find air and struggled harder against the ropes. There was no give. "Your wife won't like you doing this."

"Doesn't matter. I'm in charge. Leave her out of it. I sent her and the kid to Ridgefield for parts." His breathing rasped, the anger rising in his voice.

Jesus. I'm yours. Show this man truth.

The answer came, *Truth is a person. I want him to know Me.*

Gibson hoisted her again and left that building to stumble over rough ground and enter a smaller structure that smelled of musty, damp earth. He dropped Erika on its packed dirt floor, knocking the last breath out of her.

"My friends will come."

"Not in time. This won't take long."

"If you stop, I won't tell. You won't get in trouble."

"I don't care, and don't tell me what to do. Even if they catch me, it's worth it."

Liquid splashed, the strong odor of gasoline filled the room.

"This should do it. You'll burn like that witch, Joan of Arc. Another fool woman meddling where she shouldn't." He fumbled with the cord around her neck and ripped the coarse hood from her head, pulling strands of her tangled hair with it.

Erika lurched back.

More gasoline sloshed. The sharp smell burned her nose and pinched her nostrils. Gibson struck a wooden match that burst into bright sulfurous flame. Fire and shadows flickering over his face made him look like an evil Jack-o'-lantern. "I'll bet you're sorry you came to America now!"

Chapter Thirty-Eight

End of October, 1942
Vancouver, Washington

J osh loved being on a boat again, even on a beat-up tug like *The River Queen.* Truth to tell, any craft surviving twenty years of use and fierce storms on this river was some kind of queen.

Why did he feel such a nagging concern? Erika had insisted she'd be fine going into the Grange Hall alone. Smitty didn't have a problem with it.

Josh couldn't quit thinking about the spunky, sometimes infuriating young woman who'd invaded his life. He'd never met anyone like her. She saw beyond his weakness and was a strong, spicy new flavor he craved.

"Can we go faster, Smitty?"

"Better not. She's wide open. Any more and she'll rattle apart into a bucket of bolts."

"Okay." His fingers whitened on the rail. His head and heart were rattling apart too. Erika did that to him. She'd only be in the Grange Hall twenty minutes while they crossed the Columbia and dropped off a box of books before speeding back. Smitty wouldn't even turn off the engine. Before they left, Smitty nosed around the Pioneer Grange's point of land once more to make sure that Gibson's boat and pickup weren't there.

"He's cleared out all right," Smitty said, "though sometimes his missus drives the truck. At least his boat's gone. It's good news whenever that crazy coot ain't around."

"I get that." Josh nodded. "He sure acted tormented and mean when Johnny and I scouted around here."

"Yeah. Johnny told me. It's a shame he's that hard on his grandson. I've heard he's a nice kid."

Today the river was the smoothest Josh had seen it and with little traffic. Mr. Hodges waited right on time at the St. Helens' pier, a kindly smile lighting his face.

"The missus says hi. She for sure wants you to stop in next time."

"We'll tell Annie and do our best."

"She's not with you?"

"Not this time. Our friend, Erika's, filling in."

"See ya then." Mr. Hodges hoisted the box to his shoulder and trudged uphill to his truck.

Smitty reversed the engine and raced across the river as white water boiled out behind. They were one quarter across when he blanched and pointed.

"Tarnation! Josh, look in the alders past the point. Gibson's boat's hidden there."

Josh shaded his eyes. "I see it, but not him. So, he's somewhere on shore?"

"I hope not. If he hid it to persuade folks he was gone, that's serious."

Lord, help, Josh breathed.

Smitty's face darkened to red, hot lava. "Keep your eyes peeled. We're five minutes out."

The engine screamed as they scanned the shore and raced forward. Halfway across, they spotted Gibson's truck bumping along the road toward the Grange Hall next to the Gibson home.

"That looks like Mrs. Gibson and the boy," Smitty said. "They can help us. They're too far away to hear, so wave like crazy." Smitty leaped in the air like a baseball fan catching a hit.

"Halloo!" Josh leaped higher still, ignoring sharp pain each time his feet and legs landed. "Over here."

Young Charlie spotted them first, grinning as he left the truck and loped toward the boat. "Did you bring books?"

"Erika did." Josh pointed. "She's in the Grange Hall."

"With Grandpa? Oh, no!" Charlie dropped his grandmother's packages and bolted for the building. He popped out again, hand cupped to his mouth.

"They're not here. But there's a pile of books on the floor."

"Where's your grandpa and Erika?" Josh shouted. "Find them."

Mrs. Gibson stared, bewildered. "Annie brought books today? I didn't know she was coming."

"No, Erika did. You didn't write Annie a note?"

"No." The older woman shook her head.

"Blast!" Smitty pounded one clenched fist into his open hand as *The River Queen* nosed to shore. He tossed a rope over a stanchion. "Drop anchor and tie her up, Josh. This'll hold her until we find Erika. Do you carry a weapon?" Smitty's face was granite.

"My fists." Josh doubled his large hands.

Mrs. Gibson gasped. "Erika? The German girl? Not Annie?"

"Nope." As Smitty bent to anchor a cable, Josh leaped past him to shore.

Charlie stared, white as a ghost. "No one's here, but the back door's open." He sped through that door into the woods.

"What's happening?" Mrs. Gibson's eyes enlarged to saucers.

"Your husband's got Erika." Josh clenched his jaw.

Her face twisted. "Charles gets angry and threatens, b-but he wouldn't hurt—"

"Are you sure?"

"I don't know—" She crumpled as Smitty patted her arm and squeezed by. "Hatred may have pushed him over the edge. Josh, wait here."

"Nothing doing. I know where he's going."

Young Charlie had a head start, but Josh pumped his scarred legs and caught the boy as their shoulders crashed against the hut's wooden door.

Erika desperately worked to free her hands while Gibson's magnified shadow danced on the walls from the match's glow. His booming laugh echoed in the small building. "I'm glad to strike my own blow in this war."

Erika's heart pounded. How long had Smitty and Josh been gone? She must stay alive.

The burning match shook in Gibson's hand and then its flame caught the gas spilled on his pants. The fire whooshed along its vapor trail to the fuel can and swelled into a fiery inferno.

Erika broke free enough to deliver a fierce kick to Gibson's chest. As he roared and bent to grab her foot, she rolled fast to one side where the structure's earthen berm joined the log walls.

More fabric of Gibson's pants ignited as the door crashed open. Fresh wind and oxygen fed the flames.

When Erika rolled, her head hit the bottom support log above the berm so hard it felt like an axe split her skull. She saw lightning. And stars. Shouts and blows exploded in her head as everything went black.

"Grandpa, no!" Charlie reached for the burning man. "Drop to the ground and roll."

"Get out! Save yourself!" Old Charlie managed to hurl his good-sized grandson through the door like a bowling ball that knocked Josh aside too.

Josh stumbled but regained balance, his eyes darting back and forth to make sense of the scene. The bitter smoke cleared enough to reveal Erika, unconscious or dead against the far wall. He roared and charged like a lion.

Gibson was on fire. He blocked Josh's path to Erika. When Josh slowed to smother the man's flames, Gibson smashed Josh's jaw, snapping his head back hard.

"I did this. Leave me here."

"Why?" Josh pushed Gibson flat, rolling him and pounding out the flames that also burned his hands again, like Midway.

"Leave me." Gibson coughed, strangled. "Serves me right."

"You might deserve this, but she doesn't." Josh kept beating the fire with his blistered hands and found strength to heave Gibson toward the door.

Young Charlie burst in with burlap bags. "Use these."

Josh left Smitty and Gibson's wife working the water pump to soak bags and rushed to Erika.

No, she couldn't die. He placed a hand near her nose and mouth to find breath. She was so still. He couldn't tell.

"Erika! Dear God. Please help!"

Chapter Thirty-Nine

End of October, 1942
Columbia River

Erika's head hit the foundation log so hard, it spun and took her to another time and place. A mountaintop of golden Avalanche Lilies—glittering stars overhead—a brisk breeze—heaven?

Acrid smoke filled her nostrils. Crackling flames. Such heat—she struggled against the ropes that bound her. *The Lord is my shepherd, I shall not want ...*

Kneeling over Erika, Josh detected a wisp of breath. "Darling. Please breathe! Open your eyes. I can't lose you. Open your beautiful eyes." He grasped her arms and tried to drag her to safety. Would his legs hold both of them up?

The smoke-filled room became darker. Or was the air denser because Gibson's flames had been beaten out? Either way, Josh dragged her farther.

"Angel, look at me. I haven't told you I love you, but you have to know. Please, God. Don't take her away. Let her live!"

A soft moan rose from Erika's motionless body.

"Erika?" Did her eyelids flicker? His hand cupped her chin. Yes. Her warm breath filled his hand. Her mouth moved to form words he couldn't hear.

He brought his ear to her mouth. "Erika? What did you say?"

"If I keep my eyes closed, will you say you love me again?"

"Yes. Always. He bent further and kissed her, gently holding her to him. "Always, Darling. Every moment of every day." Her lips sweetly returned his kiss as he held her tighter.

"Josh." Her arms circled his neck as he lifted but wobbled.

He ducked his head. "Lord, help. "He lifted again and stood straight. This time he carried her through the low back door across the most beautiful green spicy bank of ferns under the blue vault of heaven.

"Thank God you came," Erika said as they sank into the ferns.

"I never prayed so hard." He cradled her tighter, rocking her back and forth, his head nestled against hers. "Thank God you're alive. I was so afraid of losing you."

She smiled. "Not going anywhere."

He held her until Smitty and Mrs. Gibson stood near.

"I think we've got him under control, and we got the fire before it ignited the house.

Josh pulled Erika close and kissed her again.

"Oops!" Smitty approached, smiling. He tilted his captain's hat back. "The fire's out without reaching the house, and Gibson's no threat now. We've got him trussed up like a Thanksgiving turkey. Serves the old coot right, trying to hurt people who never did him a lick of harm. Don't know if he deserves prison or the loony bin, but I see you two need medical care." He smirked. "I also think this story might have a happy ending after we get you some help.

"Yes." Josh smiled at Erika.

When they next looked up, Johnny also stood there beaming and covered in soot from beating out flames. "I had a feeling I was needed here. Sometimes you get a nudge, and you just know."

"Trust those instincts. They're usually right." Smitty clapped Johnny's shoulder. "I guess we'll skip the Ridgefield stop today to get you folks patched up."

"I'll say." Johnny nodded. "Smitty, can you radio Ridgefield or Vancouver to ask which doctor is closest?"

Smitty saluted. "Sure thing."

Josh tucked his scorched jacket around Erika. "I'll bet it'll be old Doc Brower. Seems only right."

Smitty soon replied. "Yessirree, that's probably who it will be!"

Chapter Forty

Early November, 1942
Vancouver, Washington

Josh waited with Erika for Dr. Brower's evaluation. He walked in fussing.

"You're not strong enough to discharge, young lady. You have a concussion."

Erika sighed. "I hope you mean I have symptoms but am well enough to go home. Sue will watch me."

"So will I," Josh insisted.

The doctor sighed. "I figured you'd say that. By the way, you were very lucky—only minimal burns. So was Gibson. Because the flames burned so hot and fast, he only suffered first- and second-degree burns. He'll stay a while in hospital, but of course his mental health is most concerning. He will face criminal charges, too, but we just got incredible news."

"What's that?" Josh stepped closer.

"The Governor's aide, Miss Pruitt, researched international agencies for us and confirmed that Gibson's son, Charles Gibson, Jr., had been captured and held in a German POW camp. But that's not the end of the story."

Erika gasped. "He's alive?"

"Yes." Dr. Brower laid down her patient chart. "Two weeks ago, resistance fighters helped Charles Junior and one buddy escape across the border into Denmark. That country is Nazi occupied but sympathetic to Allies. A Danish fisherman smuggled them to England under a load of herring in his boat." Dr. Brower grinned. "They reached freedom smelling awful, but safe."

"That's wonderful!" Erika's eyes filled.

"I've called Mrs. Gibson and young Charlie in to tell all three of them together." He glanced at his watch. "They should be here any minute. If you hear whooping and hollering, that will be us."

"And Josh and me too." Her eyes dripped.

"Guaranteed." Josh handed her his handkerchief.

"That news should help their whole family. International organizations should be able to shuttle the son back here soon. Of course, a judge must decide on a penalty for Gibson's crimes. A mental health exam has to be part of it, but knowing his son's alive should begin to make Gibson a changed man."

"I can't even imagine." Erika used Josh's handkerchief again.

He beamed and took her hand. "Finally, some good news."

As soon as Dr. Brower signed Erika's release, Josh powered her outside through the hospital's front doors in the wheelchair required for patient discharge.

As they negotiated the wheelchair ramp, Ted and Annie stood waiting next to *Henrietta Ford*. Ted handed Josh the keys. "Drive Erika home in style, Buddy. You both deserve a decent ride."

"Will do. Thanks, buddy." Josh and Ted grasped hands.

In front of the Vengeance home, Josh's parents, Johnny, and Smitty all waited, lined up in the front yard. After gentle hugs and backslapping, Johnny placed a small black box in Josh's hand. "I got this shined up and ready like you asked, in case you're ready to use it now."

Josh's face heated. "More than ready. Besides, this will make us related." The two men grinned.

Erika looked on in confusion. "What do you mean?"

"I mean this." Josh flashed his biggest smile since Midway. "I didn't count on an audience, but please be our happy witnesses." He dropped to one knee.

Erika's eyes widened. "Josh, what are you doing?"

"What do you think? Claiming treasure. Taking the pose to kneel and do what's in my heart. I won't let anyone or anything delay this." He snapped open the black velvet box holding a gold band with a small glittering diamond and took her hand. He looked into her eyes.

"Erika?" He choked up. "The Lord has brought us on a long road to each other. I didn't know anyone like you existed in this world. I never want to lose you. This ring belonged to Johnny's mother so was in your family. Johnny wants us to have it. It represents the best of the Old Country joining the new." He blinked away the moisture in his eyes and held her hand more tightly. "With all my heart, I pray to see my love returned."

Erika's eyelids fluttered.

Josh swallowed hard and continued. "Erika, I love you and want to marry you. Please accept this ring as my pledge to love, cherish, and honor you all the days of our lives to the best of my ability. Make me the happiest man in the world by saying you will be my wife."

"In the whole world?" Her face lit up. "Oh, Josh, yes. Yes, I will."

"Thank you. "That's all I wanted to hear!"

He slipped his ring on her finger and cupped his hands around hers and drew her close. His lips quickly found hers waiting. She tasted like mountain lilies. His pounding heart matched the beat of hers. "I'm the happiest man in the universe."

She held him tighter. "And I'm the happiest woman. We'll

share this new life God is giving us for a lifetime. And the ring is beautiful."

"Not as beautiful as you." He gave another tender kiss. "I can't see all of our path yet, but I know we'll follow the Lord together."

"I'm sure too or wouldn't have said yes." Her laugh rang out as she lifted her hand again to let sunshine make her diamond blaze with fire. "I wouldn't have it any other way."

Bob and Sue gathered the couple into a shared hug. Bob's eyes misted. "Welcome to our family, Erika. You've survived so much—we know the Lord will bless your lives together, no matter what is ahead."

"Thank you." Erika kissed Bob and Sue's cheeks. "I feel assurance and peace."

"For the wedding dinner," Mom chirped, "let's have a German-American feast."

Josh wiped his forehead. "Wow, Mom. How did I guess you'd go there?"

"It's a mother's job."

"I know." He hugged her.

"Hot dog!" Johnny hopped from one foot to the other. "My family's growing. You two are perfect together! I'm so happy, I might dance a sailor's hornpipe all day."

"I don't know, Johnny." Smitty pounded his back. "I think your wandering days might be ending. I figure you might get hitched too."

Johnny stood still. "Don't go planning my life for me."

"I'm not, friend, but these days there's a sparkle in your eye that wasn't there before."

"Well, it's partly that Erika's here—" Johnny blinked.

"And?" Smitty crossed his arms and waited.

"I've been thinking it might be smart to add a lady or two to our river team. Some have great observation skills."

"Especially if they're named Irene. Do you know how red your face is?"

"The sun's hot." Johnny checked his watch. "As a matter of fact, there's someplace I need to be. I'll hop in my truck and—"

Smitty slapped his shoulder. "Going to Olympia, are you? To see Irene?"

"How did you—"

"Did you forget how many years I've known you?"

"Right. But what about you, Smitty? Is there someplace you should be?"

"I'm thinking about it." He cleared his throat. "You've got me considering."

"Well, hop to it. By the way, Irene sent word that Dr. Krossner is released and heading back to Kelso. But in the future, he's advised to only donate through the International Red Cross to avoid more crisis."

"That's smart," Erika said. "My friend Oskar could help."

Smitty jabbed a thumb towards Josh and Erika. "What about these love birds, Johnny? Is their future clear? Or do they have paperwork hurdles to jump through?"

"A few." Johnny flashed a grin. "Governor Langlie says it's nothing he can't handle, and I've never seen him wrong."

When the phone gave a shrill ring inside the Vengeance home, Sue ran to answer. Several minutes later she reappeared, looking stunned.

"Erika? It's an international call from Switzerland. It's a poor connection—I only understood bits. But I think the operator said the call's from your mother."

"My mother!" Erika screamed and leaned on Josh to get into the house.

"*Mutter?* It's you? Fritz helped, and you are safe? With his mother as well? Not the Netherlands? God be praised! Give me your address and I'll give you mine. There is so much to write."

Josh brought his head close so they could listen together.

"Klaus is alive and safe also? You're sure? Thank You, dear Jesus." She leaned against Josh and burst into more tears.

"What about Dietrich?" Her voice saddened. "That's what I was afraid of. When?"

Josh concentrated and understood some individual words. Erika ended the call in a daze.

"You understood?"

"Most of it. We must tell the others. We've won battles," Josh said, "but this war isn't over."

Erika stroked his cheek. "I'll explain the hardest parts."

"I understood much through your Mother's excitement."

"I haven't heard such joy in her voice since Father left."

He rested his forehead against hers. "You sound like her, you know. Besides, it's easier to understand when you care for someone, and I do." Josh kissed her cheek and supported her back outside.

The others had waited near the front door.

"Was it really an international call?" Sue asked.

"Yes." Erika gazed at each face. "We'll give the good news first. Dietrich's courier Fritz, who helped me escape, also got both my mother and his safely to Oskar in Geneva two days before Hitler closed that border." Erika did not dry the grateful tears coursing down her cheeks. "I can picture them. Oskar will have his hands full. I don't know how, but Oskar also found that resistance men had rescued my brother Klaus and got him to safety." She bent her head and sobbed harder.

"How wonderful!" Sue grabbed her.

"Yes. That's answered prayer!" Bob pounded Josh's back.

"Somehow freedom fighters masterminded his escape from a prisoner of war camp over the border into the Netherlands and then to Scotland and England." She looked up. "It's incredible. My greatest dreams have come true. If only Father knew."

Josh tightened his arms around her. "I'm sure he does."

"You're right." She dabbed her eyes again.

"Wonderful," Bob said. "But how did your mother know to phone here?"

"Oskar again," Erika said. "Chaplain Merritt gave him your

number. He will arrange for Mother to join Klaus in England to help with Red Cross refugees. It's perfect."

When her tears continued, Josh whipped out a handkerchief.

Erika found a dry spot and blew her nose. "They will be safe there and assist others. I'm so happy yet also heartbroken." Her face crumpled. "Because Mother's other news—"

"Is what?" Josh's mother clutched her hand.

"I can't—" Erika gulped but choked. "Josh? Will you share?"

"Yes, sweetheart." Their hands welded. "We don't know the date but Dietrich was arrested by SS troops. He's in Tegel Prison north of Berlin. It's impossible to escape from there, but everyone's praying."

Josh pulled Erika closer. "One thing we know. No matter what they do to him, they can't decrease his influence on believers in Germany and beyond."

"Very true." Bob slipped his arm around Sue.

Erika took a breath. "All of us who know him can multiply his life through ours." She held Josh's hand tighter.

"We will," Josh said. "Erika, you and I've survived a wild swing of emotions in the last twenty-four hours. The same God who helped us this far will lead us and our nations in coming days."

Josh turned to his parents. "Mom? Dad? You're the best example of unconditional love I've ever known. I hope to do as well."

"It's nothing." His mom's hand darted out. "We never—"

"Believe me." He waved a hand. "You two made a huge difference, and I know what I'm talking about. I-I can never thank you enough."

"No thanks needed." Dad interrupted. "Our thanks is having you come home. We didn't want anything else."

Mom chuckled. "You know Dad won't budge when he uses that tone of voice."

"I do. The Rock of Gibraltar." Josh chuckled with her and then drew his parents and Erika into a tighter circle.

"Who would think the Lord could redeem events so full of heartache," he said.

"Amazing," his dad agreed. "But nothing is beyond Him. Look there."

Josh looked where Dad pointed.

"He's the One who created that powerful river down there."

They all gazed downhill from the Vengeance yard to the Columbia surging far below. "It flows from Canada's ice fields past Cascade Mountain peaks and then to us and the ocean. Even if we face floods or storms or future attacks, the same Savior who spoke peace to the storm on Galilee will guide us. He alone transforms strong currents into the strong hopes we need to move forward each day."

"I think I finally get it." Josh cradled Erika against his heart. "He's done wonders for us, and now for Erika's Mom and brother—and Gibson's son."

"He has." Erika gave a trusting smile. "And for thousands more we may never know about."

As scenes of Midway, and Japanese sailors invading America's coast, and one of Gibson attacking Erika flashed before Josh's eyes, he shuddered. "He's done so much and made me strong again."

"Almost well." Erika stood on tiptoe and pressed a soft kiss on his cheek.

Far below, the river flowed as smooth as glass until the current caught a massive log it tossed high like a matchstick.

"Wow! Did you see that?" Josh laughed and eased his shoulders. "Our strength is nothing."

"I did." She leaned against him. "Not compared to His."

Holding Erika in his arms, Josh gazed at the river and exhaled every tension, fear, and heartache that had crippled him. Instead, he breathed in deeply to fill his lungs with faith, and hope, and peace.

The End

Recipes

WWI Trench Cake

1 ¾ flour

½ C. margarine

1 tsp. vinegar

2/3 C. milk

¼ C. brown sugar, sugar, or molasses—any sweetening available

¼ C. currants or other dried fruit

- Pre-heat oven to 350°F or place in banked ashes.
- Grease your baking tin or line it with parchment paper.
- Rub the margarine into the flour until the mixture is crumbled.
- Add the remaining dry ingredients.
- Combine the milk and vinegar. Stir in the baking soda.
- Stir the liquid ingredients into the dry and mix well.
- Spread the batter into your greased tin and bake in a 350 F. oven. Or cover it and bank in warm ashes. Check after one hour by inserting a toothpick or

broom straw into the cake. When it comes out clean, the cake is done.

Dutch Flensje Pancakes—(thinner than French crêpes)

1 C. flour
3 eggs
1 cup of milk
1 tbsp. sugar
1 pinch of salt
1 tsp. vanilla
2 tbsp. butter

- Place flour in a large mixing bowl.
- Combine eggs, milk, sugar, vanilla and salt in a smaller bowl and mix until blended.
- Slowly stir in around one-fourth of the liquid mixture into the larger mixing bowl of flour until blended. The batter will have a runny consistency. Melt 1 tsp. butter in an 8" skillet and fry until lightly brown on one side only. Sprinkle with powdered sugar and lemon juice (or other toppings).
- Roll up, enjoy.

Spaetzle Potato Dumplings

2 C. all-purpose flour
1 tsp. salt
4 large eggs
3/8 C. milk or water depending on the richness desired

- In a large bowl, combine the flour, eggs, milk, and salt. Stir until the batter is mixed well and develops bubbles. The batter shouldn't be too thin or thick or it will be difficult to make the spaetzle. Let the batter sit for 5-10 mins.
- Place a colander in/over a bowl to drain the spaetzle once cooked. Bring a large pot of water to a boil over high heat. Add 1 Tbsp. of salt to the water. Reduce temperature and simmer.
- Press batter through a spaetzle-maker or large-holed colander and into the simmering water.
- After using each one-third of the batter, let that batch cook for 2-3 minutes until they float to the top, and stir occasionally. Use a slotted spoon to transfer the spaetzle to the colander so that excess water drips off.
- Serve immediately or sauté in butter to crisp them. If you don't serve or sauté them immediately, add 1-2 Tbsp. of butter to the hot spaetzle so they don't stick together.

Rotkohl Sweet—sour red cabbage side dish with apples and onions

1 medium head red cabbage, shredded or sliced
2-3 Tbsp. bacon fat, butter, or olive oil
1 large onion, sliced or diced
3 apples, peeled and cored, shredded, or diced
½ cup red wine (optional)
3 Tbsp. apple cider vinegar
1 tsp. salt
2 tsp. white or brown sugar
½ tsp. ground nutmeg
¼ tsp. ground cloves

¼ tsp. freshly ground black pepper

2 Tbsp. lemon juice

2 Tbsp. corn starch

- In a large pot or large Dutch oven, heat bacon fat over medium heat and lightly sauté the onion. Add shredded cabbage and apples. Continue to sauté for several minutes.
- Add 1 cup water, red wine (if using), cider vinegar, sugar, salt, nutmeg, cloves, and pepper. Stir. Bring to a simmer and cover. Simmer for about 30 to 60 minutes or until the cabbage is tender, adding more water if needed. Add lemon juice. Taste and season with more salt, cloves, pepper, sugar, and vinegar as needed.
- Mix 2 Tbsp. cornstarch with cold water and slowly stir in just enough to thicken red cabbage liquid. Serve. This also refrigerates or freezes well.

Sauerbrauten (usually beef or pork or venison) wrapped in bacon)

Rump roast is traditionally used, but also eye of round, or bottom round.

One of Germany's authentic national dishes, Sauerbraten is marinated, cooked until tender, and served with a rich and flavorful sweet-tangy gravy! Serve it with homemade Rotkohl and potatoes, Knödel, or Spätzle and you're in for a feast!

Sauerbraten requires advance planning as the meat should marinate for days before it's ready to cook. Don't shorten the marinating time. Let the meat marinate fully.

Place all veggies and herbs in a heavy stock pot or Dutch oven along with garlic, juniper berries, whole cloves, bay leaves, salt, sugar and peppercorns. Next add the red wine, red wine vinegar, and water.

3 lbs. beef rump or other roast
2 large onions, chopped
1 C. red wine vinegar
1 C. water
1 Tbsp. white sugar
1 cloves of garlic, minced
2 whole cloves (or more to taste)
3 large sprigs thyme
8 small sprigs rosemary
4 juniper berries, cracked
8 whole black peppercorns, cracked
2 bay leaves, or more to taste
2 Tbsp. all-purpose flour
Salt and ground black pepper to taste
2 Tbsp. vegetable oil
10 gingersnap cookies, crumbled

Directions

- Place roast, onions, vinegar, water, salt, black pepper, sugar, cloves, and bay leaves in a large pot. Cover and refrigerate for at least 2 to 3 days, turning meat daily. Remove meat from marinade and pat dry with paper towels but reserve the marinade.
- Season flour to taste with salt and black pepper in a large bowl.
- Sprinkle flour mixture over beef.
- Heat vegetable oil in a Dutch oven or large pot over medium heat; cook beef about 10 minutes until browned on all sides.

- Pour reserved marinade over beef, cover, and lower heat to medium-low. Simmer until beef is tender, for 3 1/2 to 4 hours.
- Remove beef to a platter and slice. Strain solids from remaining liquid and continue cooking over medium heat.
- Add gingersnap cookies and simmer until the gravy thickens, about 10 minutes.
- Serve gravy over sliced meat.

About Delores Topliff

In third grade, Delores began composing rhyming stories. Her classmates' approval encouraged her writing. Two of her four award-winning children's books are rhymed adventures.

Delores grew up near Fort Vancouver, Washington, loving its history. Before it was enclosed for safety, she crawled to the original well's edge, appreciating its stone-lined walls built by early hands. To *absorb* history, she's eaten knobby green apples from the Pacific Northwest's oldest apple tree planted by the fort's founder, Dr. John McLoughlin.

Delores married a Canadian so enjoys U.S. and Canadian citizenships. She loves her doctor sons, families, and five grandchildren, and is something she didn't think she'd be—a snowbird dividing her year between Minnesota and Mississippi.

Besides writing, she teaches university classes and enjoys

travel, photography, and various hobbies. She also loves connecting with readers and speaking to writing groups and book clubs. Find her blogs, books, and more at delorestopliff.com. Connect on Facebook at Delores Topliff Books.

Other Books by Delores Topliff

Books Afloat

Columbia River Undercurrents—Book One

Blaming herself for her childhood role in the Oklahoma farm truck accident that cost her grandfather's life, Anne Mettles is determined to make her life count. She wants to do it all–captain her library boat and resist Japanese attacks to keep America safe. But failing her pilot's exam requires her to bring others onboard.

Will she go it alone? Or will she team with the unlikely but (mostly) lovable characters? One is a saboteur, one an unlikely hero, and one, she discovers, is the man of her dreams.

Get your copy here:

Wilderness Wife

Marguerite Wadin MacKay believes her 17-year marriage to explorer Alex MacKay is strong–until his sudden fame destroys it. When he returns from a cross-Canada expedition, he announces their frontier marriage is void in Montréal where he plans to find a society wife–not one with native blood. Taking their son, MacKay sends Marguerite and their three daughters to a trading post where she lived as a child. Deeply shamed, she arrives in time to assist young Doctor John McLoughlin with a medical emergency.

Marguerite now lives only for her girls. When Fort William on Lake Superior opens a school, Marguerite moves there for her daughters' sake and rekindles her friendship with Doctor McLoughlin. When he declares his love, she dissuades him from a match harmful to his career. She's mixed blood and nine years older. But he will have no one else.

After abandonment, can a woman love again and fulfill a key role in North American History?

Get your copy here:

https://scrivenings.link/wildernesswife

Christmas Tree Wars

Christmas is meant to be a time of goodwill, but there's no peace between two neighboring Christmas tree farmers involved in a longstanding feud. Can this year be different with a bit of holiday romance tossed into the season?

When the financial planner son and forestry major niece of feuding Christmas tree farmers come home to help their families in crisis, it takes Christmas tree wars to a whole new level. As the young people seek success by competing to provide a national Christmas tree, romance fills the air and connects them like mistle to toe.

Get your copy here:

https://scrivenings.link/christmastreewars

More Historical Romance from Scrivenings Press

Window of Opportunity by Heather Greer

The Stained-glass Legacy Series—Book One

Faith and duty drive Evangeline Moore to protect her father's pristine image as a judge in Harrisburg, Illinois. Her resolve's biggest test? Dot, her childhood friend. With Evangeline beside her, Dot's desire for the Roaring Twenties' glitz and glamor leads the pair into questionable situations.

Born into a Chicago mob family, Brendan Dunne understands duty, but faith puts him at odds with his father's demands. Even when his brother James's propensity for trouble lands them in Harrisburg, the truth is undeniable. To their father, the lines he won't cross mean Brendan will never measure up.

When circumstances push Brendan and Evangeline together, unexpected events create opportunity to break free of family expectations. Will they be brave enough to forge their own path before the window closes on their chance to change?

Get your copy here:

https://scrivenings.link/windowofopportunity

Redemption's Trail by Betty Woods

Trails of the Heart—Book Two

Newly widowed with her second child due in a few months, Lily Johnson has nowhere to go until Toby Grimes, her late husband's boss, asks her to stay on as housekeeper at his ranch. Remaining in the house Mr. Grimes built for her and her husband is an answered prayer. But malicious gossips see her godsend job as a ruse for a sinful dalliance since her employer is a nice-looking, single man.

God and a lot of others turned their backs on Toby during the war, so he returns the favor by keeping to himself. Yet the need to care for and protect Lily overwhelms him. The way she tugs at his heart scares him more than going into a losing battle.

Unwilling to allow anyone to destroy a fine woman's reputation, he proposes a marriage of convenience. After much prayer, Lily accepts. Her first marriage was a love match made in heaven. The second leads down a trail only God knows. The peace she has concerning a marriage to a troubled man she doesn't love begins a walk of faith to a destination neither she, nor Toby, can guess.

Get your copy here:

https://scrivenings.link/redemptionstrail

9 781649 172549